Nodding toward the doors that led back into the gaming hell, Cassandra said, "Spend extravagantly."

"I am not given to extravagance," he said drily.

Oh, how she longed to flirt with him. To finger the diamond solitaire winking in his cravat and tell him that he wasn't always so restrained. To coax more smiles and laughter from him, those rare, intoxicating sounds.

"Try," she urged him. "For me," she could not resist adding.

"How can I deny you?" he asked playfully.

"Or risk my wrath," she teased.

"Watch me tremble." He held up his rock-steady hand.

She pushed his hand away. "Mocking a lady is poor form, Your Grace."

"Very well," he allowed. "I'll go back inside."

Her heart squeezed tightly. This was it. The last time they would see each other. She thought she understood pain, but it kept surprising her with its depth, its tenacity.

"Before I do . . ." Alex continued, "forgive me, but I cannot stop myself."

"Forgive you for—?"

Before she could finish her sentence, he pulled her into his arms and k

By Eva Leigh

The Wicked Quills of London
FOREVER YOUR EARL
SCANDAL TAKES THE STAGE
TEMPTATIONS OF A WALLFLOWER

The London Underground
FROM DUKE TILL DAWN

Eva Leigh

From Duke Till Dawn

❧ The London Underground ❧

AVONBOOKS

An Imprint of HarperCollins*Publishers*

FROM DUKE TILL DAWN. Copyright © 2017 by Ami Silber. All rights reserved. Printed in the United States of America. No part of this book may be used or reproduced in any manner whatsoever without written permission except in the case of brief quotations embodied in critical articles and reviews. For information, address HarperCollins Publishers, 195 Broadway, New York, NY 10007.

First Avon Books mass market printing: June 2017

Print Edition ISBN: 978-0-06-249941-7
Digital Edition ISBN: 978-0-06-249942-4

Avon, Avon & logo, and Avon Books & logo are registered trademarks of HarperCollins Publishers in the United States of America and other countries.
HarperCollins is a registered trademark of HarperCollins Publishers in the United States of America and other countries.

FIRST EDITION

17 18 19 20 21 QGM 10 9 8 7 6 5 4 3 2 1

To Zack

Acknowledgments

Thank you to Liz Boltz Ranfeld for invaluable input and encouragement, and to the Ladies of the Island, who are always in my corner. And, as always, much appreciation and gratitude to Nicole Fischer, Kevan Lyon, Caro Perny, and Pam Jaffee.

Chapter 1

London, England
1817

A woman laughed, and Alexander Lewis, Duke of Greyland felt the sound like a gunshot to his chest.

It was a very pleasant laugh, low and musical rather than shrill and forced, yet it sounded like The Lost Queen's laugh. Alex could not resist the urge to glance over his shoulder as he left the Eagle chophouse. He'd fancifully taken to calling her The Lost Queen, though she was most assuredly a mortal woman. Had she somehow appeared on a busy London street at dusk? The last time he'd seen her had been two years ago, in the spa town of Cheltenham, in his bed, asleep and naked.

The owner of the laugh turned out to be a completely different woman—brunette rather than blonde, petite and round rather than lithe and willowy. She caught Alex staring and raised her eyebrows. He bowed gravely in response, then continued toward the curb.

Night came on in indigo waves, but the shops

spilled golden light in radiant patches onto the street. The hardworking citizens of London continued to toil as the upper echelons began their evening revelries. Crowds thronged the sidewalk, while wagons, carriages, and people on horseback crammed the streets. A handful of pedestrians recognized Alex and politely curtsied or tipped their hats, murmuring, "Good evening, Your Grace." Though he was in no mood for politeness, responsibility and virtue were his constant companions—had been his whole life—and so rather than snapping, "Go to the devil, damn you!" he merely nodded in greeting.

He'd done his duty. He'd been seen in public, rather than disappearing into the cavernous chambers of his Mayfair mansion, where he could lick his wounds in peace.

The trouble with being a duke was that he *always* had to do his duty. "You are the pinnacle of British Society," his father had often said to him. "The world looks to *you* for guidance. So you must lead by example. Be their True North."

This evening, before dining, Alex had taken a very conspicuous turn up and down Bond Street, making certain that he was seen by many consequential—and loose-lipped—figures in the *ton*. Word would soon spread that the Duke of Greyland was not holed up, sulking in seclusion. His honor as one of Society's bulwarks would not be felled by something as insignificant as his failed marriage suit to Lady Emmeline

Birks. The Dukes of Greyland had stood strong against Roundheads, Jacobites, and countless other threats against Britain. One girl barely out of the schoolroom could hardly damage Alex's ducal armor.

But that armor had been dented by The Lost Queen. Far deeper than he would have expected.

Standing on the curb, he signaled for his carriage, which pulled out of the mews. He tugged on his spotless gloves as he waited and adjusted the brim of his black beaver hat to make certain it sat properly on his head. "Always maintain a faultless appearance," his father had reminded him again and again. "The slightest bit of disorder in your dress can lead to rampant speculation about the stability of your affairs. This, we cannot tolerate. The nation demands nothing less than perfection."

Alex's father had been dead for ten years, but that didn't keep the serious, sober man's voice from his mind. It was part of him now—his role as one of the most powerful men in England and the responsibilities that role carried with it. Not once did he ever let frivolities distract him from his duties.

Except for one time . . .

Forcing the thought from his mind, Alex looked impatiently for his carriage. Just as the vehicle pulled up, however, two men appeared and grabbed his arms on each side.

Alex stiffened—he did not care for being touched without giving someone express permission to do so. People on the street also did not normally seize each other. Was it a robbery? A kidnapping attempt? His hands curled instinctively into fists, ready to give his accosters a beating.

"What's this?" one of the younger men exclaimed with mock horror. "Have I grabbed hold of a thunder-cloud?"

"Don't know about you," the other man said drily, "but I seem to have attached myself to an enormous bar of iron. How else to explain its inflexibility?" He tried to shake Alex, to little avail. When he wanted to be, Alex was absolutely immovable.

Alex's fingers loosened. He tugged his arms free and growled, "That's enough, you donkeys."

Thomas Powell, the Earl of Langdon and heir to the Duke of Northfield, grinned, a flash of white in his slightly unshaven face. "Come now, Greyland," he chided. A hint of an Irish accent made his voice musical, evidence of Langdon's early years spent in his mother's native County Kerry. "Is that any way to speak to your oldest and dearest friends?"

"I'll let you know when they get here." Alex scowled at Langdon, then at Christopher Ellingsworth, who only smirked in response.

Alex took a step toward his carriage, but Ellings-worth deftly moved to block his path, displaying the speed and skill that had served him well when he'd fought on the Peninsula.

"Where are you running off to with such indecorous haste?" Ellingsworth pressed. He held up a finger. "Ah, never tell me. You're running back to the shelter of your Mayfair cave, to growl and brood like some big black bear in a cravat."

"You know nothing," Alex returned, despite the fact that Ellingsworth had outlined his exact plans for the rest of the night.

Ellingsworth looked at Langdon with exaggerated pity. "Poor chap. The young Lady Emmeline has utterly shattered his heart."

Alex shouldered past Ellingsworth, only to have Langdon move to stand in his way.

"My heart is not *shattered* because of Lady Emmeline," Alex snapped. At least that much was the truth.

"But why shouldn't your heart be strewn in pieces throughout Regent's Park?" Langdon mused. "You courted the young lady for several months, and you told Ellingsworth and I that you'd already received her father's grateful acceptance of a marriage offer."

"She never agreed to anything," Alex said flatly.

"A modest girl, that Lady Emmeline." Ellingsworth nodded with approval. "She wouldn't have said yes right away. They never do. Nothing to be alarmed by."

"How would you know?" Alex's voice was edged. Ellingsworth had little experience with offering for ladies' hands, committed as he was to a life of reckless pleasure.

Langdon added, "It'd be unseemly for an earl's daughter to eagerly snap up a marriage proposal the moment it was offered."

Alex scowled. Despite the fact that, at thirty-eight, he was sixteen years her senior, they would suit well as a wedded couple. Lady Emmeline had been perfectly trained in the responsibilities of an aristocratic wife. Though he wished she stated her own opinion rather than constantly agreeing with him, there were worse faults one could find in a prospective bride.

They could marry at Christmas, eight months from now. It would be a small but elegant wedding, followed by a lavish breakfast and a wedding journey in the Lake District. And then, if everything went well, in less than a year, Alex and Lady Emmeline might welcome their first child—hopefully a boy so the line would be secure. It would've been precisely the sort of match Alex's father would have approved, considering Lady Emmeline's faultless background and her spotless reputation.

"Look at him now, mooning away," Langdon sighed, smugly thwarting Alex's attempts to step around him. "He looks poorly."

It would be bad form to knock his friend to the ground. Damn the social niceties that dictated a man couldn't punch another without repercussions.

"Perhaps he should be bled," Ellingsworth suggested with his habitual smirk. It was his constant companion since returning from the War, as if he refused to take anything seriously.

"I am perfectly well." Alex looked back and forth between these two rogues whom he called friends. "No need to call for a quack."

"He's already had an amputation," Langdon noted, raising a brow as he always did. "One prospective bride—gone." He made a sawing motion at his ankle, as if cutting the shackles of matrimony.

Alex glanced down at his own lower leg, as if he could see the invisible links that might have bound him to Lady Emmeline. He'd come so close to becoming a married man and sharing the rest of his life with one woman—the faultless duke his father had bred him to be. It hardly mattered that Alex felt nothing for the gel other than a sense of distant respect. She would have made a fine duchess.

"We were at White's yesterday when we heard about what happened," Langdon said with disapproval. "Didn't even tell your two closest friends that Lady Emmeline had run off with a cavalry officer. No, we had to hear it from Lord Ruthven, of all people."

Alex didn't need reminding that the whole world knew about his embarrassment. He'd been ensconced in his study reviewing land reports from his holdings when the butler announced a surprise visitor. Lady Emmeline's father came into the chamber, pale and shaky and full of abject, groveling apologies. He'd handed Alex a note written by his daughter that stated she'd run off to Gretna Green with a poor but dashing cavalry captain. Alex had stared at the short missive for a good five minutes, trying to understand its significance.

"You should have come right to us with the news,"

Ellingsworth drawled. "So you could spare us the humiliation of learning about it secondhand."

"Forgive me for failing to consider *your* feelings in all this," Alex snapped.

What could he say to his friends that would make them understand how the pain he felt was mostly embarrassment, not sadness? He wasn't even certain he desired their understanding.

He was a duke. The holder of countless profitable estates and assets. A prime mover in Parliament. A frequent advisor to the Prince Regent—though the profligate fool almost never took Alex's advice. Marriage to the Duke of Greyland would be considered a huge coup for any young lady of gentle birth. But Lady Emmeline had thrown away a chance to be a duchess . . . for love.

That's what her note had said. "Forgive me, Your Grace. But I love him terribly, as he loves me. You deserve better than a wife whose heart belongs to another . . ."

"Ah, he's well off without the feckless chit," Ellingsworth insisted. "Had no backbone, that girl. She trembled like a willow whenever he spoke. A fearful lass can't be very amusing in bed."

"Don't talk about Lady Emmeline that way," Alex said, but there wasn't much heat in his words.

He backed away from Ellingsworth and Langdon, thinking perhaps he could dodge around them. But they were clever, curse them, and Ellingsworth edged behind him, blocking him in.

Ah, damn and damn.

Alex scowled at his friends tormenting him in the depths of his ill humor. While he felt no loss of affection from the girl's elopement with another man, pain lanced him at her desertion. Was there something about him . . . ? Something that made women flee from him? Was he truly that intimidating? Was he—was he unlovable?

But that word, that concept—*love*. He'd never felt it at home, though he'd heard it existed. He'd seen it in the way cottagers at the family estates acted with their children—the fond looks, the touches and smiles. Love was real, but it had been in short supply for the Duke of Greyland's children.

His jilting brought back that same, gnawing question. If his own mother couldn't show him affection, perhaps there was something about him that was fundamentally unworthy of love. An absence, a lack of a key inner component that would cause someone, anyone, to feel for him.

Lady Emmeline would have been a fine mother, raising sons and daughters in a way that befitted their station. She wouldn't have loved him, but that wasn't a requirement for marriage. They could have gotten along with mutual respect. If he felt a cold emptiness from this thought, he shouldered it aside. He'd gotten this far without love in his life. He could exist without it now.

Alex still smarted at her desertion but the greatest

damage was sustained by his pride. At least neither Langdon nor Ellingsworth looked at him with sympathy.

"He's definitely going home to sulk," Langdon said disapprovingly.

Ellingsworth looked horrified. "I never spend a night at home, unless I'm too ill, and even with a scorching fever, I go to the theater."

"I've had a meal out, and now I'm heading home to read a new translation of Euclid's *Elements*."

"You see, Langdon," Ellingsworth noted. "He's got a romping good time already planned. He's no need of us."

"Right about one thing." Alex grabbed hold of Langdon's shoulders and forcibly moved his friend aside. He stepped up into his carriage, but to his annoyance, Ellingsworth and Langdon followed, seating themselves opposite him. "I *don't* have need of you." He rapped on the roof of the carriage, and the vehicle began to merge into traffic.

"That's where you're wrong." Langdon grinned in the semidarkness of the carriage's interior. He pulled a flask from inside his coat, then took a swig. "Stewing at home is for spinsters."

"I've done my duty," Alex said in a clipped voice. "Paraded my carcass on Bond Street so everyone could get a good eyeful of me, let them know that Lady Emmeline's sudden marriage has not one speck of impact on me."

Ellingsworth grabbed the flask from Langdon and took a drink. "You did right by that, old man." He leaned over and jabbed his knuckles into Alex's shoulder—as close to showing affection as Ellingsworth ever got. "But your night's not finished." He held the flask out to Alex.

But Alex didn't take the flask, much as he craved a drink. "It is." He swayed with the movement of the carriage. "I can't stomach a ball tonight, and I'm not interested in going to the theater, or anywhere else I've got to show a good face in wake of—" He glanced out the window. "In wake of everything that's happened."

"We aren't going anywhere respectable," Langdon said with a wink. "The people there won't give two figs if you were jilted by a goat."

Alex curled his lip. "I'm not going slumming."

Jabbing a finger toward Alex, Langdon said, "Nothing but the highest company tonight. The most stylish. The most esteemed. But they'll be too busy calculating odds to worry about whether some girl dropped you."

"Are you drunk already?" Alex demanded. "I don't understand any of the gibberish flapping from your lips."

"He means that we're going to a new gaming hell," Ellingsworth explained. "It's so new and fashionable it doesn't have a name. Langdon and I were there last night, after we heard about you at White's. The hell's been open for a fortnight. People queue up around the block to get in." He leaned forward. "You have to go.

It's going to be open for just a month. Then it closes shop and disappears like a faerie kingdom."

"Haven't heard of any new gaming hell," Alex muttered, crossing his arms over his chest.

Ellingsworth rolled his eyes. "You've been embroiled in *le scandale de la Mademoiselle Emmeline.* Doubtful that you'd know if St. Paul's burned down. Which it hasn't, by the by."

"Come on, Greyland," Langdon cajoled. "I guarantee that a night at London's most à la mode gaming hell will raise your spirits. Wine. Cards and dice. An abundance of pretty ladies." He said this as though the presence of lovely females was the ultimate trump card. "Join us there tonight, even if only for a few minutes."

"What's your alternative?" Ellingsworth added. "Geometry? Calculating the surface area of a sphere?" He feigned a yawn.

Indeed, what *was* Alex's alternative? Home was huge and empty, a reminder that his attempt to fill it with a wife and children had been an utter failure. And it was in moments like this—quiet, introspective times—that thoughts of The Lost Queen couldn't be held at bay. They flooded him like a monsoon in a tropical climate. If he didn't keep moving, he'd drown.

He growled, "Give my driver the direction of this den of iniquity with its wine and dice."

"And ladies," Langdon added with a grin. He and Ellingsworth wore matching smiles of satisfaction. "You'll have no cause to regret your decision."

Regret. He'd done everything right. He always played by the rules, never forgetting the importance of his ducal role. He shouldn't regret anything. But tonight, he'd loosen his grip on the reins of his ducal propriety. After all, what had being proper ever gotten him?

A SPRING drizzle settled over the streets, calling forth scents of wet stone and manure. The slick cobbles gleamed like onyx as pedestrians and horses picked their way over the uneven stones. London grew loud with the rain as people shouted to each other and hooves clattered.

The gaming hell was situated in a slightly raffish part of Piccadilly. It nestled between other stone-faced buildings, sporting a colonnade and the slightly overdressed look of a prosperous banker. Heavy velvet drapes concealed the windows. True to Ellingsworth's word, well-dressed prospective guests were queued up on the curb, waiting for the doorman to admit them entrance. No one seemed to care about the rain—they were far too busy craning their necks to see how much farther they had to go before being admitted entrance.

Alex had never seen such a thing in his many years of sampling London's entertainments. He didn't know he could still be surprised—which was both alarming and intriguing.

The carriage drove past the queue on the way to the front door. He, Langdon, and Ellingsworth got out of the vehicle, then stood in the street, looking at the latest in gambling establishments.

"I'm not getting in line," Alex stated flatly. The very idea that a duke would queue up like a clerk buying his luncheon was utterly foreign.

"That's not a concern," Langdon assured him. Leading the way, he ascended the front steps and approached a man in green livery.

"Back of the line," the doorman said without looking at Langdon.

Langdon scowled. "I was here yesterday! With my friend." He shook Ellingsworth by the shoulder.

"Back of the line," the servant intoned. "Got to make room for fresh faces, fresh blunt."

"We brought a new face with plenty of blunt," Ellingsworth insisted. He pointed at a very irritated Alex. "This is the Duke of Greyland."

At last, the doorman's impassive façade cracked. His eyes widened as he reached behind him to open the door. "Right this way, Your Grace."

"And my friends," Alex said coolly as the other people in the queue shifted and muttered in discontent.

"May of course enter." The doorman waved them forward.

Alex climbed the steps, then entered a foyer where another liveried servant took his coat, hat, and walking stick. The servant performed the same task for Ellingsworth and Langdon.

"Ah, Your Grace! My lords!" A man of middle years

with silvering hair and an extremely amiable countenance came striding forward, his hands outstretched as if welcoming old friends even though Alex had never met the man before. Somehow, word must have already reached him from the front of the house that a duke and two other noblemen were in attendance. "Welcome! All of you are most welcome to my humble establishment."

Humble wasn't quite the word Alex would have used to describe the place. From the foyer, he could see into a large chamber adorned with crystal chandeliers, shining brass fixtures, equestrian paintings, and curtains fringed with gold braid. It was a cross between Carlton House and a brothel—though the two weren't all that different from each other.

"I am Martin Hamish," the proprietor continued, a hint of Scottish burr in his voice. "And this institution of fortune is at your disposal." Hamish snapped his fingers, and a footman appeared with three glasses of sparkling wine, which Langdon and Ellingsworth immediately seized. Alex slowly picked up the remaining glass and sipped at the wine. He was pleasantly surprised to find it of an excellent vintage.

Hamish waved his hand toward the main gaming hall. "We have hazard, *vingt-et-un,* faro, which was quite favorable toward Lord Langdon. Plenty of excellent food and drink. I employ a cook straight from the court of poor Louis XVI. Lord Ellingsworth most particularly enjoyed our lemon cakes yesterday." He beamed at them. "Trust me, Your Grace, my lords, you will find no more pleasant way to spend an evening than under my roof."

Alex nodded at Hamish, then ambled toward the large gaming hall.

Ellingsworth turned to him. "Stake me a hundred pounds."

"What? No," Alex said immediately. He had the money, but he'd seen his young friend lose cash like raindrops in a cupped hand. Ellingsworth went through his quarterly allowance at an alarming rate.

"Then give me five thousand pounds," Ellingsworth said easily.

"Did you secretly imbibe a cask of whiskey on our way here?" Alex demanded.

His friend rolled his eyes. "I'm sober." He thought about it for a moment. "Mostly." He exhaled. "The hundred pounds would set me up at the tables so I could win that five thousand."

"Which you need because . . . ?"

"I have a project I'm working on." Ellingsworth grinned. "A secret project."

Alex could just imagine what folly his friend wanted to finance. "An expensive secret."

Langdon dug into his coat pocket and produced a hundred-pound note. He held it out to Ellingsworth. "Enjoy, old man."

"My thanks." Ellingsworth grabbed the money and hurried off toward the tables.

"First of all," Alex said with exasperation, "what the hell are you doing walking around with that much cash on your person? You're a duke's heir."

Langdon shrugged. "Most underground gaming in London is cash only. They're not interested in my vowels, duke's heir or no. Your other question . . . ?"

"Why on earth did you give Ellingsworth the hundred pounds? He's just going to lose. He usually does."

"He's my *friend*, Greyland." Langdon smiled faintly. "It costs me little to make him happy for a few hours. Mayhap you ought to consider the price of your own happiness." With that, Langdon ambled off.

Shaking his head at his youthful friends, Alex stood alone and surveyed the chamber. Unlike at some gaming hells, this unnamed one permitted women as well as men to risk their fortunes. Jeweled diadems and plumes were as plentiful as stickpins and Brutus-styled hair. Perfume, sweat, and alcohol scented the noisy air as the guests clamored at the various card and dice tables. More servants in green constantly moved through the room, bearing trays of food and drink.

He moved deeper into the room, taking his time, assessing. Perhaps Alex might be able to carry through with his plan and forget himself for a while in this place. Let slip the tether that always bound him.

By nature, he wasn't a man given to gambling. It was the curse of his class, the need to wager outrageous sums on nearly anything. The betting book at White's was proof of that. And this gaming hell was, too.

The large vaulted chamber was packed with patrons eager to know the thrill of a bet, the highs of winning and the crushing despair of a loss. Boredom ran riot amongst aristocrats, especially now that Bonaparte had been exiled to St. Helena, never to escape again. That boredom bred a need for sensation, for emotion. Alex had never felt this ennui, too busy with his responsibilities, but he knew several who did. Ellingsworth and Langdon were two of many men hungry for experience in the midst of privilege. Langdon, especially, seemed to thrive on challenge and danger.

Alex was slightly older, and perhaps he flattered himself to think he was wiser, too. But what had that gotten him?

He took a step toward the hazard table. The hell with it. Time to give up some of his control. Sink his teeth into the meat of life.

Yet before he made it to the table, he saw more than a few of the patrons looking in his direction. Some of them were whispering behind hands and fans. A few glanced at him with that dreaded emotion: pity.

He threw back the last of his wine. Damn and hell, was there nowhere he could go to feel at ease?

If they wanted something to talk about, by the devil, he'd give them enough ammunition to set their chins wagging for the next decade.

He stalked to a *vingt-et-un* table. People's gazes and whispers followed him. The Duke of Greyland *never* gambled. Tonight, he would.

He wagered wildly, heedless of his cards. Wins and losses piled up, until he no longer cared how much money he'd lost or gained. It could have been a pittance, or a fortune. What did it matter?

A small crowd gathered, watching with barely concealed amazement.

"He's gone mad," someone whispered.

"The chit broke his sense," another answered.

He moved to place another substantial, careless bet. A voice behind him made him freeze, however. It planted him like roots from an oak, and he couldn't move under its memorable feminine, familiar spell.

"Won't you play another hand, my lord? I'm certain the house will give you credit. Come, I shall fetch you a glass of wine."

He knew that voice. *Her* voice. The Lost Queen.

Yet it couldn't be. Had to be another illusion, like that woman's laugh at the chophouse.

"Are you hungry, my lord? Cook has just prepared a superb *steak avec poireaux vinaigrette*."

No—this was no illusion. Two years melted away like ice in a fire as Alex slowly turned around, uncaring that he was in the middle of a game. His body roared with pain and pleasure.

There she was. Achingly unforgettable. Devastatingly beautiful. As slim as a birch tree, with pale golden hair framing a face of shattering loveliness. Dressed in a bronze satin evening gown, her hair held up with amber clips, she stood next to Lord Coleman, smiling at the old earl in her winning way. Her hand rested lightly on his sleeve.

She wasn't one of the patrons. She . . . worked here. But how? Why? What did any of this mean?

"Cassandra." The word came from his lips like a rasp, as though his body was a cavern that had been closed for a millennium.

He didn't speak very loudly—at that moment, he couldn't. Yet she looked up at once. Her hazel gaze met his.

For half a heartbeat, her expression registered joy, longing. Then horror.

He blinked, and both expressions were gone from her face. She looked smooth and unreadable. It was as if he'd imagined her emotions.

He felt both numb and acutely aware of every nerve. His heart pounded and his mouth went dry.

"Alex?" she whispered.

It truly was her. Cassandra Blair. The Lost Queen. The woman who'd shattered his heart two years ago.

Chapter 2

$\mathcal{F}$or several moments, Alex and Cassandra stared at each other, as if frozen. The only thing that moved was Alex's heart, pounding like a steam engine in the center of his chest.

He barely noticed Lord Coleman looking back and forth between them. "I'll, ah, investigate the *vingt-et-un* tables," the older man muttered before ambling away, leaving Alex alone with her.

He'd had lovers and mistresses before—women who enjoyed pleasure and were eager to share it with him—and while he acknowledged he'd been attracted to sundry women, his hunger for Cassandra had been sudden and obsessive. He'd seen a flame smoldering beneath the coolness of her exterior and it called to him, like a fire seen through a long, dark night.

He'd been drawn in by her quiet dignity, so different from the forced frivolity of debutantes in search of husbands. When other women looked at him as a collection of wealthy estates, awed by the age of his title and his prestigious lineage, she had spoken to him and looked at him as though he was a man, not just a duke. There had been tragedy in her eyes and understanding in her smile born from years of lived experience. And—he couldn't deny it—the carnal awareness she displayed in her movements stoked a fire in him he'd never before known. He'd burned to touch her, to taste her kisses, to know the feel of her body against his.

Now the woman who'd carved a hollow inside his body and brain stood before him, two years older but as powerfully stunning as she'd been back in Cheltenham. Seeing her again seared a hole right through him. He'd be reduced to ashes in a moment.

All the details of her returned to him in an instant, from the arch of her eyebrows to the birthmark on the inside of her thigh. A birthmark he'd kissed.

Someone at one of the faro tables shouted, snapping Alex back to the present moment, to this place. Cassandra, too, seemed to wake, blinking and furrowing her forehead.

He could not speak to her as he longed to do in the middle of a gaming hell.

"Your Grace?" the card dealer behind him tentatively asked. "Do you wish to continue playing?"

"No," Alex snapped over his shoulder. "I—"

His words died as he looked at Cassandra. Scanning the room, he noticed a secluded corner, partially shielded by an enormous Chinese vase holding palm fronds. The middle of a gaming hell was no place to talk to her. No place to *see* her.

Before Alex could think, he took her uncovered hand in his own ungloved hand. The feel of her skin against him was a hot brand upon his heart, both a balm and an agony.

Wordlessly, she followed him to the corner, where Ellingsworth and Langdon couldn't cast their curious gazes in his direction. Even in a gaming hell, where guests engaged in numerous vices, people gossiped.

Her familiar fragrance of rose and warm vanilla drove thorns of heat through his chest. Though her expression remained unreadable, the long line of her throat revealed the quick pulsation beneath her flesh. His fingers itched to stroke along that silken column, as he'd done before. Or press his lips to the spot at the juncture of her jaw and neck, to taste her again.

Her eyes widened slightly, as if she could read his thoughts.

Very slowly, as if defusing an incendiary device, she untangled her fingers from his. But she didn't put more distance between them.

"Alex," she whispered.

"Where did you go?" he demanded lowly.

She didn't speak. Yet her gaze never left his.

"I woke up," he continued, "and you had disappeared."

Her gaze slipped to the side, as if she had trouble looking him in the eye. Was she ashamed?

He pressed. "No one at the hotel knew when you'd left or where you had gone."

Her lips tightened regretfully. "I know." She glanced back at him, and a wealth of misery shone in her eyes. "I'm . . ." She drew a breath. "I'm so sorry."

Her apology was only a trickle of water upon the hot wound of the past. The words were too meager for the immensity of his feelings, broad and vast as a jungle, and just as dangerous.

He couldn't stop the words that tore from him, revisiting that dark time. "And then no word. Not a letter, not a note. Nothing." Anger and fear pulsed beneath his words. And relief, to find her again after so long, after he'd believed the worst.

"I looked everywhere for you," he went on. "Every inn between Cheltenham and London. My solicitors scoured the country for word of you."

"England is a vast place," she whispered. Her face was pale, her eyes wide.

"It always seemed too small to me," he gritted. "Until I tried to find you. It was as though you were made of smoke. You vanished utterly."

She looked down at her clasped hands, her knuckles white as she gripped her fingers tightly.

He gazed at the crown of her head, shining softly gold like something deeply precious. "I thought—" His voice thickened. "I thought you'd been hurt. Worse. That you'd . . ." He couldn't even say the word, though he had proof at last that his greatest fear had been unfounded.

"Oh, God, no," she breathed. She glanced up, and then her eyes briefly closed. "I had hoped that you'd forget me. Go on with your life as if we'd never met."

"How can you say that?" He realized his voice had grown louder. Alex carefully lowered his tone so that they wouldn't be heard above the noise of the gaming hell. "It's not my habit to seduce impoverished widows at spa towns." Sharp, cutting feelings threatened to overwhelm him once more—in Cheltenham, he'd reached toward her like a plant finding sunlight. And when she'd gone, he could only think that again, he was unworthy of love. The sun disappeared.

"Nor is it my custom to become a duke's lover," she said, barely audible.

The words *seduce* and *lover* reverberated between them. Her pupils widened, darkening her eyes. Her gaze darted up and down his body. A flush stole into her cheeks. She blushed like that when she came.

He couldn't think of that now. Not here. Not when there were too many unanswered questions and raw emotion nearly engulfed him.

"Please," she breathed. "Forgive me. I acted out of self-protection." She pressed her hand against his thundering chest. "The money you gave me—so honorably—it was enough for me to go home. To contest my wicked cousin." Her brow furrowed and her mouth turned down. "The villain. The clever, shrewd villain. He kept my creditors hounding me. I had to leave for home in the dead of night so they wouldn't pursue me. I had to vanish utterly to keep myself from the Marshalsea."

The thought of Cassandra imprisoned there shot frost through him. The infamous debtors' prison was a miserable place, full of desperation and sorrow. Alex had once been there to visit an old school friend, who had refused to allow him to pay off outstanding debts. The Marshalsea was a warren of sad, cramped rooms and hopeless people spending interminable hours in squalor.

"Damn it," he said gruffly. He barely cared that he'd sworn in her presence.

She smiled sadly. "I know." Her smile faded. "I reached home, also in the dead of night and found my ancestral home barred to me. No place to go, no friend to give me shelter. I applied to the local magistrate." She shook her head mournfully. "Too late. My cousin had taken control of my entire fortune. I hadn't two groats in my pocket. I had nothing, and nowhere to go."

He shook with the force of her revelations. The trials she had endured. Faintly, he heard the shouts of the men and women at the gaming tables, the click of dice, and harsh explosions of laughter. They seemed so far away, so frivolous compared to what Cassandra had faced.

"You could have come to me," he rasped. Her hand against his torso recalled that night, two years ago, when they had gone to bed together. She'd dug her nails into his chest, urging him on, as he'd moved within her.

A merciless storm of desire and emotion pummeled

him. He wanted to rage against it like a mad king shouting at the tempest, yet it had him. All these years had passed, and his hunger for her—his need for her affection—hadn't dimmed. Not at all.

"Already, you'd done so much for me. How could I ask for more?"

He felt his cheeks darken. "What's the use of my bloody fortune if I couldn't help you?" Rage at her faceless cousin was an acid in his veins. "Tell me that bastard's name and I'll wring your fortune out of him." He'd never meant any words more than these.

She shook her head once more. "He took my money and went to the Continent. Aix-les-Bains, Vichy, Montecatini Terme. He could be at any spa, or any city. There's nothing anyone can do." Her lips tightened. "It was difficult enough to ask you for money to get me home. I couldn't come to you with my hands outstretched." She moved her hand from his chest. "I know you. You're generous. You would have given me what I asked for, because of the strength of your honor."

Another flush stole into his cheeks. He'd been complimented many times in his life—a matter of course for a duke—but none of those flattering words had the impact that hers did, perhaps because he genuinely cared what she thought of him. She gave out compliments because she meant them, not because she was obliged to.

She exhaled in a short burst. "If I was to survive, it would be through my own strength, my own will."

He nodded, even as he cursed the very thing he admired so much about her.

They'd come to know each other during that fortnight in Cheltenham. She'd married too young to a man of hot blood—but emotion had been her guiding principle when she'd accepted his proposal. When he had died of a fever contracted after a hunt, her strength had carried her through.

It didn't matter how dire her circumstances might be, she was determined to succeed on her own merits. She was no lost damsel in need of rescuing.

He thought it would just be a few dull weeks at the hotel while recovering from a riding injury that had hurt his shoulder. He'd come into the hotel's elegant, marble-clad foyer and seen her. All thoughts of his injury fled. Her proud, assured bearing had drawn him in, and beneath that, an elusive sensuality. She'd eaten alone in the dining chamber, with its vaulted ceiling and echoes of murmured conversation.

Alex had never believed in fairy tales, but she seemed an elfin queen in exile. Her pale hair, the clearness of her gaze, the sleekness of her limbs all recalled the stories he'd heard from his nursemaid about the fairy folk who lived in the woods behind his home. So he'd dubbed her The Lost Queen. He'd been unable to resist her allure.

He'd had the hotel's manager introduce them. They'd talked about fairy tales and old legends and the wish to sail away to far-off places. It was as though idle conversation was unnecessary, and they'd spoken directly from their hearts. He'd never met anyone who could be so reserved and yet so incisive at the same time. Her contradictions wove themselves into a web, ensnaring him.

When he'd learned of her plight, he had decided at once to give her money to help. They'd been in the hotel's conservatory, warm and damp and green, and he'd seen a trickle of perspiration work its way down her neck to nestle in the folds of her fichu.

She had tucked the money there. Not in her reticule. "For safety," she'd explained, but he had been too distracted by the sight of that gleam of sweat to pay close attention.

He'd taken her to bed soon after. Not as a man purchasing a woman's favors, but as further proof of his heart. For the first time, he'd allowed himself to feel soul-deep emotion, believing that at last it would be reciprocated.

She'd gone away instead. He'd been so hurt by her— but now he knew why she'd been so quick to put distance and silence between them. The wounds could at last heal.

"What can a woman alone do," she explained, "but make her way in the world."

"What did you do?" He was half-afraid of the answer, because there was always a particular option available to women.

She gave him a wry smile without much humor. "Became a lady's companion."

He exhaled.

"Yet you're here now." He glanced behind him, at the crowded gaming hell full of men and women drinking and wagering.

She blushed deeper, as though ashamed. "Mr. Hamish needed a woman of gentle birth to keep the people at the tables, and I had no choice but to accept his offer of employment. The last woman who'd retained my services was a bitter, angry widow—a dowager countess. She resented my youth. Accused me of stealing. She planted jewelry in my possessions. I left her employ with a blight on my name and without a character reference. Finding more work as a lady's companion became impossible." She spread her hands, an expression of rueful acceptance on her face.

His heart ached with pity. His beautiful, proud Cassandra, brought to this. He couldn't reproach her for not informing him of her whereabouts or circumstances. Had he been in the same place, he would have acted as she had.

Yet they were here together again. After two years of fruitless searches, and the resulting despair when he couldn't locate her, providence had seen fit to have them meet again. He didn't know how or why, only that it was a gift he wouldn't toss aside.

"Cassandra—"

She glanced worriedly over her shoulder. "I have to get back to work. Mr. Hamish will notice I'm not on the floor, and I cannot afford to lose my position here.

And . . . I'm sorry to hear about what happened with Lady Emmeline."

He grimaced. The news was one-day old and everyone knew, even a woman he hadn't seen in two years.

But he didn't want to think of his fruitless wooing of another woman. He took Cassandra's hand in his. "Don't go."

"I can't stay." She pressed a quick kiss to his knuckles—to his shock and pleasure—then slipped away, back into the heat and chaos of the gaming hell. He stepped out from the corner, watching her go as though she was the last glint of light in the darkness.

Ellingsworth and Langdon appeared suddenly, flanking him.

"Who was that?" Langdon demanded.

"You never mentioned a blonde," Ellingsworth accused at the same time.

Alex cleared his rusted throat. "That's a story I won't be sharing."

His two friends exchanged glances. Ellingsworth had, despite his vocal disavowals to the contrary, done very well at university. His mind was nimble, perhaps overly so. "The unknown lady."

"What of her?" Alex snapped.

"Lady Emmeline was never truly your goal," he deduced. "You courted her, yes, but it was *she* who held pride of place in your heart."

"Ellingsworth—" Alex said warningly.

Yet his friend wouldn't be scared off. "The wooing

of Lady Emmeline was merely a way to overcome heartbreak."

"Stop reading your nieces' sentimental novels," Alex muttered, but he couldn't outright lie and tell Ellingsworth he was wrong.

"Cheltenham," Langdon suddenly exclaimed.

Alex jerked in response. "The hell are you talking about," he growled.

"You're right," Ellingsworth said with surprise. "You went away to Cheltenham, and when you came back . . . you'd changed. Turned even more serious—if such a thing was possible. And there was . . ."

"What?" Alex snapped.

"Pain in your eyes." Ellingsworth looked nearly embarrassed to have noticed this much.

"There wasn't," Alex said lowly, but his friends were too perceptive. He grabbed a drink from a passing servant, and his friends did the same. Alex threw back his wine, but Langdon and Ellingsworth sipped at theirs.

Ellingsworth continued, "It was her. The blonde. She had to have been at Cheltenham, too. You weren't yourself when you returned. Shoulder had healed but you'd been wounded another way. Took months before you came out of that cloud—and when you did, you started looking for a bride. Lady Emmeline. A girl to fill the gap left by the Cheltenham blonde."

"Enough of your fancies," Alex muttered, but there was no denying how close his friends were to the truth.

He tipped his glass back for more wine, but it was empty. Moodily, he set it on another passing servant's tray.

"Oh ho," Langdon crowed. "A crack in the ducal defenses."

Alex scowled, glancing away.

Langdon and Ellingsworth shared another look, this one fraught with unspoken words.

"Let Ellingsworth and me take you somewhere else," Langdon urged. "There's a fine tavern in Leicester Square that hosts knife-throwing tournaments. Plenty of pretty wenches to turn a man's head, too."

"No," Alex said at once. "I'm in no humor for wenches or knives or anything else." He craned his neck, looking once more for Cassandra.

A thrill of panic juddered along his spine. Had she disappeared again? No—she was by one of the windows, smiling and talking with a gentleman and two ladies. The vise of his fear loosened. He took an instinctive step toward her.

"Don't blame you," Langdon said, keeping pace beside him. "She's a striking woman. Got a queenly aura about her."

Alex wheeled to face Langdon. "She's not to be leered at."

Langdon's brow raised as he held up his hands in surrender. "Not a glance. Not a peek in her direction."

"Why don't you go to her?" Ellingsworth asked quietly.

Alex felt his jaw harden. "It would jeopardize her employment here."

"She *works* here?" Langdon exclaimed.

In response, Alex glared at his friend. He knew he was being churlish to Langdon and Ellingsworth, but there wasn't a damn thing about this situation that he liked.

Ellingsworth placed his hand on Alex's shoulder. "Come on, old man. Let's get you home. Nothing good will come of lingering."

A swell of gratitude built in Alex's chest. His friends were impetuous and pleasure seeking. Ellingsworth continually made gibes and jests, and Langdon was always in search of gratification. Yet they clearly wanted to protect him from himself.

He nodded stiffly, then turned and headed toward the exit. It took every ounce of his self-possession to keep from looking back. Toward Cassandra.

From her vantage near the windows, Cassandra Blake watched the duke's wide shoulders as he left the gaming hell with his friends. His posture was just as upright and proud as ever—a duke down to his very marrow, despite the shock he'd had tonight.

She moved through the crowd, nodding, smiling, urging people to play. Yet her thoughts were leagues away.

Alex wasn't the only one who had been stunned by the night's developments. Coming back to London, she'd braced herself for the possibility that she might, just might, see him again. Excitement and dread had fought within her, like two cats scrapping in an alley.

Please let me see him, she'd think when falling asleep each dawn. *Please, let our paths never cross,* she'd think as she traversed London's streets.

Cassandra had heard through the usual gossip networks that he'd been seriously wooing a young woman of gentle birth. A strange, unexpected—and unwelcome—pain had lodged in her chest at that news. Then, yesterday, that lady had jilted him publicly.

God, how he must be hurting. She ached for him, even as she secretly rejoiced that the stupid chit hadn't possessed the good sense to make Alex her husband.

A duke had to marry, but there wasn't a single woman alive who was his equal.

She'd seen the worst of humanity, its greed and self-ishness and stupidity. She'd never known anyone who didn't demand reciprocity in some fashion. Even saints wanted their halos admired.

But Alex . . . he came by his integrity honestly. He never said what he didn't mean. He gave of himself because he wanted better for others, without expecting anything in return. It wasn't weakness—it was true gallantry.

That had been her undoing.

She shoved at the tempest of emotion battling within her. "There is a spot open at the hazard table, my lady," she told a flush-faced woman with graying hair. "I understand the dice favor women."

"Do they?" the lady trilled. She walked on somewhat-unsteady legs toward the gaming table.

Cassandra stifled a sigh. The tables were honest, but the players didn't always have the best sense. *Not my concern.* She couldn't stop people from being fools, and the more rash they became, the more her own profits would go up.

People came to gaming hells because they wanted to forget themselves. They dropped their dignities at the entrance in exchange for the chance of winning significantly.

Not Alex. He was a proud man. He'd never allow anyone to see him as anything less than flawless. He certainly didn't want anybody to observe him hurting. After Lady Emmeline's rebuff, Cassandra hadn't known if he would hide. Or make himself visible as a way to let the chatterers know he wouldn't be felled by a lady cutting him loose. Both were possibilities.

Cassandra had mentally braced herself, but that had done almost nothing to shield her from the storm of feelings—happiness, terror, pleasure, sorrow—that hit when she saw him again. When he'd spoken her name. When he'd looked at her as though she'd truly come back from the dead.

Or when he gazed at her as though he wanted to carry her off to the nearest bed and make love to her for days.

She now pressed a hand to her chest, willing her heart to slow. It was always an unruly creature and refused to calm, still pounding away even though Alex had gone. Her feet wanted to run after him. Her body ached for his touch.

Cassandra hadn't taken a lover in two years. Not since Alex. Maybe that had been foolish. Now there was nothing between her body and the memories of him, his dark hair mussed, the hard square line of his jaw tightening as he thrust into her. She wouldn't have believed such an honorable, principled man would make love to her like he was born for the task. As though his only desire was to give her unending pleasure.

No. Those memories served no purpose. They only put her at risk. But heaven and hell, how she ached for him now. Her knight, her lover.

"The Duke of Greyland?" Martin Hughes, alias Martin Hamish, asked at her shoulder.

She turned to him, and saw his upraised brow. Martin was curious. Fifteen years of knowing someone allowed you to recognize their every mood like a farmer knew the shifting weather.

He jerked his head toward the office, and she had no choice but to follow. They entered a darkened corridor off the main gaming hall, where Martin used a key latched to a watch fob to unlock one of the doors, then stepped inside. Part of Cassandra wanted to flee. She dreaded reviewing her history with Alex, but there wasn't a way around it.

Seating himself behind a large oak desk, Martin opened a case and pulled out a cheroot. As he lit the end, Cassandra breathed in the familiar scent of his tobacco blend. Instantly, she was back standing in the yard of one of countless coaching inns, with Martin securing passage to their next destination, their next job. Always, always, they kept moving, for staying in one place meant a greater chance of detection and capture.

Martin took several draws off the cheroot. He studied its smoldering end. Taking his time. Cassandra stood and waited, her hands clasped in front of her. Trying to hurry him would only make him irritated, and there wasn't anything to be gained by that.

She glanced at the safe standing behind his desk. It held the entirety of their profits, which would be paid back to their staff, investors, and, ultimately, themselves. The safe held her future, one that would free her from this life of dishonesty.

"Not a word from your lips about the Duke of Greyland," Martin said. His Scottish accent vanished the moment he crossed the threshold of his office.

"It was two years ago," she noted. "What went on between us didn't seem important to what you and I are doing now."

"And what *did* transpire between you and His Grace?" he asked pointedly.

"Nothing strange. It was in Cheltenham." She needed a distraction, so she ran her hand along the carved edge of the desk, feeling its curves and hollows with fingers that could still pick a pocket without the slightest trouble. "Played the Desperate Widow gambit."

"You take him?" Martin asked mildly.

"For five hundred pounds."

Martin grinned. "That's my lass."

She couldn't curb the bubble of pleasure from his praise. It didn't matter that they hadn't worked together in nearly a decade. He would always be the one she wanted to please.

"I got his blunt and disappeared. Hardly worth discussing." She wouldn't tell him about going to bed with the duke, and she surely wouldn't mention the fact that her body still hungered for Alex's touch. Or that her heart yearned for his understanding, his compassion. She would have given anything to see one of his rare smiles. That cautious flash of a grin spoke of how uncertain he was in allowing himself a moment's amusement. She imagined that someone, long ago, had told him that dukes didn't smile. Or laugh. Or take pleasure in anything.

He deserved to let himself feel happiness and a respite from the duties pressing in on him from every side. He was worthy of love.

But she wasn't the woman to give that to him. She never could be.

"Looks like he's still panting for you," Martin noted. "Especially after losing that gel to the cavalry officer."

Naturally, Martin knew everything about everyone. He was a library's worth of information.

She shrugged, even as her heart leapt.

"Why not keep him on the lead for a while?" her

mentor suggested. "Get a few hundred pounds more out of him."

"He's just smarting because that girl eloped," she said flatly.

"Perfect!" Martin exclaimed. "No better time to gull someone. Isn't that what I taught you?"

The rules for running confidence schemes were carved on Cassandra's heart the way others knew their Bible. But the Bible didn't put food in her belly or keep her in silk stockings. The Bible didn't care when she was a child, alone and desperate.

That desperation never left her. She'd probably go to her grave feeling its claws around her throat.

"I've been at the confidence game for sixteen years," she said, keeping her voice level. "You've taught me everything I know."

"Rule Number One?" he pressed. He liked to quiz her sometimes. As if he was still her teacher.

"Keep yourself clean," she recited. "No tangles, no mawkishness."

Acting very educational, he pressed, "Because why?"

Cassandra exhaled, slightly annoyed. She wasn't a fifteen-year-old girl in need of training. At thirty-one, she'd learned everything she needed, and had kept herself out of the law's hands. Not once had she been brought before a magistrate. That wasn't about to change as a result of Alex, regardless of how she felt about him.

"Because," she said, recalling Martin's earliest words

to her, "the most risky scheme a swindler can do is the one they pull on themselves."

"And caring about our marks is the most perilous thing that could happen to us," he finished, jabbing his cheroot toward her for emphasis. Then he smiled. "But you're a clever girl, cool and hard as diamonds. Get more blunt out of the duke, why don't you?"

"Didn't you tell me not to run two games at once?" she returned. "I can't do my job here and string him along at the same time." Her heart withered and her stomach soured at the thought of taking more money from Alex. She was done with that life. Done with hurting people. Hurting him.

She crossed her arms over her chest. "I don't see why we couldn't have set up this gaming hell in Edinburgh or Dublin. Safer that way. Less chance of either of us running into prior dupes."

"London's a proper banquet," Martin explained. "Best action in the world is here." He ran a hand down the front of his embroidered waistcoat, candlelight catching on the rings adorning his fingers. He could never resist a bit of flash. "And I'm nothing if not generous. I could've summoned any of a dozen swindlers to run this place with me. But I chose you."

"I'm grateful for it," she answered sincerely. Even lawful gaming hells made profit hand over fist. "But it's not like you to run a legitimate business."

"This will be my last scheme," Martin insisted for the hundredth time. "I wanted to end my career on the level. That way, there's no chance of being hauled in before the law. You'll see," he vowed. "Won't take but a blink and we'll be swimming in cash." He eyed the safe meaningfully.

Cassandra couldn't contain her restlessness any-more. She paced the room. "Just a month. You prom-ised. We'll run the hell for a month, and then decamp."

"A month is the perfect amount of time," Martin said smugly. "Keeping something around for a short while ensures the toffs will come running. They'll throw blunt at us, knowing we won't be here forever."

"All our debts paid," Cassandra added. "Including George Lacey's investments." Lacey was the sort of man wise people avoided, particularly when it came to money. She'd been set against making Lacey an inves-tor, but Martin had said it would be fine.

"Paid in full," Martin said with a munificent expres-sion. "Even to Lacey. And there will be enough left over to set us up for the rest of our lives. Think of it, my lass." He beamed. "No more schemes. No more swindles. Just high living for the rest of our days."

How wonderful would that be? Ever since Chelten-ham, she'd become so bloody tired. Of running from one place to another. Of using men's better feelings against them. Of always being someone other than her-self. She hadn't wanted to keep scamming them, but she'd had no choice, no way of earning her coin. When Martin had written her, it had been like a sign from the heavens. She could earn money through legitimate means, and use that to set herself up for the rest of her life.

Cassandra had no idea what she would do if she didn't need to deceive anyone anymore. But that open future didn't frighten her. She'd find something, somewhere, to do. Maybe she'd open a hat shop in a coastal town. Or she'd go to Italy and try to learn how to paint. It didn't matter. All that was important was that she'd be done with fleecing and scheming and pretending.

She stopped pacing and examined a framed print of a country estate. Oh, maybe, maybe, if she allowed herself to dream . . . Alex could be beside her as she ran that hat shop. Or he'd gaze over her shoulder as she painted a Roman ruin and kiss her neck, praising her work.

Such lovely dreams.

But that's all they were. He was a duke. She was a swindler. What would come of their association? Nothing good, to be sure. She could lose everything she'd worked so hard for. If he ever found out the truth . . . She would be brought to trial. Transportation was the usual fate for those guilty of fraud. Months at sea with hard labor to follow.

She looked down at her hands. They were smooth and youthful. But they'd grow hard and cracked and old—just like the rest of her—if she was sent to Australia. *If* she survived the journey. *If* she could endure the punishing labor. Many didn't.

Thank God Martin had trained her well. She'd stayed ahead of the law for a long time.

"Don't think I'm not grateful," she said. "I am. But I don't see or hear from you in seven years. Seven years on my own. Out of the depths of the void, your letter arrives, telling me to come to London. You *left me*."

Martin rolled his eyes. "Don't say you're still wounded over that. You survived. You even took a duke for five hundred pounds." He grinned.

She bit back a sigh. Martin would never admit that he was in the wrong, even as the noose slipped over his neck. And she couldn't stay angry with him. Not when he was the one who got her out of that wen of a Southwark flash house when she was a grimy girl picking pockets.

He showed her how good she could have it—mingling with toffs, drinking wine instead of gin, sleeping on feather mattresses instead of filthy hay. Showing her how to play the pretty widow instead of becoming just another tart walking the street.

Her loyalty would always be to Martin.

She did truly owe everything she had to him. She wouldn't be an ingrate and turn her back on him. Besides, if Martin's predictions for the gaming hell came true, she could leave behind her shadow life and finally step into the sun.

She wouldn't have to cheat good men like Alex anymore.

And she'd never see Alex again. A rift of pain opened up within her at the thought, but she ignored it, as she always did.

"Time to get back to the floor." She moved toward the door, then exited the office. Shouts and laughter and the smell of spilled wine greeted her in the corridor.

The evening had only just begun, and there was money to be gotten from the countless aristos cramming themselves into the gaming hell.

At least Alex wouldn't be one of them. Her heart clutched at the thought of seeing him once more. She couldn't be disinterested whenever she beheld his sternly handsome face, or when she looked into his dark eyes and saw concern and caring, *real* emotions. He was as honest as she was deceitful. Like all untrustworthy creatures, she longed for what she wasn't.

And her body warmed, grew soft and supple from just the feel of his hand in hers. Two years ago, he'd been a creative and talented lover, leaving his brand upon her. Had anything changed? Would they be as good together as they had been so long ago?

Did he still care for her, the way she ached for him?

She could never find out.

Chapter 3

❧

$\mathcal{A}$lex stared out his bedroom window, his hands braced on either side of the glass. The chamber over-looked the garden in the back, but at this late hour, there wasn't anything to see. Night's shadows thickly covered the hedges and trees. He strained to observe something, anything, to distract him—yet nothing emerged from the darkness.

Unlike his antecedents, Alex often suffered from insomnia. It was family lore that the first five Dukes of Greyland could sleep the undisturbed slumber of the just, even if someone decided to use cannons and trebuchets to rip down the walls of Greyland House—the dukedom's seat in Suffolk. Alex's own father slept through his predawn birth, despite the efforts of several large footmen trying to shout the old duke awake.

Alex's mind could never be so easy. It often kept him awake late into the night, no matter how physi-cally exhausted he might be. He frequently sat up until the small hours of the morning, thinking over how he might have spoken more eloquently in Parliament, or if he was taking the correct path by ordering a field flooded, or whether or not there was enough grain for his tenants.

Am I doing the right thing? The thought always stalked him, from his earliest years to now.

Tonight was no different. He'd left the gaming hell and, escorted by Ellingsworth and Langdon, gone immediately home. He dismissed his friends as soon as he'd arrived on his doorstep, then retreated to his study to pore over estate ledgers and review petitions. Anything to stop him from thinking of Cassandra. To keep away from her, even while he longed to claim her as his own.

He knew that was out of the question. Though Cassandra came from a noble background, his father would have looked askance at her impecunious circumstances. Alex had enough fortune for them both, "But," his father had said more than once, "a bride must bring wealth and influence with her. Neither can be neglected when selecting a wife."

Lady Emmeline had possessed both. She had been the perfect candidate for a wife.

When it came to potential duchesses, Cassandra had neither wealth nor influence. All the emotions he'd tried to bury after her desertion now roared to life. His chest actually ached. She could have given him what he'd feared would never be his—love. But he'd never have that now. He'd never have *her*.

When the clock chimed one, he'd sent his remaining staff to bed. Tried to do the same for himself, but to little avail. Lying in bed, staring up at the canopy, he wished for shackles to keep him bolted to his mattress.

Alex scowled now and pushed away from the window. He tugged on the bellpull, then threw on his clothing heedlessly. His legs urged action. As he dressed, his sleepy butler arrived, wearing a hastily donned robe.

"Your Grace?" Bowmore asked.

"Have my horse saddled," Alex answered in a clipped tone.

Bowmore was too well trained to ask where Alex planned on going at this hour. "Which one, Your Grace?"

He wanted speed, wildness. "Sirocco." Though the horse was a gelding, he'd never lost that spirit Alex needed right now.

The butler bowed and retreated silently. Alex finished dressing, shoving his feet into tall boots. He didn't bother with a hat. Whoever saw him on the streets at this hour cared less for decorum than he did at the moment.

He pounded down the front stairs and out the door to the street, where a groom waited for him, Sirocco dancing on the end of the lead. Without a word, Alex mounted the horse and took up the reins. He'd give the groom an extra day off to compensate for being awakened. A guinea would go to Bowmore, too.

But he'd worry about his servants later. Now he needed movement. He urged Sirocco into a trot, then a canter, finally a gallop, tearing through London's dark streets. Directions meant nothing. He had no purpose, his mind trying to empty itself of thoughts as his body moved in time with the horse.

But the thoughts wouldn't stop their churning.

Hell, he wished Cassandra had come to him when her cousin had cheated her out of her widow's portion. It would have been so very easy to bring in his own legal counsel and restore her lost fortune. If that had been unsuccessful, and she had refused any financial assistance, he could have readily found her employment with any of a dozen fine families looking for companions and chaperones for marriageable daughters or elderly aunts. He could have *done something*.

"Damn it," he growled to himself. "Do *not* go back."

Because he could do something now. He could get her out of that gaming hell, could try to recoup the money her cousin had cheated from her. Or gain her a position with a good aristocratic family. If he, the damned Duke of damned Greyland, gave her a reference, she would have no trouble finding honorable employment.

The night was cool, and his breath showed in puffs as he rode. If it were a more decent time, he'd go to his fencing or pugilism academies and work through the frustration pulsing through him. But neither were open for several more hours.

Cassandra would refuse any offer of help he extended to her. Her pride matched his own. Much of her life remained a mystery to him, but he knew that much. At Cheltenham, she hadn't let him pay for her meals whenever they had dined together, though that meant she ate plain boiled meat and broth. Unable to feast on rich roasts and succulent vegetables while she nibbled slowly on her miser's meal, Alex ate boiled meat and broth, too. Then he had consumed a second dinner in his room, because his appetite had barely been sated by such scanty food.

If he'd been in her position—friendless, penniless— he, too, would reject anything that implied a handout.

Yet she was a woman, and therefore at the mercy of a brutal and indifferent world. She wasn't a girl, either, but an adult woman, and one of gentle birth. There were so few options available to her.

He had to help her. Even if they did not rekindle their affair, it was his *duty* to make certain she was safe and cared for. He couldn't let her traverse this callous world without offering her some kind of security. Being a duke meant he had to see to the welfare of those less fortunate. Cassandra didn't need to demean herself by inveigling wealthy gamblers at the gaming hell. Surely anyone deserved better than that.

And if his heart beat faster at the thought of her, if a thrill of anticipation crackled through his body knowing that he would see her again, hear her voice and watch the candlelight shine upon her hair and skin—if any of that happened, he would suppress those feelings like turning down a lamp's flame. Their time together had passed. He wouldn't mourn what was never to be.

He pulled his horse up sharply. The animal wheeled in circles as Alex stared at the front of the gaming hell.

She was in there. And he'd brought himself to her door without thinking.

"Hellfire," he bit out.

A powerful tug in the center of his chest commanded him to dismount, stride into the gaming hell, and carry Cassandra out.

Instead, he urged his horse into a gallop, taking him away.

From her.

THE gaming hell's doors opened tonight, as they always did, at eight o'clock. The first surge of genteel gamblers flooded into the main area in a wave of diamonds, tobacco, and glassy-eyed excitement.

Cassandra stood in the middle of the hall, wearing a modest gray silk dress and her most welcoming smile. She murmured, "Welcome, my lord, my lady," over and over again. "The hazard table is looking very promising this evening. Do help yourself to our excellent wine. Lovely necklace, my lady."

She wasn't used to playing the shill this way. Her swindles were usually more complex, involving at least a week of planning and planting seeds to gain the desired outcome—namely, a nobleman giving her a heap of money for various reasons, and then her disappearance.

The oddest aspect of Martin's gaming hell was its legitimacy. None of the dice at hazard were weighted. The cards for faro and *vingt-et-un* were unmarked. The dealers had been instructed to work with absolute honesty. Very likely, this gaming hell was the most trustworthy establishment of its kind within fifty miles.

Everything had to be on the level, or else she would walk. That had been her most important condition when accepting Martin's proposition. To her surprise, he'd readily agreed.

Her taste for the swindling life had soured after Alex. She'd gotten by these past two years running small schemes on dishonest men, men who wanted to cheat the system. Ambition and greed never waned. She could always rely on those darker hungers to put food on her plate and a roof over her head.

Alex had never been one of those men. She'd assessed him at dinner one night, in the grand dining hall. He'd been dining alone. A few discreet inquiries had revealed that he was a duke, one of the wealthiest and most influential in the country. She'd been struck by his good looks—surely rich, well-bred men didn't have such angled jawlines or shoulders that could fill a doorway. The way he held himself revealed a lifetime of horsemanship and fencing, as well as lessons in dancing and decorum.

Men with strong morality were not drawn to people

who bent the rules. She'd seen that about him right away. And so she'd formulated her strategy. Instead of playing the beseeching, helpless female, Cassandra had tailored her role to match his pride with her own. She'd forced herself to eat the most pallid, cheap food with the air of a deposed monarch. She'd avoided nearly everyone's company, making sure he saw her taking solitary walks with an aura of pained dignity.

Her plan had worked. He'd been drawn to the strong, resilient woman she had pretended to be.

"Will you blow on my dice for luck?"

With a polite, mildly reproving smile, Cassandra turned to a young buck. He grinned at her as he held out a handful of ivory cubes.

"I fear that if I do," she said, "the same request will resound from every corner of this establishment, and I'll have no breath left for myself." She continued to smile. "Turning blue would hardly be attractive, don't you agree?"

"You would be lovely no matter your hue," he answered with an attempt at gallantry. "You would start a fashion for maidens to paint their own cheeks blue."

"And you are keeping the table waiting, my lord." She said this gently, nodding toward the other hazard players who observed the buck's flirtatious efforts with annoyance.

With a carefree laugh, her would-be wooer returned to the hazard table.

Cassandra silently exhaled. There had been a time in

her life when she would've relished wrapping that lad around her finger, amusing herself with seeing just how much she could manipulate him. She could praise his signet ring and touch his hand. He'd be captivated by the brief contact and stammer out some compliment, which she'd blushingly disavow. It would be a simple matter to draw him further along, flattering his needy self-image with a slight hint of her own superiority—a powerful lure for young men with too much money and not enough purpose.

But she wouldn't do that.

Her weariness of the game had to be because of her age. The things that excited and interested her at twenty—including controlling a rich young man—didn't have the same appeal anymore. She didn't have a girl's excitement about the possibilities of the world. But then, she'd never had that luxury.

What would it be like, to spend an evening not worrying about her next meal? Not agonizing about how long she could safely call someplace home?

And if she was spinning dreams . . . What if she had someone of her own, who knew precisely the kind of woman she was? And accepted her anyway?

A dark-haired, brown-eyed man with a hawkish nose and unshakable integrity . . . ?

The need for such a man was so powerful that it was like a second heartbeat. Wanting him was a dream, a foolish fantasy she couldn't dismiss as a girlish infatuation. He made her feel safe, cared for, respected. No one had ever given her as much.

And no one would again.

Yet, as if she'd conjured him from wishing, Alex appeared at one end of the main hall, looking devastating in black evening dress, his hair slicked back, his cheeks freshly shaven. Her imagination must have fabricated this illusion of him. But no, the image of Alex looked right at her, causing her heart to jump. As he began walking toward her, she realized he was no illusion, but real. He stopped in front of her.

She swallowed hard as he gazed down at her with his unwavering dark stare. Had he been speaking to people? Somehow learning her secrets? Her mind hastily slapped together stories, excuses, explanations.

He gazed at her, and she could only look back, like a doe being spotted by a wolf.

But his eyes were warm as he gazed at her. "Cassandra," he murmured.

Her body heated in response to hearing him say her name in his low, gravelly voice. Her pulse stuttered, and that hot, bright gleam of happiness and hope cut through the darkness within her—just from having him near.

"Staying away is impossible," he went on. "Not when I know you're here."

Her heart leapt again, damn the stupid thing.

She glanced around. Martin was busy in the foyer,

greeting guests. He had to know that Alex was here, which meant he would try to urge her to gull him again.

What should she do? Send Alex away? That would be wisest.

Her fingers wove between his—thank God, he wore gloves tonight, so she wouldn't face the temptation of his skin against hers—and she led him toward the back of the main hall. She tried to quiet her thundering pulse, and almost physically shoved aside the hope and excitement swelling within her.

A set of doors opened out onto a small, secluded terrace. The heat lessened here, while intimacy increased. In the shelter of the darkness, Cassandra could pretend that she truly was a woman of quality, without a blight on her name, and that she could have a future with a man like Alex. Self-deception was chancy, however. She needed to remember that, especially with so little distance between her body and Alex's, and his scent of soap and sandalwood casting a cunning spell.

Having him near was too painful. She ached with the desire to be something she wasn't—a real lady of gentle birth, the kind of woman with whom he truly belonged. He thought she was, but she knew differently. If he ever felt anything for her, it was all an illusion, based upon her lies. What would he do if he knew she was only a fabrication? Would he forgive her and pull her close, promising to make everything all right? Or would he angrily push her away and walk off without a backward glance, leaving her to collect the fragments of her heart?

She knew the answer, and it made her hurt throb all the more. Better to head off that pain before it could take hold and ruin her.

Her only consolation was the end of her career as a swindler. Once the gaming hell closed shop, she would be free. Free to live as just a woman without pretense. It would be a solitary life, but she was alone already. The isolation couldn't be much worse than what she now experienced.

She turned, and her hands lightly rested on the stone balustrade. A neat enclosed garden slept behind the building.

"I cannot be out here long." She rubbed her hands against the stone to remind her of who she was and what she needed. "I'll lose my position if Mr. Hamish thinks I'm not attending to the other guests."

"It's for that reason I've come back," Alex said softly. "It doesn't need to be like this."

Her pulse kicked, and she couldn't stop herself from turning around to face him, leaving only a foot's distance between them. Cassandra had to tilt her head back to look into his eyes—unusual for her, given her height.

"And what do you propose?" she challenged. "There are not many honorable ways for a woman to earn her coin. I am a lady's companion, not a gentleman's."

Though it was dark on the terrace, she thought a

flush stained his cheeks. It was as close as she could come to saying the words *courtesan* or *mistress* in his company.

"Is that what you are suggesting?" she pressed.

"Cassandra," he said roughly, "I'd never insult you that way."

Of course he wouldn't. Alex was too much a gentleman to suggest anything so impolite. Yet she'd tasted the fires of his passion, felt him groan against the skin of her belly. He wasn't as cool or removed as he believed himself to be.

Yearning welled up. To break open the dam that held back his desire. See him wild with need, loosened from the role he had to play. To let herself be wild with him. To be truly herself with him.

Here. In this dark space where no one could see them.

Had she picked this spot on purpose? Was she guided by her own unknowing hand?

A dangerous game. There were times for risks, and times for sticking to what was known. Her mind had to be firmly turned to the running of the gaming hell and the goal of financial freedom. She couldn't let her needs or the demands of her heart dictate her direction. If she did, she may as well tie stones to her feet and walk into the Serpentine.

"I know you don't mean any insult," she murmured. "I'm not the first female to find herself in . . . dismal circumstances."

"They needn't be so dire." He clasped her hand between both of his. She wanted to tug herself free. She
wanted to sink into the comfort he believed he offered.
"I have the ear of England's best families. Say the word.
I'll find you a good, respectable position with any of
them. Girls in need of a chaperone, or dowagers who
require companions. Stay in England. Travel abroad.
See the world, now that we have peace. Anything you
want, Cassandra, and it's yours."

"And you can guarantee that?"

"You know I can."

His absolute certainty broke her heart. His longing
to be her savior was obvious, like a thick blanket that
warmed and suffocated. She had no doubt that he could
and would give her whatever she desired.

Not everything.

Damn, but hearts were fragile, easily wounded
things. They needed protecting. Armor. Yet if she let
someone slip past that armor, that meant the chance
of a terrible wound. One she might not survive. It was
hard enough, to endure having Alex so close, with his
desire to rescue her. But he didn't realize how impossible it was for him to play her savior.

She'd seen her own father waste away in the Marshalsea, more heartbroken over his wife's desertion than his
own debt-riddled circumstances. She'd watched countless men and women in London's dismal corners suffer
and fail at affairs of the heart. Why? Because they'd
put their faith, and love, in someone else.

The brokenhearted haunted Whitechapel and South-wark, the ghosts of the lovelorn and wretched.

Wisdom was a hard-won gift. She'd become wise at a very young age.

Send him away, her mind whispered. *Protect yourself.*

Never let him go, cried her heart.

But who would she listen to? Her heart or her brain?

Sadly, she knew the answer.

"I made a promise," she said at last. "Mr. Hamish is relying on me."

"He's using you," he answered bitingly. "He's thinking only of himself, not your honor. Not your welfare."

Part of her already understood this. Martin had been kind to her, but only as far as it benefitted himself. She couldn't fault him for his selfishness. Generosity for its own sake didn't exist, not in her experience. Though it did—with Alex. It was one of the reasons why she'd gone to his bed.

"I know," she replied. "But I gave him my word, and I am always true to my word."

A muscle flexed in Alex's jaw. She knew he didn't care for her response, even if some part of him respected her code of ethics.

"How long do you intend to work here?" he demanded.

A little bit of truth helped shore up a lie. "Mr. Hamish doesn't plan on keeping the hell open for more than a month. We've got thirteen days left, and then the operation closes. He intends to use his earnings to open a more-permanent establishment in Edinburgh."

"You'll follow him to Edinburgh?" He seemed to push these words out as if rubbing sand into an open wound.

She shook her head. "With my saved wages, I plan on going to a town somewhere up north and teaching deportment to mill owners' daughters."

"Every step is planned out." He released her hand and crossed his arms over his chest.

"Life is a chess game." She pursed her lips. "All moves are thought out well in advance, or else disaster follows. I made that mistake with my cousin, and it can't happen again."

He exhaled as he glanced away. "This . . . is intolerable. You must allow me to help you."

The duke was completely in her control. She could ask anything of him now, and he'd give it to her.

She imagined the luxurious apartments that could be hers, silk and satin and beauty everywhere she looked. Jewels for her ears and throat. Food cooked by her own French chef. Plenty of fine things to wear or look at. Every one of her youthful dreams brought to bear.

She didn't want any of that anymore. Where once her mouth might have watered with greed, now she tasted ashes.

"Must I?" She smiled.

He looked rueful. "Of course, you have to do what you think is right."

"Thank you."

A corner of his mouth turned up, the most she had ever seen him smile. What would it take to get him to grin, to laugh aloud?

She wouldn't know. She shouldn't know.

"I have to do *something* to assist you," he insisted.

Nodding toward the doors that led back into the building, she said, "Spend extravagantly."

"I am not given to extravagance," he said drily.

Oh, how she longed to flirt with him. To finger the diamond solitaire winking in his cravat and tell him that he wasn't always so restrained. To coax more smiles and laughter from him, those rare, intoxicating sounds. But why torment herself with what she couldn't have? That way lay pain and disappointment—two emotions she knew too well.

"Try," she urged him. "For me," she could not resist adding.

"How can I deny you?" he asked playfully.

"Or risk my wrath," she teased.

"Watch me tremble." He held up his rock-steady hand.

She pushed his hand away. "Mocking a lady is poor form, Your Grace."

"Very well," he allowed. "I'll go back inside."

Her heart squeezed tightly. This was it. The last time they would see each other. She thought she understood pain, but it kept surprising her with its depth, its tenacity.

"Before I do . . ." Alex continued, "forgive me, but I cannot stop myself."

"Forgive you for—?"

Before she could finish her sentence, he pulled her into his arms and kissed her.

Chapter 4

Cassandra couldn't move. Her thoughts halted in place, too. For a moment, she could only stand frozen with shock as Alex kissed her. The sane part of her mind fizzled like water on a candle, until it burned away. Because her body knew just what to do, and what it wanted. Need and hope and happiness swelled within her, until she felt she would burst with the press of emotions.

It had been so long. Too long.

He kissed her with the hunger of a man long denied. She echoed his need with her own, their mouths hot and open and searching.

She pressed close to the unyielding span of his body, curving into him, finding all the places where they fit. Her fingers wove through the thick silk of his hair, angling his head to give her better entry to his demanding, velvety lips. He made a low, animal sound as she deepened the kiss, his hands fitting to her waist and urging her closer still. No more decorous duke.

He was a man letting his carnal self go free, a self that demanded to be known.

This is a mistake. A bloody mistake. It opened the dam of her own wants and desires. She wanted him, in every way—his soul, his body. His proud, honorable heart. She wanted him so much it made her eyes burn. So much that she wanted to say to hell with the gambling and Martin and money and the promise of a secure future, to simply sink into the storm of passion that couldn't be held back or refused.

They continued to kiss, even as he walked her back into the deeper darkness of the balcony. She followed his lead.

Dreams long denied swirled to the surface. He could carry her away, and they would be together, fully together in every way. Her past would mean nothing. The future didn't matter. They would revel in the now.

Yet Alex was a complication she couldn't allow. Everything he made her feel threw obstacles in her path.

She couldn't make herself break away. She kissed him hotly, giving in to desire and fantasy. *Just this once, let me have what I truly want.*

He was the one to pull back, his chest heaving, his gaze sharp and fierce. Slowly, his hands slid away from her waist, leaving her aching with need.

She lowered her hands from where they cupped his head. But she didn't move to put a safe distance between them. She stayed where she was, the air thick with hunger, the scent of him all around her.

He opened his mouth to speak.

She interrupted. "Is this the part where you apologize for insulting me like that?" Her voice sounded breathless. "Because if you do, I may truly slap you."

"Gentlemen don't kiss ladies without express permission." His own voice was a dark rumble, going against the politeness of his words. "I behaved like a rogue."

The word *ladies* almost made her laugh. She was no lady—but he didn't know that. And she preferred his rogue's kiss instead of the well-mannered, bloodless kiss from a gentleman.

"Then we're both scoundrels," she said, continuing to fight for breath. She sounded much calmer than she felt. Her mind and her body shouted for more. More of him. More of the dream he offered.

She tried to take a step back, but had nowhere to go, the balustrade pressing into her spine.

"Never say such a thing about yourself," he growled.

"Let's both accept responsibility," she said with more confidence than she had, "and agree that it will never occur again." If it did, what came next would be certain. She'd throw herself into his bed and never want to leave. And sooner or later, the truth about who she truly was would surface. He would learn that she was no widow, there was no villainous cousin, that she was nothing she'd claimed to be. It would be a complete disaster. And the heartbreak that would surely follow would devastate her.

His jaw flexed, as it always did when he was angry. Yet she knew his anger was entirely for himself. No matter what she said to him, or how she had reacted to his kiss, he'd still believe that he'd behaved like a beast, in a way utterly unbecoming to a duke.

The sudden desire to muss his hair and tear open his clothes grabbed her. She wanted to see him completely naked, watch him lose his treasured self-control. He'd come very close when they'd had their one night together. He'd pinned her hands to the bed—to her excitement—but had released her almost at once, as if afraid of crushing them both with his need. His touch had been careful, almost humble, verging on too gentle . . . though she'd seen fierce desire in his gaze and the flare of his nostrils. Even then, he'd kept part of himself back, as if afraid of hurting her with the full force of his hungers.

It had been just one night with him, yet she still felt every part of it, the memory never fading.

Now he seemed close to letting slip the tether that bound his urges. His words were barely more than growls, and his chest rose and fell with hard-drawn breath.

"But you need to leave," she concluded. "Now."

He didn't move. "I want to see you again."

She exhaled, and glanced away. Shards of invisible hurt stabbed themselves into her chest. "That would be ill-advised." Turning back to face him, she added, "Women on the margins don't have much reputation.

What little remains of mine would be obliterated by your continued presence. People would see us. They'd know we had been lovers. I'd be ruined."

It wasn't a fair thing to say, striking him just where he was most vulnerable—her respectability. But in the world where Mrs. Cassandra Blair was an upright, well-bred widow, she spoke the truth.

A shadow crossed his face, painful and fierce. But he quickly ruled his feelings and was in control of himself once more.

"You're right," he said. "We cannot see each other again."

How she hated hearing him say those words, even if they were the truth. Feeling like a rusted machine, she held out her hand. To her aggravation and fear, her fingers trembled. "Shall we part as friends?"

"I'm always your friend, Cassandra." His hand engulfed hers. Vulnerability flickered through her. He could crush her easily. "If you ever have need—please find me."

A hard ache formed in her throat, and she found herself blinking furiously.

"I will," she said, with no plan of ever doing so.

Instead of kissing her knuckles, he released her quickly, as if holding her too long would make him act wildly. He took a step back. Then another.

Her chest hurt. Everything hurt.

"Goodbye, Cassandra," he said lowly.

And then he was gone.

She whirled around to stare blindly at the dark garden. A jagged throb clenched in her chest, and her throat burned.

Swindling was the only life she knew. Though she'd been tempted to find more honest work in the two years since Cheltenham, she had no skill in any trade other than running schemes. The few times she'd applied to shops, the proprietors had stared at her with hard, cutting gazes, and demanded references. Once, to work at a bookshop, she had fabricated a letter of character, but it had all fallen apart when she'd been quizzed thoroughly on her knowledge of authors and their works. The shop owner sneered with contempt as she'd slunk out.

If she had the capital to start her own business, that humiliation wouldn't be repeated. No one would deride her or snicker.

But to make that dream happen, she couldn't go after Alex. She had to stay here.

She ground her knuckles into her closed eyes, forcing back anything that resembled a tear.

"Move forward," she whispered to herself. "Always forward."

But that didn't sound as good as it once had.

*H*is heart still thundering from his hard morning ride, Alex stood in the stables behind his home, with Sirocco tethered to an iron ring set in the stone wall. The horse's velvety sides glistened as Alex sponged cold water over its sweat-coated body. He'd already walked

Sirocco at a steady, slow pace for several minutes after they had finished their ride. The horse needed further cooling, however. And while the job might be more suited to one of the stable hands rather than the master of the house, Alex took some soothing comfort from the routine.

Anything was better than brooding and stewing over last night. Reliving the kiss again and again until he fairly throbbed with wanting. But he couldn't stop the bitter taste of Cassandra's definitive dismissal. Yet another woman showing him the door.

The sting of Lady Emmeline's rejection was nothing compared to what he experienced now. Sharp agony pierced him when he recalled the feel of Cassandra's lips against his, her body lithe and snug to his own. The bright intelligence and dignity in her gaze. She could coax a smile from him, too, when even his closest friends accused him of being overly somber, exceedingly dignified.

That gravity vanished whenever he was around Cassandra. He'd kissed her on the terrace of a gaming hell—hardly the actions of a gentleman.

He didn't miss his poise. He only wanted her. Wanted, and couldn't have.

He ran a wet, cold sponge along Sirocco's neck, over the horse's back and down its flanks. The animal snorted, dancing slightly, but it held itself mostly still, happy to be cooling off.

Alex needed the same service performed for him.

He'd had another restless night as his mind churned and his body steamed with thwarted hunger. A cold bath might suffice, snapping him out of his roiling turmoil. How was he to go on as normal, with her a short ride away? How could he keep his distance—especially knowing that in a brief time, she'd disappear again. He'd assured her that he wouldn't go near her, but as each minute apart from her ticked by, that task seemed more and more impossible. With Cassandra in London, he had no tolerance for his ducal duties, the mountains of papers to review, the men of consequence to see. Knowing that she was close by, he throbbed with impatience to be near her.

"Were I the scribbling sort," Ellingsworth drawled as he strolled up, "I would pen a burletta called *The Duke's Disguise,* about a nobleman who masquerades as a stable lad. I'm still trying to decide if it's a comedy or a tragedy. Someone should marry the horse before the final curtain." He leaned against the wall and folded his arms across his chest, his usual smirk firmly in place.

"Lady Marwood is ashen with fear of losing her place as London's most celebrated playwright," Alex answered without looking up from his task.

"She's married to a viscount, so I'm not overly concerned about her revenue stream being curtailed."

Alex stopped what he was doing and pulled out an engraved watch from his waistcoat. His discarded coat lay on a bale of hay in the corner, and he worked only in his shirtsleeves.

"This timepiece needs repairing," he noted. "It states the hour as being half past ten, yet here you are, awake."

Ellingsworth yawned hugely. "Am I, though?"

"That's always debatable." Slipping the watch back into his pocket, Alex resumed rinsing off his horse.

"I'm in desperate need of tea with a liberal amount of whiskey in it. Come with me to White's," Ellingsworth offered. "Let the servants finish your work here."

Alex shook his head. "I always complete what I start."

"Naturally." Ellingsworth rolled his eyes. "Ever the principled duke, never the scoundrel." He paused. "But you haven't *always* been principled, have you? For example, during your time in Cheltenham."

Alex stiffened. "You look like a man of gentle birth," he retorted, "when, in fact, you behave like a gossiping orange girl."

Ellingsworth took no offense. Instead, he stepped forward, careful to avoid ruining his boots in the puddles on the ground.

"There's a thunderous cast about you," he noted, "and evidence that you've ridden your poor horse like a demon. Since the gaming hell the other night, you've been more dour than usual. Hypothesis—you're pining for Madam Cheltenham."

"Her name's Mrs. Blair," Alex said through clenched teeth.

"Ah," Ellingsworth said with appreciation, "the fair

Mrs. Blair has wrought some kind of spell on you. She's got you dangling and jerking like a puppet at the end of its strings."

"She's no master manipulator." Alex wrung out the sponge over Sirocco, then tested the temperature of the water running off the animal's side. It was still slightly warm, so the beast needed further cooling.

"Greyland," Ellingsworth said soberly, "I can see you're troubled. Speaking of it might provide some relief."

He stared pointedly at his friend. There was no sense in prevaricating, not when Ellingsworth proved both perceptive and determined. He needed to speak of Cassandra to someone, and Ellingsworth was here, waiting for him to unburden himself. "What I say to you can go no further than this stable."

"I'm as silent as our equine friend here," Ellingsworth said with a grin, then he grew more serious. "Truly, Greyland, I'll say not a word to anyone. Not even Langdon, if you wish."

"I do," Alex said.

"Very well." Ellingsworth's brow creased with a rare display of concern for someone other than himself. "Are you in some kind of trouble? Is she making herself problematic? There isn't . . . a child?"

Cold alarm shot through him. "God, no." Though he wasn't entirely certain. There was always a possibility. But Cassandra would have told him, had their one night together produced a babe. She might be proud, but she wouldn't condemn a child to a life of poverty simply for the sake of her self-worth.

"She and I . . . became lovers," he finally managed. "In Cheltenham. We went to bed together, and the next morning, she'd vanished. Until I saw her the other night at the gaming hell, I'd heard nothing from her for two years."

Ellingsworth's brows climbed in surprise. "Who is she?"

"A gentleman's widow. Her husband's cousin cheated her out of her widow's portion. I . . ." He cleared his throat. "I tried to help, but to no avail. She has nothing and no one. She's orphaned, and her sodding cousin ran to the Continent." Simply stating these words aloud filled Alex with fury, that someone as decent and gentle as Cassandra would have been treated so abominably by a man who was supposed to help protect her.

"Thus the necessity of employment at the gaming hell," his friend deduced. "Not the most suitable work for a respectable woman. Surely she'd accept you as her protector."

"She isn't that kind of woman," Alex snapped.

Ellingsworth's mouth was wry. "There is no *that kind of woman,* Greyland. Morality is a fragile, illusory thing that men invent to keep women tractable."

Alex dipped his head in acknowledgment. "Suffice it to say, that path is not one she chooses to follow."

"And yet . . . ?" Ellingsworth prompted.

"And yet . . ." Alex took the bucket and strode toward

the pump in the courtyard. He pulled on the handle, and fresh, cold water poured from the spout. When the bucket was full, he brought it back to the horse and resumed his work.

"You went to her," Ellingsworth exclaimed.

"I kissed her," Alex admitted.

"Judging by the look on your face right now, it wasn't very good."

Alex opened his mouth to speak, but his friend cut him off.

Ellingsworth continued. "The kiss wasn't *very good*—it was a thing of unequaled magnificence."

Heat bloomed in Alex's face. He wanted to deny it, but then nodded in acquiescence. Everywhere he was hot, even thinking about what it was like to taste Cassandra again. The desire between them was fiercer than before.

Ellingsworth clapped his hands. "Langdon owes me a hundred pounds!" He grinned. "He was convinced you'd simply walk away from the woman, but I had faith your blood wasn't made of sleet."

A flare of outrage blossomed, that his friends would actually bet on him. But he should expect no less from two rich, idle men.

"Take your hundred pounds and damn the both of you," Alex muttered.

Ellingsworth raised his hands in a gesture of surrender, then lowered them. He peered closely at Alex. "There are no scratches on your face."

"What of it?" Alex demanded.

"She must have enjoyed the kiss."

"Was that another bet?"

Ellingsworth didn't bother looking affronted. "For a man who kissed a beautiful woman, and she took pleasure in it, you're terrifically choleric."

"She did enjoy it." He'd felt the way she'd opened for him, the tight press of her body against his, her frantic breath. He'd seen her passion-glazed eyes and swollen lips.

He struggled to push those images away. "But it matters not, because I can't have her."

His friend straightened. "Whyever not? You're a duke—the Prime Minister hangs on your word. Dozens of noblemen will leap like jackrabbits to obey your command. Anything you want is yours."

"That's why I can't have Mrs. Blair." Alex tested the water coming off the horse again and was satisfied to find it cool. He wanted to dump the rest of the bucket over his own head—or maybe throw it at Ellingsworth.

Instead, he grabbed some drying cloths from a peg and wiped down the animal. "A genteel widow with nothing to her name. No possessions. No family. She's at the mercy of the world." His jaw tightened. "All the power belongs to me. I could ruin her with my attention."

"What if," Ellingsworth posited, "your attention was more honorable. Take her as your mistress."

Alex straightened. His hands clenched into fists. "What?"

Ellingsworth appeared to warm to the idea. "You can remain lovers. Have new kisses of unequaled magnificence—and more. And you'd keep her generously supported. A house of her own, jewels, servants, a carriage. Women love carriages," he added confidingly. "More than jewels."

It took every measure of Alex's control to keep from punching his friend. "How the hell can you suggest that?"

Ellingsworth held out his hands as if even discussing the topic was ridiculous. "Lady Emmeline is an earl's daughter. Who is Mrs. Blair's father?"

Alex struggled to recall, but his mind came up with nothing but haze. "Can't remember. Some landed gentleman who must have been the son of a baronet. I'm not certain."

"Exactly my point," his friend said, aiming his finger at Alex. "She was working in a gaming hell, for the love of Christ. It's not as though she has outstanding prospects. Becoming your mistress would be an advancement for her."

Alex tossed down the cloth he held and strode over to Ellingsworth. He gripped his friend's neckcloth in a vise and gave him a shake.

"Don't ever insult Mrs. Blair again," Alex said through gritted teeth.

Ellingsworth's eyes were round with shock. "It's not an insult," he managed to gasp. "It's realism."

"She'd never sell herself that way."

His friend struggled to pry Alex's fingers from the silk around his neck. "Have a care. My valet will pillory me if I return to him with a destroyed neckcloth."

Alex released Ellingsworth with a shove. The younger man stumbled back before regaining his balance.

"Women have few ways of making their way in this awful world," Ellingsworth said, trying to smooth out the mass of wrinkles at his throat. "We don't let them use their brains, so the only resource they have is their bodies. It's a bloody shame, but it's the way of things."

"There are other ways to help her besides paying for her bed," Alex muttered.

"Like what?" Ellingsworth pressed. "The only other option you have is marriage, and that's an utter impossibility."

The word itself—*marriage*—struck Alex like cannon fire hitting a fortification. He steadied himself.

It was absurd. Impossible, as Ellingsworth said.

But was it . . . ?

Ellingsworth stared at him. "You can't possibly be thinking of taking Mrs. Blair as your *wife*."

Almost at once, Alex wanted to deny it. Yet the thought kept returning to him again and again like a bee revisiting a flower. What if he did marry Cassandra? She would have his protection, his *true* protection. She would be elevated in the eyes of Society and never want for anything again. No more work as a lady's companion, no more smoke-filled gaming hells. They would fall asleep together at night and rise together in the morning. And they would never have to be apart. They could be seen in public without scandal.

She could give him children. Perhaps even love. Alex and Cassandra would live out their lives, side by side.

He felt something strange and shining unfolding within him. Happiness. Genuine joy.

Hell, he thought. *I've gone wild.*

Ellingsworth gaped at him. "If you want to permanently tie your name to someone, her breeding has to be impeccable. Society expects nothing less." He shook his head. "Precisely the reason why I *won't* be taking a wife. I'm a third son. Nobody cares who I marry, no family name relies on me."

"But you can dole out advice to me like a coster-monger selling me a pear," Alex answered drily. "You can't even keep a mistress for more than a few months without losing interest in her."

His friend dismissed the idea with a sniff. "That signifies nothing. You, my dearest Greyland, are a different kettle of sheep."

"Don't you mean kettle of fish? Or sheep of a different fold?"

Ellingsworth shooed the thought aside. "What matters is that you're in a very different position from me. From the rest of the country. You're a pillar of England, et cetera. You have *obligations.*"

Alex's anger renewed itself in an acidic wave. "Why

shouldn't I marry someone I have feelings for, regard-less of who her father is? She has feelings for *me*." He drew himself up, heedless of the towels in his hand. "I'm a bloody duke. I can do whatever the hell I please."

Color drained from Ellingsworth's face. "So you're actually thinking of marrying the widow from Chel-tenham." He sputtered. "She brings nothing to the table. No alliances, no money. Nothing."

"She brings herself," Alex angrily corrected.

Everything within him blazed to life. The thought was absurd, preposterous. And yet marrying Cassandra felt right. They cared about each other. They had mutual desire and passion. And she was from a good family, even if they weren't listed in the Domesday Book. He'd have a greater chance of happiness with Cassandra than Lady Emmeline. And he would make it his life's work to ensure Cassandra was very, very happy.

There was a prospect of love. He had to seize that possibility while he could, for it might never come his way again.

To hell with what his father had decreed. The late duke couldn't rule Alex from beyond the grave. This was Alex's *life*.

"All my years," he ground out, "I've played by the rules. Done exactly what was expected of me. Acted the dutiful heir, listening to everything my father told me. What did I get for my troubles? Jilted by Lady Em-meline. But this time . . . this time, I'm going to go after what *I* desire."

"I . . . I . . ." Ellingsworth blinked. He fell silent. Then, "If this is what you truly want—"

"It is." He'd never felt more certain of anything.

"And what of Lady Emmeline?"

"She made her choice, and I make mine. This time, I will marry a woman I care for. Who cares for me. No more mutual toleration. I will have what I want."

"Then I support you." He stepped closer and clapped a hand on Alex's shoulder. "Felicitations, old man. You will make her quite happy."

"She still has to say yes," Alex said with a wry smile.

"How can she say anything else?"

He felt like a furnace ready to explode. But he would be calm. He would be in control. Tonight, he would go back to the gaming hell and ask Cassandra to be his wife.

Chapter 5

Cheers and the clink of glass rang out across the gaming hell. The sounds of revelry and joy were everywhere, echoing from the coved plaster ceiling, reverberating off the columns lining the walls. The night was early. Nobody had lost heavily—yet. The groans and curses would come as the hour grew later.

Cassandra welcomed those sounds of unhappiness. Every sound of pleasure or joy grated on her like handfuls of stones running up and down her spine. But a moan of dismay meant someone had lost to the house—increasing profits for her, Martin, and the other investors in the gaming hell. One month of business might not seem like much, but in a gambling-mad place such as London, with a genteel clientele, heaps of money could be made in a short time.

And she had no taste for cheerfulness tonight. She felt raw and angry from turning Alex away once again. Much as she wanted to hide in her private rooms upstairs, she couldn't. She was needed down here, wheedling and charming guests into playing longer and deeper. Their loss was her gain. She had to remind herself of that.

She stood near a faro table, a smile affixed to her face like a shield. "Have another go, my lady," she urged an older woman in yellow satin. "I'm certain that luck will be on your side this time. Don't you think so, my lord?"

The man, who was as much a lord as Cassandra, nodded vigorously. Younger than the lady by at least two decades, he was pomaded and polished, his grin as practiced as the caresses he gave to his female patron.

"Indeed, you cannot stop now, my love," he cried with an affected wave of his hand. "You promised me diamonds purchased with tonight's winnings."

"So I did." The dowager patted the man's face. "I cannot deny you anything, pet."

A wave of stifling anger passed through Cassandra. Everyone got what they wanted—but her. She'd deliberately pushed away the one man who'd been truly good to her, who cared about her. There was no comfort in the fact that she'd had no choice in refusing Alex, that she'd been acting in both of their best interests.

Keeping her smile tacked in place, she moved away from the couple. It was so hot in here tonight! So crowded. If only she could sneak off to the balcony to refresh herself with a little solitude and darkness.

She pressed a hand to her temple, willing a headache to subside. She glanced toward the doors leading to the terrace. Should she go outside? The cool air might do her a bit of good. But if she went to the balcony, reminders of Alex would stab her like needles. He already haunted her thoughts in the main hall. And when she walked on the street. And when she lay herself down for sleep every morning.

It didn't matter where she stood. She felt his lips against hers now. Tasted the passion she and Alex had created. Had he kissed like that in Cheltenham? The fire between them had only grown stronger these past two years. She wanted him so badly her body ached—and hated that she craved him so much.

She saw the warmth and concern in his dark eyes, too, in shadows and in sunlight. Always close by, but forever out of reach.

More sounds of gaiety punctured her thoughts. Looking at the nearby faro table, she saw the wild joy in the guests' eyes, the carefree air that verged on madness. To be on the other side of the table. To forget the burden of her many identities and the constant need to endure. If only she didn't have to cozen and swindle for her survival.

If she ran into any of her old marks—a distinct possibility—she would simply tell them what she'd said to Alex. None of them would pursue her with the same single-minded purpose, however. They were feckless men in search of the next amusement. So unlike Alex.

"A word, Mrs. Blair?"

Startled, Cassandra whirled to face Martin, standing behind her.

"Apologies, Mr. Hamish," she murmured. "I didn't see you there."

Martin gazed at her sadly. "Unlike you." He placed a hand on her back and gestured toward an alcove off the nearby hallway. "A word?"

Dread pooled in her stomach. Whatever it was he had to say, she was in no humor to hear it.

"Of course," she said brightly.

She permitted him to guide her toward the alcove, making certain that her face didn't betray her edgy wariness.

Once they were safely hidden in the nook, Martin faced her, his back to the room. He was a somewhat tall man, with a broad torso and she couldn't see past him, which made her slightly anxious. A full view of any room was good. She craved the sight of windows. Damn those early years with her father in the Marshalsea. It didn't take much for her to feel choked and uneasy.

Martin's eyes were concerned but alert. Despite their privacy, he didn't drop his Scottish accent. "I worry for you, my dear."

"There's no need for concern," she answered.

"You say that too quickly," he noted. Always a keen observer, that Martin. "Didn't even ask me what made me worried about you."

She shrugged warily.

"You're drifting through the place like a low-lying mist," Martin said.

"I've brought dozens of people to the tables tonight alone," she replied defensively.

Martin held up his hands. "Never suggested you weren't doing your job. But I'm a bloke whose known you since you were a Southwark urchin, picking pockets for coin and handkerchiefs. That smile of yours looks as counterfeit as Dusty John's forgeries, and your eyes just as dull as the coins he makes in his basement."

A wash of heat flooded Cassandra's cheeks. She should be more difficult to read, but then, as Martin had pointed out, they knew each other well. Too well, perhaps.

"Maybe it's regret that makes you so distant tonight," Martin speculated gently.

"I've got nothing to regret," she replied automatically. Only when the words left her mouth did she realize that wasn't entirely true. She wished she'd never selected Alex as a mark, and she wished she'd never come to London.

What was up and what was down? Left and right?

She'd find her bearings again, once she had her share of the profits from the hell. When she left London, she'd never look back. And let heartbreak be her constant companion.

Alex had no idea how easy his life was, or the comfort and security of his existence. A peculiar resentment bubbled up at the thought, but she forced it down. She'd never see him again, and he could go back to his sheltered life, leaving her to the peril of her own.

"No?" Martin pressed. "Not even a grain of remorse for letting the Duke of Greyland slip through your fingers?"

Her breath deserted her and an ache settled between her ribs.

At her silence, Martin continued, "He was a grand pigeon. Didn't you tell me you got five hundred pounds off him?" He whistled. "A juicy plum to take from a single mark. Don't you think," he continued, "you ought to go back to that tree once more? See if you can't pick some more plums?"

Cassandra forced breath into her lungs. "I'm done with the duke," she said gruffly. "Got what I wanted and moved on." She drew herself up. "Now's the time to think about what we're doing right now. To think about the future."

Her mentor looked disappointed. "Is this my bold Cassie? The same gel who swindled twenty pounds from a vicar?"

She didn't like remembering her early jobs, when she'd been brash and hungry. "I'm thinking about the now, Martin. The gaming hell. Everything else is a needless distraction. Including His Grace."

"You're a woman grown, and I have faith in your judgment," Martin said, "but I'd think again about Lord Greyland. The iron is hot, Cassie."

"Pigeons, trees, irons," she muttered. "He's a man." She crossed her arms over her chest. "Is that why you brought me here, to set me to chiseling the duke again?"

"I'd hate for any of us to lose an opportunity," he answered. "You never know what's around a corner. It's called a Wheel of Fortune because it turns."

She narrowed her eyes. "Something coming up I should know about?"

He smiled at her. "Just life, Cassie. It comes around and rips out our throats if we're not careful." Martin gently chucked her under the chin. Then ambled out of the alcove to take up his position as the master of this establishment.

Cassandra leaned back in the alcove, using the wall to support herself. *A little longer.* Just twelve days before they could shutter the club and divide the profits. Her new life awaited her. One free of burdens, freed from the past. She thanked the heavens now that they'd picked such a short duration for the club's existence. Six months or a year in London, having Alex close at hand but completely unreachable, was a torture she couldn't endure.

She had to get through this span of time. If it didn't go as planned . . . she'd lose everything.

With a rough exhalation, she straightened, preparing to go back on the floor.

Alex stepped into the alcove. Without touching her, he angled his body to corral her back into the niche.

Her sigh stopped, strangled in her throat.

The look on his face . . .

She took an instinctive step back, her hand flying up to shield herself. Which was stupid, because he was much stronger and bigger than her, and if he wanted to hurt her, there was very little she could do to stop him.

His jaw was iron hard, his cheeks dark, and his brows had drawn down into a chevron of anger. Pure, unfiltered rage was in his face. He was barely stopping himself from throttling her right there.

Her worst fear had come true. He'd heard her and Martin. Referring to Alex as one of her marks. The revelation that neither she nor Martin were who they'd claimed to be. He knew it all.

Horror, misery, and shame welled as the scab of her lies was scraped off. She wanted to crawl into a chasm and never emerge. But that wouldn't change the fact that he knew who she was, what she was. A creature beneath contempt.

Her heart splintered apart. He was beyond her, now and always.

There was only one way to play this, one way to protect herself—and him.

"So," she said frostily, drawing anger and iciness around her like a cloak, "now you know. Thank God."

SHOCK and fury ricocheted through Alex's body like a bullet but his injury was invisible, all-consuming. How was he still standing?

Thoughts and feelings crashed against each other, no end and no beginning. Only disbelief and rage, pushing against the seams of his body so that he nearly exploded with the force of it all.

He wanted to rip down the columns lining the chamber. He clenched his fists to keep from flipping over the gaming tables, sending cards and dice and people scattering everywhere like leaves shaken from a tree. His gaze burned into Cassandra, who stared back at him with an ashen face. The face he had hoped to see every day for the rest of his life.

He'd come intending to make her his forever. Instead, he found himself flung into the depths of a jagged hell.

Someone had finally loved him. But that wasn't true. None of it was. He was as unworthy of love as ever, and the one person he thought had cared for him had been pretending the whole time.

Pain pushed him from the inside out, shoving against his muscles, his bones, in an all-consuming agony. Sorrow and fury smashed against each other like craggy cliffs, crushing him between them.

"Trickery," he finally managed to say through clenched teeth. "All of it. Every word from your mouth." His gaze flicked to her lips, full and rosy even though they were set in a grim line. "Every glance from your eyes." He looked into those green-brown depths gleaming with wariness. She was afraid of him. Good. "Each touch and whisper. Nothing but deceit."

She didn't cry. Didn't rage and scream or faint. Instead, she simply looked back at him, with that damned cool façade of hers that had enticed him in the first place. Yet her jaw looked too firm, as if she was forcing herself to keep from shouting.

Was that also part of her game? Would she play this as a wronged woman? She'd already spun one tale; she might again. Would she try to convince him that everything he thought he heard had been misinterpreted? He couldn't pick the gold from the straw and was left wondering what was true and what was illusion.

"Survival," she said tightly. "That's all I try for."

He stared at her. She didn't even attempt to refute her duplicity. Merely accepted it as the truth. Damned brazen wench.

"You sleep soundly each night, knowing that you're a parasite?"

Her eyes blazed, though she held herself perfectly still. Her face changed. The cool wall of her dispassion dropped, and anger simmered to the surface. Her lips were cruel, her eyes glittering. "Words from a man who doesn't do a drop of work and lives on the lifeblood of his tenants." She looked briefly horrified at her words, as if she'd lashed out without thought, but then that shock was hidden behind more hostility.

He stared at her, shocked by her transformation. Gone was the proud but noble widow. In her place was a wrathful woman whose words cut like blades. Her accent changed, too. It was harder now, more of the streets.

Did he know her at all?

He pointed a finger at her. "Do. Not. Dare."

"You think to judge me, yet you know nothing of who I truly am."

"I should bring you before a fucking magistrate," he growled.

More color left her face at his curse. She pushed past him—possibly seeking safety in the crowds—and he gave chase. He caught up with her between the tables. The throng had grown thicker now. No one saw that he grabbed hold of her wrist in an iron grip.

"Get your hands off me," she said through clenched teeth.

"You're not going anywhere," he said lowly. "Not unless you want me to shout to these people that this hell is crooked. That would be pretty, wouldn't it? A duke's accusations of cheating. Who do you think they'd believe? A base-born nobody, or me?"

She swallowed as hectic color bloomed in her cheeks. "Come with me."

He didn't let go of her as they made their way toward a corridor. Her pulse hammered beneath his fingers. She tested a handle, and then opened the door to reveal a cramped storage room. Tables and chairs and cheap statuary were heaped in random piles, and a print of a fashionable couple hung on the wall, its glass cracked and the gilt on the frame peeling.

She stepped in and he followed, closing the door behind them. There were no candles or lamps, but light crept under the doorjamb and cast him and Cassandra as ghosts in a chaotic Purgatory.

"How many others?" he demanded. "How many men have you ensnared with your stories? With your body?"

She sucked in a sharp breath. "I could say the night is black and you wouldn't believe me," she shot back. "So why should I tell you anything now?"

Why wasn't she begging for his forgiveness? Her feral strength shocked him—and came as no surprise at all.

"Give me the truth," he snarled.

"This city is full of thousands of women scrambling to keep alive. Survival by any means—that's how we live. If that means picking a wealthy gent's pocket, we'll gladly do it."

"You get a man to take off his clothes before picking his pocket, is that the way of it?"

Something bright and feverish smoldered in her eyes. "I only take what I'm given freely." She firmed her jaw. "I am no thief. I might've been, when I was small, but Martin showed me there was another way. A better way. Where I was warm and fed and didn't fear the noose."

It was impossible to tear his gaze from her now. "Who are you, really?"

"Why should I tell you?"

He pointed toward the door and the gaming hell beyond it. "Because if you don't, I'll go out there and bellow that this place is marking cards and using weighted dice."

A long pause followed his threat. Then, "Cassandra Blake."

"There was no Mr. Blair."

"I've never been married," she admitted.

His head spun. He remembered so clearly the feel of

her in bed, the honey-sweet sighs that feathered against his skin, the warm, delicious yield of her body. The press of her lips against his. And the words, so many words. Avowals of those who had wronged her, of her own respectability, her *honor*.

Her dignity, her integrity, that beautiful, proud tilt of her chin—they were untrue, as false as the connection they'd shared. She'd looked at him and spoken to him with such candor, but that, too, was part of her trickery.

And the caring in her eyes, the gentleness of her touch, her understanding and compassion . . . that had been an illusion. One he'd fervently wanted to believe.

None of it was true. Everything he'd felt for her had been built upon lies. He thought he'd vomit.

"Goddamn you," he rasped. He realized then that he still held her wrist. She felt fragile in his grip, but that was false, too. Nothing could break her. He let go, shoving her away.

She looked resigned. "I've seen the worst of the world. Been called every name, too. Your curses mean nothing."

He took a step toward her. She backed up, putting protective distance between them. "You *swindled* me. And God knows how many others." Now he truly felt ill, thinking of himself as just one in an endless stream of gullible men beguiled by her. Who'd been entranced by her beauty, and lured into bed for her own gain. "You deceived for *profit*."

"To survive," she said.

She was so lovely, so wicked and beautiful. His chest ached as he looked at her. But her beauty was just a lure. He'd thought her the loveliest thing he'd ever beheld, but that loveliness was an illusion. It was like drinking from a crystalline, pure lake, only to discover it full of poison.

He'd never felt himself a bigger fool, and he hated that she had made him feel that way. He'd been nothing to her but a means to gain five hundred pounds. That was the price of his heart. Five hundred goddamn pounds.

Alex had reached for love, thinking he'd finally found someone who truly cared for him. Yet that had been a Trojan horse of deceit. Now the enemy had swarmed in, laying waste.

If he survived this devastation, he would build a fortification around his damaged heart and never let anyone past its barrier.

"Was nothing between us real?" he snarled.

She did not answer, her gaze flitting to the side.

"I really should call the constabulary," he said coldly, brutally. He wanted her afraid.

Her gaze flew back to him. "And have me arrested on what charge? You gave me money of your own volition. That's no crime."

He felt his cheeks burn as his blood turned to acid. "I am a *duke*. I can do whatever I damned well please."

She went very still, like a cornered doe.

He couldn't feel any victory.

"You'd never hurt anyone, Alex," she said after a long moment.

"It's *Lord Greyland* or *Your Grace*," he said bitingly.

"I know you, *Your Grace*."

"Like I knew you? What are my secrets, Cassandra?" He took another step toward her, aware of how big and menacing he could make himself appear. "How far will I go to see you pay for what you've done?"

"You won't do anything," she said, "especially to me." There may have been uncertainty in her voice—he couldn't tell.

"Think about that tonight," he said lowly. "Tonight and every night. What will I do? When will I strike? You'll never know. But it will be coming. Don't doubt that."

With a choked sound, she scurried past him, then out the door. It hung open as light and noise poured into the storage room.

He let her go, even as his father's voice crowed in his mind.

I told you, I told you.

A STEADY, pattering drizzle fell over the streets of London, making the roads muddy and slick. Everyone seemed irate and annoyed, shouldering their way through the city, growling or cursing at one another.

The gray gloom shrouding London perfectly suited Cassandra's mood. She'd been unable to sleep after the club had closed, lying in her narrow bed and staring at the ceiling of her room with dry, gritty eyes, her stomach churning with worry, until circling thoughts drove her to rise and dress. She left the gaming hell with no particular destination, only the thought that if she walked fast enough, she could outpace Alex's disgust, his anger, and his threats. Every face she saw was a mirror of his—hurt and anger in every stranger's eyes, everyone plotting her downfall.

She'd never before had to confront one of her marks after a swindle, not when that same mark *knew* they'd been taken. For all her experience in the game, she wasn't prepared for the hurt caused by Alex's wrath. It scoured her, hot and acid.

Whatever they had once shared, it was destroyed now, at her hands. She could only sift through the debris and mourn what would never be. The anger and reserve she'd wrapped around herself protectively during their confrontation were gone. All she had was regret and misery.

And fear, too. He'd given her a warning that he'd seek retribution somehow, some way. When it would come, she didn't know. But she didn't think a man like him lied, especially when it came to handing out threats. This was a side of him she'd never seen, and it terrified her. Anxiety was a continual jangle through her body, pulling her tight, ready to snap.

Despite the mud and slick cobblestones, her pace was swift. She was dressed too finely to run, though that's just what she wanted to do. Run and run until she no longer remembered the raw agony in Alex's expression, the suffering in his words, or his vows to hurt her. Speed away as if she could outpace her own pain.

Only when she reached the cheerful front of Catton's bakery and sweet shop did she realize where her feet had taken her.

After waiting in line, Cassandra bought herself three cinnamon and sugar pastries, wrapped up in a little blue parcel with brown satin ribbon. But she didn't want to wait. Instead, she found herself a table and devoured all three pastries, one after the other. She ignored the curious and somewhat scandalized looks she received from the other elegant customers as she licked crumbs from her fingers. To hell with them. To hell with everything and everyone but this moment.

Her anxious gut didn't care for her eating the pastries, though. A wave of nausea swam up from her belly.

After pushing herself up from her table, she left the shop. She needed to find her bed, and sleep. It would be another long night tonight, made longer if she didn't get some rest before the doors opened. Maybe that would help the uneasy sickness that overwhelmed her. But with Alex's look of shocked betrayal burning her mind and his words of retribution ringing in her head, she wasn't sure she'd be able to sleep.

She allowed herself one more indulgence and hailed a cab. Women of good reputation didn't ride in cabs alone, but who cared? Happiness was beyond her. All that was left were small, useless pleasures. After giving the driver the destination, she settled back against the threadbare squabs, her eyes closed against the watery ashen light of day.

Alex's words swam through her thoughts. They repeated themselves over and over.

Trickery. All of it. Every word from your mouth. Every glance from your eyes. Each touch and whisper. Nothing but deceit.

Was nothing between us real?

She told herself again and again that it was all part of the swindle. Every look she cast in his direction, every time he made her smile, or her heart beat faster—they were nothing but illusions she built to draw him deeper and ensure the final outcome. His thoughts and feelings shouldn't matter to her.

But they did. Goddamn everything, they did. She'd been foolish enough to let real feelings for him grow. Now she reaped the bitter harvest of her folly. Would this pain never cease?

She rubbed at her face, forcing back the tears that willfully gathered in her eyes. There was no room in her life for weeping and softness. That was the clear path to destruction.

How far will I go to see you pay for what you've done?

Fear covered her sorrow like clouds over a burning sun. He could have her arrested at any moment. Dragged before a magistrate and tried for any reason. She'd be transported.

Would he really do that to her?

His rage told her yes. Yes, he would.

The cab jolted to a halt. "Here we are, madam," the driver called down to her.

She shook herself to alertness, paid the man, then mounted the stairs to the gaming hell. Instead of knocking for one of the skeleton staff they employed for the day, she let herself in with a key.

Inside, all was silent readiness for the next wave of gamblers. The front hallway stood clean and quiet. A maid polished one of the mirrors hanging in the foyer. She glanced at Cassandra with wary surprise. It was rare for the masters of the house to be up and about at this hour.

Cassandra gave the girl a small smile. But instead of going up the stairs to her room and the distant possibility of sleep, she strode into the main hall.

The tables were set for the night's activities, with fresh cards and polished dice lined up and waiting. In contrast from the noise of the night, during the day, the hall was heavily silent and disturbingly empty. She glided between the tables, running her fingers along the wooden edges and over green baize.

These tables would buy her a new life. One where she'd never again witness naked suffering and betrayal in someone's eyes. Or feel this kind of agony.

Never see Alex again.

Her chest throbbed, and she pressed her hand between her ribs to stop the pain. But it didn't stop, only grew stronger and stronger until she bit back a gasp.

It didn't matter if she saw him again. He knew now who and what she was. He hated her. Hated her so much, he threatened her with God knew what kind of revenge.

Needing relief from her painful thoughts, she glanced around the hall. There was enough room between the tables to add a few more, and increase profits. More profits meant greater security against her ever having to run another swindle. She could hide from Alex, and from her heart.

She ought to tell Martin about her idea for more tables. He was likely asleep, but he'd be interested in hearing her proposal to increase their blunt.

Cassandra left the hall and climbed the stairs to the private apartments two floors up. Less care had been spent on furnishing this part of the building, with some carpeting coming up from the floor and faded wallpaper lining the hallways, but it was warm and clean and a far cry from the filthy flash houses she used to call her home in London.

Reaching the door to Martin's rooms, she knocked softly. No answer. She pressed her ear to the door, listening for Martin's snores. When they'd worked together, posing as father and daughter, she'd always been able to hear him snoring through the thin walls of countless coaching inns.

Today, however, there was no sound. She knocked again, louder this time, but after waiting a few more minutes with no word or sound, she slowly opened the door.

The sitting room was neat and tidy. No books or papers lay strewn on the table or floor. Maybe a maid had been through, since Martin was notorious for the messes he made of his personal space. Cassandra recalled forever cleaning up after him, which he considered a vulgar habit of hers.

The door to the bedroom stood open.

"Martin?" She took a tentative step. "You awake?"

No one answered her.

Hesitantly, she made her way into the bedroom. She prayed that Martin wasn't entertaining a female guest. But there was no sound coming from the bedchamber and Martin never mentioned any woman with whom he kept company.

Cassandra stood in the doorway and looked into the room. The bed was made, and the doors to the wardrobe stood open.

It was empty.

Hurrying inside, Cassandra went through drawers and cabinets. Not an article of clothing remained. Not his prized engraved shaving set, nor pairs of shoes, or neckcloths.

Prickly fear gripped the back of Cassandra's neck. A terrible, awful sense of doom smothered her, building upon the layer of fear she already felt from Alex's threats.

In a moment, she was back downstairs. The maid had finished polishing the mirror and was now working on dusting picture frames.

"Mr. Hamish," Cassandra said without prelude. "You seen him?"

"No, madam."

Cassandra turned and walked as quickly as she could toward Martin's office. She banged open the door, then staggered back.

The safe in the corner of the room. Its door gaped wide, revealing an empty interior.

"Bloody hell," Cassandra cried, covering her mouth with her hand. To keep from being sick.

Martin had taken all the money from the gaming hell and run.

He'd *betrayed* her.

Chapter 6

❧

A gasp sounded from behind Cassandra. She whirled around to find not just the maid, but a footman and one of the faro dealers standing in the hall, staring with horror at the empty safe.

John, the faro dealer, looked from Cassandra to the safe, and back again.

"Where's the money gone?" he demanded.

What could she tell him? That Martin had disappeared with everything?

"We're going to get paid, right?" the footman asked in alarm.

"Everything's fine," Cassandra answered, raising her hands like she was calming a pack of street dogs.

"You said this place was on the level," John accused sullenly.

"It is," Cassandra was quick to assure him. "You'll get paid, but we can't let anyone else—"

Before she'd finished speaking, both John and the

footman had dashed off. Most likely to tell the rest of the staff that there wasn't any cash in the safe, which meant the whole operation was ruined.

Cassandra exhaled and shut her eyes. Word was going to get out that Martin had run off with the money, likely reaching the ears of the swindlers and underworld figures that made up her investors—people she shuddered to cross.

"What should I do, ma'am?" the maid asked.

Cassandra opened her eyes. "Go home," she said tensely.

"But my wages . . . ?"

"I said you'll get them," Cassandra snapped.

"When? I got a Mam and sisters at home, and the youngest is sick and needs a sawbones, but what am I going to do if I don't get my wages?"

"Tonight," Cassandra heard herself say. "Come back tonight and I'll pay each and every one of you."

What had possessed her to say that? She'd have to find Martin in less than ten hours. If she didn't, she'd have nothing to give the staff. They'd tear her apart if she told them they worked all this time for free.

The maid looked uncertain, but nodded and untied her apron. She tiptoed into the office and set the apron on Martin's desk, then scurried out as if afraid Cassandra might bite her in two.

Alone, Cassandra leaned against the desk and rubbed her face. The room spun. She shook her head. There wasn't time to cave in or surrender to fear. Martin had to be found. That wouldn't happen if she stood here wringing her hands and bleating in panic.

In an instant, she was out the door and back on the street. She hailed another cab, heedless of the expense. Cost didn't matter with something this urgent.

A driver pulled his vehicle over. "Where to?"

"The King's Doxy in Soho." Her words were clipped as she climbed into the cab.

"Sure you want to go there on your own, madam?"

"Just drive." She closed the door and stared out the window, lost in thought, as the cab drove off. Her thoughts spun and her head ached. A hard, angry knot formed in her stomach. How could Martin do this to her. To *her*? She'd known him for most of her life. He'd been the one to show her the what's what of the world. How to speak like a toff, how to bat her eyelashes at men, how to appear like she was refusing money even as she tucked it into her reticule.

He'd been more of a father to her than poor, sad Michael Blake.

And he'd *deceived* her. Like she was nothing more than another pigeon. How *could* he?

Acid climbed up her throat. She swallowed bile and clenched her jaw.

Whatever his reasons, she'd get that damned cash back from him. She'd make him pay back everything, all that he owed her. Because he did owe her. She had been the one who'd gone with him to all the investors, smiled prettily at them and made promises about all the wealth the gaming hell would pull in during its limited engagement. No formal documents existed with her name on them—no swindler ever wrote down anything—but it was known across London and beyond that both she and Martin were guaranteeing the success of the gaming hell.

The investors and staff had trusted her. And she had trusted Martin.

She'd faced other hurts before. One couldn't grow up on the streets without confronting betrayal. But those were small insults and injuries that everyone experienced in life. This, however . . . this was another realm.

Was this what Alex felt? This bitter, choking sensation that made the whole world look gray and covered in smoke? How did he stand it? How did *she*?

The cab came to a stop. "Soho," the driver called down.

She got out and paid him, noting that he drove off quickly, not lingering to pick up a fare or asking if she wanted him to wait. The streets of Soho looked more like the streets where she grew up: narrow and crooked, full of people, filth, and desperation. She'd vowed never to come to these neighborhoods again, not when she'd tasted the soft and elegant life. Now she had no choice.

The sign for the King's Doxy showed a crude portrait of the actress Nell Gwynn, who'd been the mistress of King Charles II. Nell's painted red lips curved in a coarse smile of invitation. But the windows, grimy as they were, had all their glass, and no one slept in a puddle of their own sick on the front step.

Martin had a silly attachment to this place. He'd spoken of it happily, telling tales of his youth swindling drunks. For some reason, he didn't despise his early years, the way she did. He thought of them fondly, and often said, "It was easier then. Modest and simple. Before things grew complicated." Then he'd sigh and order another pint.

Someone inside laughed harshly. Then voices were raised. A glass broke.

No decent woman would go into a place such as this on her own.

Cassandra walked in.

She stopped just inside the doorway. Low, smoke-stained timbers crowded overhead, and the floor looked sticky. Tables were scattered here and there throughout the dim room. It was early enough in the day to host the most dedicated drunkards, men dozing next to their greasy pints or having rambling conversations with people who weren't listening. A thin, rib-ridged dog slept in front of the fire. The room stank of stale beer and sweat.

Cassandra fought a shudder of disgust. She knew this place—not the King's Doxy in particular, but hundreds of other grimy taprooms filled with hollow-eyed ghosts barely scratching out an existence in a cold world. Her vow not to return meant little when she needed to find Martin.

Walking farther into the pub, she ignored the few curious or outright rude stares that followed her. Everyone here thought she was a lady, with her fine ladies' clothes and years of aping a lady's behavior. She wasn't any better than the sullen barmaid slouching in the corner, picking dirt out from beneath her nails. A road split many times, and a person's life changed completely depending on uncountable choices they made over a lifetime. Cassandra had made decisions that brought her here, now.

She looked for the man who'd all but raised her. The man who'd betrayed her.

A wave of burning fury and fear spilled through her. She shoved it aside. Now was the time to be in control. She had only herself to rely upon.

A tall, stooped man in an apron stood behind the bar, mechanically wiping out pewter mugs with a dirty rag. He looked at her like she was a flea crawling up to the bar.

"Slumming today, madam?" he asked insolently.

She paid no heed to his rudeness. It couldn't touch her. "Does this place rent rooms?"

"It does."

"Did a man calling himself Hughes or Hamish or Halford or Hall take a room today?" She held out her hand to a little over her head. "Stands about this tall? Likes to wear loud waistcoats. About fifty years of age."

"Maybe," the barkeep said as though he couldn't be bothered to think. "He done you wrong?"

She barely held back a bitter laugh. "Is he here or not?" she pressed.

"You want to dance, slumming lady, or are we going to come right to it?" he answered. He held out his hand and waited.

She ought to have known he'd want a bribe. Nobody did anything for free in this kind of place. She couldn't even be angry about it. That's just how business went in the slums.

Pulling a coin from her reticule, she held it up but away from the barkeep's grasp. "I don't like dancing. Give me what I'm looking for."

The barkeep eyed the coin eagerly. Without taking his eyes from its dull shine, he said, "Nobody took a room today."

Shoving aside disappointment, she asked, "What about this week?"

"Just a young, poxy lad. And a sea captain, tan as a pair of boots with a big black beard. No one else."

Martin never affected disguises, sniffing that they were for actors.

Plummeting defeat threatened to drag her to the filthy floor. He wasn't here. This place was her best lead. Beyond it, she grasped at smoke.

She dropped the coin to the counter, and gripped the bar tightly to keep standing.

"Miss Blunt?"

Cassandra Blunt was one of her many aliases, the one she used when interacting with London's underworld. She turned with a wary look to behold a portly man with thinning hair coming into the tavern. His clothes were worn but of good quality, and he carried an ebony walking stick topped with a brass figure of a serpent's head.

"Mr. Lacey," she answered, forcing a bright smile.

Damn damn damn.

George Lacey leaned on the bar beside her. At once, a full, clean tankard of ale appeared next to his hand. He didn't waste time thanking the barkeep, but drank down his pint in a few gulps as if it was his due.

"Surprised to see you on this side of Town," Lacey said after belching softly.

"Business can take me many places," she answered. "You know how it is."

He chortled. "I run myself ragged jaunting from one corner of London to the next. Always some shopkeeper refusing to pay for protection, or someone reneging on a loan. Interest rates don't pay for themselves." He chuckled again.

Maybe he was too much of a gentleman to mention the whorehouses he owned in Whitechapel and Seven Dials.

"I need to get back to Piccadilly," Cassandra said.

"You've got time for a drink with one of your investors." It was a command, not a request.

Cassandra smiled thinly. She didn't want anything from this midden heap of a taproom, and she didn't want to spend another minute in Lacey's company.

Nobody in London was as well informed. Any and all news came to him almost as quickly as it happened.

"How fares the gaming hell?" he asked, then sipped at another ale. "Got a little over a week left before we shut the doors for good, yes?"

She silently exhaled. He didn't know about Martin running off with the money. Not yet.

"It's grand," she answered. "Can't keep the toffs out. They line up thick as flies outside, panting to get inside. Martin and me, we'll have your investment paid back in a trice. With interest."

"Of course." Lacey's smile cracked at the edges.

The barkeep banged a tankard in front of Cassandra, slamming it down so the foam sloshed over the side and onto the wooden surface of the bar. With an insolent look, he slouched away.

She picked up her drink and pretended to sip from it. She'd rather swallow water from the Thames than this bilge.

"How are your daughters?" she asked, straining for something to talk about. Nerves strung her tight. Martin was still somewhere with the money, and time was running out. She'd either have to pay the staff or else go into hiding.

Lacey shook his head. "Slatterns and whores, the lot of 'em."

"Ah," was the only response she could come up with.

A thin shadow appeared in the doorway. "Mr. Lacey!"

"Aye," he answered, turning toward the newcomer. It was a lad of about fourteen, ragged and alert in the way all street children were, as she'd been as a child.

The boy approached but looked warily at Cassandra. A spark of fear glowed at the base of her spine. She eyed the door. Could she make a break for it? How far would she get before someone caught up with her?

"Go ahead and state your business, Jem," Lacey declared. "I don't pay you to wipe up the spit from your gaping maw."

"Yes, sir." The lad leaned close to Lacey, cupping a hand over his mouth as he whispered in the older man's ear. Jem kept glancing at her as he spoke.

She could run. Run right now and never look back.

If she was cornered and caught, they'd cut her first. A swipe of a blade across her cheek. They always did that to the pretty girls.

She watched the look on Lacey's face. It went from mildly bemused to outraged in a heartbeat. He glared at her with a fury that could burn down Bethnal Green.

Cassandra's heart pounded. *No.*

She started to edge toward the door.

Lacey's hand shot out and grabbed her elbow. His grip was strong and cruel, tightening enough to bring a sting of tears to her eyes.

"You fucking slut," Lacey snarled.

"Please, Mr. Lacey—George—" she pleaded. "I didn't know. I had nothing to do with it."

"The devil's bollocks," spat Lacey. "Never trusted either of you. A pair of adders."

She felt the color leave her face. "I was looking for him. Ask the barman."

The barman in question shrugged. "She came in just before you. Searching for some bloke. I don't know who."

Cassandra pled, "I swear to you—"

"Shut it!" He gripped her tighter, his fingers digging into her flesh. "For all I know, you're going to meet that bastard in Glasgow and split the lot between you."

"No—"

"Listen careful and close, trollop." Spittle formed in the corners of Lacey's mouth, and his face was a vivid red. "You get me my goddamn money. You get it *now*, understand?"

"As soon as I find Martin, I swear I will. Pay you back with interest," she added.

"You fucking better," Lacey hissed. "It's my bloody business to hurt people who cross me. Don't think I won't on account of you being a female. I'm especially clever when it comes to hurting women."

She didn't doubt that.

"I'll get your money," she gasped, struggling against the pain.

"Try to run," he vowed lowly, "and you won't be able to show your face in any city in England. Got connections abroad, too. No place will be safe for you. Remember that."

"I will." Fear was white-hot, combining with the pain Lacey inflicted, nearly blinding her.

"Now get the hell out of here before I find some other way for you to pay me back."

He released her quickly, and she caught herself on the bar before falling to her knees. She stumbled outside, into the street, her breath coming hard and fast as the throbbing continued where Lacey had held her.

She ran down the street. But there was nowhere she could run. Lacey's reach was everywhere. He'd find her, no matter where she went.

What am I going to do?

Martin had to be somewhere. He couldn't have gone far, could he? Or maybe he was already halfway to Dover, and then onto Calais and the Continent.

If Lacey knew about Martin, then all of London understood what had happened. The entire city would turn its back on her. With nowhere to go, and no place to find shelter, she was alone.

Completely alone.

There was one person, however, who was trustworthy. One man knew who she truly was.

She just prayed he wouldn't throw her out into the street, as she deserved.

"Your Grace, I don't believe you've heard a word I've said."

Sitting at the desk in his study, Alex stared at the papers stacked before him. Numbers and words covered the sheets and folios, but to him they resembled nothing more than a child's illegible scrawl in the dirt, drawn with a twig.

"Perhaps we should adjourn for the day, Your Grace."

Alex's gaze swung up to the concerned yet bland expression of Greene, his man of business.

"Yes, what?" Alex asked distractedly.

Greene merely gave Alex a pale, soft smile. "We've been going over the latest reports from your Northumberland estate, Your Grace. But, forgive me if I am importunate, it seems as though your thoughts lie elsewhere today."

"Slept poorly last night," Alex muttered, rubbing at his eyes, though he didn't owe Greene an explanation. He didn't mention that, since Cassandra had exploded back into his life, he hadn't slept much at all. Every waking moment was spent either working, riding, or fencing as he fought to keep his angry, aching thoughts from her. The things she said. The things she'd done. When he did sleep, his dreams weren't the place of restful refuge. Last night, after learning of her betrayal, his dreams had him chasing her across a shadowy plain, always just out of his reach, her laughter trailing like ghosts. He was never certain in those shadowy reveries what he would do if he caught her. Alex didn't like any of his impulses.

That is what happens when you ignore my directives, his father intoned grimly in Alex's mind.

That beautiful goddamn liar had played him false in Cheltenham. To make matters worse, she'd done it to him again two years later. He'd been so ensnared by her lies, he'd been a hairsbreadth away from asking her to be his wife. How many men had she enticed into bed for the prospect of money?

She was no different from a strumpet. Except he'd been the idiot who believed she actually desired him. She'd spread her legs for his wealth.

At least with courtesans, he'd known precisely what it meant to sleep with them. It was a simple exchange of money for sex. But Cassandra had used sex as a tool to get what she wanted: five hundred pounds. Half a thousand pounds was the price of one night with her. Did she charge more for the privilege with other men, or was he the sodding lucky bastard who'd been taken for such a sum?

Damnation. He was a fool. Brutal pain sliced through him every time he thought of her face. Whenever he revisited their kiss, their lovemaking. The tender look in her eyes that he'd mistaken for love. Rage soon followed, thick and hot and viscous as molten rock, leveling everything in its path.

"Shall I have tea brought in, Your Grace?" Greene inquired politely. "Wine?"

"Coffee." Alex wasn't the sort of man to drink himself into oblivion. That was a choice for cowards.

Greene rose and went to the bellpull. When he

tugged on the cord, a liveried footman appeared moments later at the door. "Coffee and something to eat for His Grace," Greene told the servant. "I trust that is acceptable, Your Grace?" he asked, turning back to Alex.

"Fine," Alex answered with a preoccupied wave of his hand.

"Shall we conclude our business for today?"

He shook his head. He would not give Cassandra the victory of controlling him. She'd gotten five hundred pounds from him, but she wouldn't get anything more. The money was inconsequential in comparison to his vast holdings and wealth. It wasn't money he desired.

He wanted justice. Vengeance. Anything to take away this rage and hurt.

Not once last night had she said she was sorry for what she'd done. She'd been defiant the whole time, never groveling or asking for forgiveness. Those flashes of sadness or regret in her eyes had likely been more illusions.

On top of everything else, he deserved a bloody apology. He wanted to see her beg. Craved the sight of her humbled and repentant, pleading with him for absolution.

Which he wouldn't give her.

"We'll review the crop yield reports," he said to Greene, trying to corral his thoughts. "Then we can move on to the petitions for repairs."

"Of course, Your Grace."

Yet the moment Greene began talking of corn and

barley, Alex's mind snapped free of its tether and ventured into dangerous territory.

There had to be some means, a sense of conclusion or retribution or *anything* to ease the terrible ache and anger that threatened to tear him apart. The way things ended with her last night, nothing felt finished. All he had was the weeping furious wound of his pride and heart, with no physician or cure.

Alex forced himself to stare at Greene's moving lips, though his heart thudded with renewed fury just thinking of Cassandra.

He needed to shove thoughts of her from his mind and body. Ellingsworth and Langdon teased him mercilessly over his discipline and control. He called on that self-restraint now. Each day would grow easier and easier, until all memories of Cassandra faded like a painting pulled off the wall and left in the sun.

A tap sounded on the door. The footman who appeared looked apologetic.

"Forgive me for disturbing you, Your Grace," the young man said. "A woman is here and insists on seeing you."

"I'm not at home to visitors," Alex answered.

The footman reddened. "As I told her, Your Grace, but she was most insistent. She had no card, but she told me her name was Miss Blake."

"I don't know a—" Alex abruptly halted.

Good Christ, he meant Cassandra.

His first impulse was to have the footman throw her

out. Bodily, if need be. But a voice whispered at the back of his mind. *What could she want? Why would she come to me?*

He rose, and Greene immediately shot to his feet. "Where is she?"

"The Cameo Drawing Room, Your Grace."

"I'll see you tomorrow, Greene," he said to the waiting man.

"Of course, Your Grace." Greene gathered up the papers, tucking them into a large portfolio.

Alex left him there and strode quickly down the hallway to the drawing room. He caught himself rushing and deliberately slowed his steps. Damn. He should have kept Cassandra waiting. An hour, at least. He could go back to his study, but Greene was already packing up, and going anywhere else in his home would only smack of desperate time wasting.

After tugging on his waistcoat and adjusting the folds of his neckcloth, ensuring his most ducal appearance, Alex approached the Cameo Drawing Room with a leisurely pace. He paused for a moment to gaze at a portrait of his ancestor, the third Duke of Greyland. What would this grave-eyed man think of his descendant being swindled out of five hundred pounds by a common criminal? Taken to bed and robbed like a sailor with a thieving doxy? Would he be disgusted? Or laugh with derision?

A fresh wave of anger bloomed at the thought. Furious with her, and with himself, he turned from the portrait and headed for the drawing room doors. He pulled them open the way one pulled an arrow from one's body—swiftly and ruthlessly.

"The audacity you've got, coming to me now," he thundered.

Cassandra whirled to face him, caught in midstride. She'd been pacing. Her hair was untamed, coming loose from its pins, and her eyes were equally wild as she beheld him. She looked breathless, lost.

More of her tricks. He wouldn't be moved by them. He didn't give a bloody damn.

But . . . it was the first time that she truly looked less than controlled. She was stricken, her face pale and hands shaky. Alarm rose in a red-edged wave, with anger close at its heels.

"What the devil is going on?" he demanded.

"I . . ." She swallowed audibly. "I've got nowhere to go, no one to take me in."

He started at her sudden admission. "Seek the comfort of your friend, Hamish. If that's his name."

"It's Hughes," she choked out. "Martin Hughes. And I can't."

"Cheated him, too, did you?" he sneered. "Did you fuck him, too?"

She shook her head, but not before a look of disgust crossed her face. "He's gone." She strode to the window that faced the street and peered out from behind a curtain, as if keeping watch for someone or something. "Taken all the money from the gaming hell and disappeared."

For a moment, Alex could do nothing but absorb this information. Then he snapped back to reality. "Another swindle."

"Go back to the gaming hell and look for yourself if you don't believe me." She swung around to face him, looking positively feral. "He took his clothes, his shaving set, and every bloody penny from the hell. There's nothing to pay back the investors, to pay the staff. To pay *me*. Everything vanished with him."

Alex scowled. "Why come to me?" he demanded. "I'm not your friend."

"I know," she said bleakly. A flare of pain gleamed in her eyes, and she turned away. "I'm . . . hunted."

The word sparked a blaze of apprehension. "The hell does that mean?"

"Without the money, I'm either dead, or I'll wish I was dead." She paled. "They want my *blood*."

"Who does?"

"The staff, the investors. George Lacey—a man you don't want to make angry. I didn't want to go to him for any funding," she said quickly. "A bad reputation for taking his pound of flesh, that Lacey. But Martin said it would be all right. We couldn't fail. We'd be safe." She knocked her fist into her forehead. Hard. "God, why did I listen to him?"

"A pair of thieves and liars, the both of you," Alex

spat. "You'll find nothing here. No help." He opened the door. "Get out."

She took a step closer. "You're the only person in London I trust."

He stared at her, appalled. Secretly gratified. He shut the door.

In his silence, she rushed ahead. "There's not a thing I've done to merit your trust or forgiveness. Nothing at all. But if you turn your back on me . . ." She couldn't finish the sentence and clenched her jaw as if to hold back more words—or tears. "Without Martin and the money he took, I can't pay back the investors. I can't pay the staff. Lacey will find me, and he'll . . ." She squeezed her eyes shut and shuddered.

If she was playacting, she was doing a fine job of it. Visceral terror radiated from her, fear at what fate lay ahead of her.

He wouldn't be fooled again. "How does any of this concern me?"

"I sank three hundred pounds of my own money into the gaming hell," she said. "That was all I had in the world. Everything. I've got nothing to pay anyone."

He refused to allow himself to feel any pity for her. "Go find shelter in Southwark, or any of the hundreds of thieves' dens infecting the city."

She blinked hard. "No place is safe for me now. Nobody's going to stand against Lacey."

Alex walked quickly to the sideboard and poured a whiskey. Part of him thought to offer a drink to her, since it looked as though she could clearly use one. But she didn't deserve the kindness of a whiskey. The drink burned, but not nearly enough to erase the acid of his own wrath and shock.

"As you pointed out last night," he said tightly, "I'm a duke. Not the sort of criminal class you associate with. There's nothing I can do for you."

She drew a deep breath, as if readying herself for a difficult task. Finally, she spoke. "Help me find him."

He started in surprise. "What?"

Cassandra took several steps toward him. "Help me locate Martin," she said carefully, the way one might negotiate with an armed brigand. "I'll need to look in some . . . less savory places. But if I have you at my back, no one will try to hurt me. I'll be safer in the shadow of your title. Even in the underworld, dukes are respected. And once I—*we*—get hold of him, we'll get all the money back from him. I can repay our backers and staff. I'll get Lacey's fingers off my throat." She drew another breath. "Then . . . I'll pay you back."

Alex stared at her. "You'll *what*?"

Warming to her topic, she said quickly, "Five hundred pounds. That's what you gave me in Cheltenham. And I'll give you back every penny, every pound. With interest," she added. "We'll be even, then. You'll go on with your life and forget I ever existed."

"That's unlikely," he answered darkly.

She spread her hands. "Consider it a step in the right direction."

Alex raked his hands through his hair and pondered this. Personally, he had no use for the blunt. It was barely a fraction of his wealth. Yet recovering his five hundred pounds—plus interest—could offer some recompense for the deceit she'd practiced. Money could never suture the wound, but it was *something*. It had weight and meaning for her. He could control that. Control her.

He asked, "What of the staff at the gaming hell? And the investors? They'll need to be informed."

"Lacey knows and he'll tell the investors. As for the staff . . ." A sheepish look crossed her face. "I bolted as soon as I figured out what Martin had done. I didn't think they'd want or believe anything I said."

"Head back," he directed, "and pay them."

She raised her brows. "With what? If I cash everyone out, that's three hundred and fifty pounds." She patted her reticule. "Still empty."

He strode to his desk, opened a drawer, and pulled out a locked ebony box. Using a key he took from his waistcoat pocket, he opened the box. Stacks of currency filled the box. He counted out three hundred and fifty pounds and held it up so Cassandra could see it.

"This should cover it," he said.

"With this amount being added to the five hundred I already owe you," she noted.

"Of course."

He didn't want to notice that she trembled slightly as she gave a small nod, then held out her hand for the money. But he didn't step forward to give her the cash.

"This stays with me." He tucked the pound notes into an inside pocket in his coat. He put the box back in its secure location.

Her eyes widened. "What are you doing?"

He walked to the bellpull and tugged on it. Within moments, Bowmore appeared.

"My coat and hat," Alex said to the butler. "And have my carriage brought around."

"Yes, Your Grace," Bowmore answered.

"You may go now," Alex said.

When Alex turned back to Cassandra, she was gazing at him with a studious, contemplative look. "What?"

"Nothing," she said at once.

"Tell me," he demanded.

She looked reluctant to speak, but then she said softly, "Pull a cord, a man appears to do your bidding. A carriage to take you from one end of the city to the other instead of walking on patched secondhand shoes. I'm sure you could tell Bowmore you're hungry, and in ten minutes, you'd have a feast ready to be devoured."

He spoke bitingly. "I know acutely the privilege of my position."

"But do you know the misery of others' lives?" she asked.

"I won't apologize for being born into my life," he rumbled.

"And I won't apologize for trying to survive in mine," she answered.

"For someone without a single ally and in desperate

need of a friend," he replied, "you have thorny comportment."

She pressed her lips together tightly, her gaze on the floor. Then, she said softly, "I'm . . . sorry."

He waited for a glow of pleasure at hearing her apologize, or the lifting of some burden from his chest. No relief or gratification came.

"Words mean nothing," he said brusquely. "Only deeds."

"There's not a thing I can do that will ever make you trust me," she answered without a trace of self-pity. "Nothing that will make you hate me less—or keep you from taking your vengeance."

"You underestimated me once," he said softly. "And I misjudged you. You thought you could play me for a dupe, and I understood you to be a woman of honor. Neither of those mistakes will ever be made again."

She stared at him, her eyes huge in her face. She looked both brittle and strong, like a slim tree in a gale. But he knew that she would bend before she would break. "I believe you."

A tap sounded at the door. Bowmore appeared with a footman carrying Alex's caped greatcoat and hat. "Your carriage awaits, Your Grace."

The footman held Alex's coat as he slipped his arms into the sleeves. After donning his coat, Alex turned to Cassandra. She stood with her hands on her elbows as if cold. "You have a pelisse?"

"Just the clothes on my back. I left in a hurry," she

explained, but he heard the underlying meaning. She'd been afraid.

Her fear jabbed little needles of worry into his chest. And anger at himself, that he should be at all concerned whether or not she'd been frightened.

Dusk was falling, and with it came a soft rain. Were there any coats in the house he could lend her? Some old castoffs belonging to one of his sisters? The youngest had taken everything with her when she had married nine years ago.

Why should he be troubled if Cassandra was cold? The lying swindler could secure her own comfort.

"Are you really coming with me to pay the staff?" she asked suddenly.

"They have to house and feed themselves and their families, don't they?"

"That's . . . kind of you."

He bared his teeth in an approximation of a smile. "Kindness has nothing to do with it."

Chapter 7

❦

Silence weighed heavily in the carriage as they rode to the gaming hell. It would be stupid to try any small talk or chitter chatter with a man who held her life in his hands. *Bit of rain tonight. When are you planning on stringing me from the yardarm?*

Out of the corner of her eye, she watched Alex cautiously. Night was falling, and street lamps and storefronts traced the hard lines of his profile as he stared out the carriage window. His hands rested on the brass head of his walking stick planted between his feet. He took up space without trying. She shoved herself into the opposite corner of the carriage. Cassandra tried without success not to let their legs touch.

There was no way not to be aware of him. On every level. His forbidding presence was bigger than life.

Every one of her nerves was stretched tight as a fiddle string, ready to snap. On all sides, she was being pulled. Lacey and the investors, the staff of the gaming hell, her reputation in the underworld as a plain dealer. And Alex. Him most of all.

His anger was a living thing, all teeth and bristles. It crouched between them, snarling, terrifying. There was no one to blame for the beast's existence except herself. Her heart pitched low every time she glanced at him, seeing the distance between them that she had created.

And beyond his bitterness, there was also his vengeance. At some point in the future, he'd wreak his retribution against her. What would it be? When would it happen? She feared it. She wanted it to happen *now*, just to get it out of the way.

She rubbed at her neck, trying to push back the panic that threatened to choke her. She'd never had to confront an angry mob before. If she'd had her way, she never would.

This must be what thieves felt on their way to the gallows. She'd seen hangings before—they made for a good harvest when picking pockets, with everyone's attention turned toward the figures jerking and twisting on the end of a rope. They were supposed to be warnings, those executions, threats against those who broke the law. Death was their future. But that threat stopped no one. It was either steal or starve.

She was now heading to her own possible hanging. If the staff ripped her to shreds, she wouldn't be surprised. No good fate awaited her in any direction. Lacey, the staff, Alex. Doom on every side.

Even as a child on the streets of Southwark, her life hadn't been this hopeless.

She shivered. The cold forced its way through the fabric of her dress. No spencer or pelisse offered her protection from the chill.

Alex glanced over at her, opening his mouth as if to speak. She held herself in suspension, waiting for what cutting remark he might have for her. But he only shut his mouth and pointedly looked away. As if she wasn't worth the effort of words.

Which was worse? Sitting here in this carriage with him and his hatred, or the fate that awaited her at the gaming hell?

Finally, the coach pulled up outside the club. It was early enough that no crowd had formed outside, waiting to get in. Tonight, and every night after, all they'd find was disappointment.

Her heart thudded painfully. Someone shouted on the street, causing her to jump. But there was no turning back now.

A footman jumped down from the carriage and hurried to open the vehicle's door. The servant reached in to help her out. She slid her hand into his, but couldn't take the first step. Her body froze as her mind whirled.

Alex was there to pay the staff, which should have given her some relief from anxiety. But she wasn't used to facing angry mobs.

"Go on." Alex's voice reverberated from the dark.

"I'm trying." But she still couldn't move. "Not eager to put my neck on the block."

"No one's chopping off anyone's head," he answered. "Not while I'm around."

Her worries frayed to the breaking point. "Is that supposed to be a comfort?"

"It's the truth. Whether or not you're comforted by it isn't of concern to me."

"Ma'am?" the footman asked.

She jumped when something large and warm cupped her lower back. Alex's hand.

"Easy," he said quietly. "I'm right behind you."

"You want me to suffer."

"As long as I'm with you," he said steadily, "no one will hurt you. I give you my word."

"Am I safe from *you*?" she asked pointedly.

"I won't harm you physically while you're under my protection."

It wasn't a complete acknowledgment of her safety, but it was something. Her muscles relaxed, starting where he touched her. Despite every reason to the contrary, she believed him. If anyone could guarantee her security, it was Alex. The future was unknown, but for now, she was protected.

Taking a deep breath, she stepped down from the carriage. She smoothed her rumpled skirts as Alex climbed out of the coach. Compared to his clean, handsome elegance, she resembled a rag left out in the rain. No one would listen to a word from her mouth, not looking as she did. But maybe his presence—and money—might give her avowals some weight.

One thing about executions—it was key for the condemned to put on a brave face. That meant stepping up to the rope with shoulders back and chin held high. No fear. No blubbering or begging. Go gamely. Once, she'd seen a woman who had killed her cruel husband go to the gallows with the proud air of a queen. No tears streaked the condemned's cheeks as the rope was slipped over her head. That bravery had amazed a young Cassandra, never to be forgotten.

She straightened her own shoulders, summoning all the regal grace she could. *Don't show fear. They'll cut you down where you stand if you're afraid.*

And Alex was with her. That gave her a peculiar, irrational relief.

She mounted the steps, Alex right behind her. The door was unlocked, and she pushed it open. A crush of noise and angry voices met her. Half of the staff had crammed themselves into the foyer, lying in wait for her. A sea of enraged faces glared at her.

All of them demanded answers. Pay. Blood.

She held up her hands, asking for silence. "Where's everyone else?"

"In the main hall," one footman spat. "Bitch."

She ignored his comment, though Alex didn't leap into the fray to defend her.

"Come on, then." She pushed through the mob. They didn't want to get out of her way, so she shoved and jostled a path for herself. She glanced behind her. Everyone moved out of Alex's way, parting before him, quieting their complaints as he passed through.

Typical. A duke and a lowborn woman were different animals. One gave nothing to a scavenging rodent and respected the noble wolf.

At last, she made it to the main hall. More people gathered there, and a huge outraged cry went up the moment she appeared.

She climbed up onto one of the faro tables and motioned for quiet. A minute went by as the crowd settled into angry silence.

Alex stood at the rear of the crowd, his expression stony.

"You all deserve an explanation," she began. Furious murmurs of agreement rumbled from the mob. "As of tonight, the gaming hell is closed."

"We were promised a month of work!" shouted a serving woman. "It's been half that."

"What about my wife, my kids?" demanded a faro dealer. "Can't pay my landlady with broken promises."

"I know." Cassandra tried to speak above so many enraged voices. "I . . ." She struggled to speak. "I'm sorry." Two apologies in one night—a new record for her.

"Don't want any 'sorry,'" the first serving woman yelled. "I want my blunt."

"You'll get it," Cassandra said.

"How?" It was the maid from earlier in the day. "I

saw the safe. It's cleaned out. You're just feeding us more lies."

Cassandra scanned their faces. Hatred and hunger burned in each one of them. The mob was a hairsbreadth away from rending her limb from limb.

"I've got the money," a male voice announced calmly.

Everyone turned to look at Alex, who stared back with cool authority, as unruffled as a gentleman in a drawing room.

"Who are you?" one burly footman asked timidly.

"The Duke of Greyland," Alex replied icily. "And you'll address me as 'Your Grace.'"

The footman wilted. "Yes, Your Grace."

Alex strode to the foot of the table on which Cassandra stood. As she clambered down, he took her hand to assist her. It was a natural gesture of courtesy, done without thinking. Still, he kept her from falling. His grip was tight, however, almost bruising.

"Now be quiet," he told the staff once she was beside him. "Line up, and I will pay you your wages. Then you will all disperse."

A wave of silent disappointment moved through the deflating crowd. They had hoped for blood, and it was denied them. But money was just as important. The mob meekly obeyed, arranging themselves in a queue without a word of complaint. Of course, Alex could do that—command an unruly mob to do his bidding as easily as he breathed. This crowd that would murder her would scurry like insects to obey him.

"Tell me their names as they approach," Alex said to her, "and what they are owed."

For the next thirty minutes, they ran through the entire staff. Cassandra stated each person's name, their position within the establishment, and how much they were due. Alex paid each and every one. And gave them five pounds extra.

"God bless you, Your Grace," many said after glaring at her. Five pounds could house or feed a person or family for a long time.

He waved off their praise, focusing on the rest of the staff.

Most noblemen had stewards or land managers who dealt with financial matters. It was vulgar to handle actual money. Yet Alex didn't appear to care. He had a task to accomplish, and nothing seemed to stand in his way of getting it done. Would he be horrified if any of his highborn friends saw him now? Embarrassed?

At last they'd gone through everyone and the gaming hell stood empty, except for her and Alex.

She struggled to push the words from her lips. "Thank you."

He appeared unimpressed by his actions and her gratitude. "A month without pay must be a long time."

"I remember." As a child, she'd gone weeks at a time without a coin crossing her palm, which meant she had to steal everything she'd eaten, and slept in dirty alleyways.

He glanced at her, assessing. But she wouldn't tell him more about herself. He didn't ask, and she didn't owe him the story of her life. Besides, he already thought her the worst sort of criminal. Why prove him right?

"Are there a few pounds left over?" she asked.

"I'm not giving you any money," he answered.

"I can't sleep here—Lacey will come looking for me. But I'll need something to pay a boardinghouse."

He tugged on his coat, ensuring that his appearance was flawless—as usual. He checked his pocket watch as if time was his to master. "Go up and pack. I'm giving you fifteen minutes."

"Where am I going?"

"While we look for Martin," he replied levelly, with no fear of being contradicted, "you're staying with me."

CASSANDRA woke as she often did—not knowing where she was. It was a habit born from years of moving from place to place, never the same location for more than a week. This morning, that familiar fear lurched in her stomach. *Where am I now?*

An embroidered canopy curved overhead, little yellow flowers sprouting all over the fabric. Stretching out her hand, she felt soft, smooth sheets, and the gentle weight of a down blanket pressed lightly on her body.

Her surroundings were right grand. The bedroom was big enough to sleep half a dozen people, the walls were covered with paintings of pretty girls dressed like pretend shepherdesses, and thick patterned carpets covered the polished floors. A fire already burned in the hearth. The room smelled of beeswax and lavender, so clean and sweet it nearly brought tears to her eyes.

This was Alex's home. Was it shelter, or a cage? Either was a possibility.

Nothing was what she expected anymore.

Anger choked her throat when she thought again of her mentor's betrayal. She'd *trusted* Martin. He'd thrown out their long history together like so much slop from a chamber pot, uncaring who got hit with the splatter.

Cassandra rubbed her face, then sat up. A pair of slippers—not hers, since she didn't own any—waited beside the bed. She slid her feet into the slippers and was unsurprised when she discovered that they fit. They cushioned her feet perfectly, softness caressing her skin. They were of green satin, delicate little things never meant to touch the pavement outside. She'd never owned anything as fine as these tiny slippers.

Rising from bed, she tugged her patched robe on over her threadbare nightgown. It had never made sense to spend her money on good quality sleep things, since no one ever saw her in them. And, if by some chance a mark did see her in her nightclothes, it was explained easily enough by the widow Mrs. Blair's chancy financial situation. With the money she was going to get from the gaming hell investment, Cassandra had planned to get lovely cotton nightgowns, a silk robe, even replace her underthings with fancy little pieces.

But that would never happen. Not unless she found Martin.

She strode to the window and drew back the heavy velvet curtain. Lemony sunlight poured into the room. The bedroom overlooked a giant garden with hedges and trees and flowers—it could have served as a public park, but instead it belonged to one man, and was for his personal enjoyment.

This kind of overflowing luxury could never be commonplace to her. But to Alex it was everyday.

She padded in her borrowed slippers to the washstand and poured some water from a china pitcher into a matching bowl. No chips in either piece, no cracks or spots from age. She quickly bathed, splashing cool water on her face and using a cloth to clean under her arms and behind her ears and neck. Her minimal luggage had been unpacked at some unknown point. Last night, she and Alex had returned late from her trip to the gaming hell, bearing her few bags.

The housekeeper, Mrs. Neville, had escorted her to this bedroom. A bath had been waiting, its warm steam smelling of roses.

"I didn't ask for this," she'd said.

The older woman had smiled kindly. "His Grace ordered it for you. There's supper waiting, as well." She'd waved her hand toward a table at the side of the room, laden with covered dishes, and the air smelled unmistakably of roast pheasant and potatoes. Only then Cassandra had realized she hadn't eaten anything for a whole day. Had Alex known that? Did he know that the sight of a fresh bath brought a confusing wave of gratitude and anger?

Or was this his way of saying she was dirty, and that he didn't want to dine with her?

Everything was exquisite, and as she bathed, then ate, a protective bitterness rose up within her. She'd been denied these luxuries her whole life. They meant nothing to him. Enjoyment of her bath and food became impossible when presented with the monument of her privation and his privilege.

It was far easier to be angry than allow herself the full measure of grief over all that had been lost, over the man whose heart she'd destroyed, and the cost of her survival.

She'd fallen into bed, and plunged into a dreamless sleep.

The bath had been carted out at some point in the night. Same with her supper dishes. Unnerving, the way this house ran like one of those silent clockwork automatons she'd seen once at a traveling fair.

A gentle tap sounded at the door.

"Come in," she called.

The door opened and a young maid poked her head in. "Good morning, ma'am. Shall I help you dress?"

All of Cassandra's clothes fastened up the front because she'd never had the means to afford her own maid. It was difficult, too, to trust an abigail. It would only take one slipped word in the servants' hall to bring everything down.

This maid would most likely report back to the housekeeper about her behavior, her words. Mrs. Neville would surely tell Alex everything. Servants loved to gossip.

Lord knew what they were saying about her belowstairs.

Oh, God. She was so tired of second-and third-guessing herself.

"Not necessary," she answered. "Am I eating in my room again?"

"Breakfast is waiting downstairs. But if you wish, I can have a tray brought up."

Eating in her room would be the coward's way out. She hadn't survived to the ripe age of thirty-one without taking chances.

After dismissing the maid, she took as much care as she could with her appearance. After donning her best blue dress with a darker blue spencer, she put her hair into some kind of order. Pinning up the mass of it into a simple chignon showed off the curve of her neck to good advantage. She was at Alex's mercy in this house.

It never hurt to have some charm and prettiness in her arsenal.

One final glance in the mirror showed that, given the shakiness of her circumstances, she looked rather well. Her eyes were cool instead of showing the terror she felt. She gave her cheeks a light pinch, just to put some color there. Cosmetics were for the demimonde.

After asking a footman for directions, she found herself outside the dining room. Cautiously, she peered in through the doorway. Alex sat at the head of a giant table that resembled a galleon. He didn't seem to notice her as he went through a stack of letters and absently took a bite of toast.

The morning light turned his hair dark ebony and traced the forms of his handsome, somber face as he frowned over what he read. His fingers absently brushed at his lips.

Her heart scampered up her throat and her pulse gave a jolt. She pressed her hand to her chest, willing everything in her to calm. He couldn't know that her attraction to him still burned, or that her heart still ached whenever she looked at him, thinking of what they'd once shared and the mistrust between them now.

All of her power would be stripped away if he realized the effect he had on her.

The threshold to the dining room seemed vast as a desert. God, but it was hard being here, so close to him. Wearing her armor every moment of every day.

Showing weakness is the way to disaster. Or so

Martin had told her—if she could trust anything he'd ever said.

She'd never had trouble fleecing men out of money on the pretext of helping a poor widow—yet now that she needed true help, now that she needed to ask *him* for assistance, she felt tight and angry and sad all at the same time.

The sooner she got on with things, the sooner she could find that bastard Martin, get the money, and return to her plans of life after swindling.

Drawing back her shoulders, lifting her chin, she glided into the dining room as if she belonged there. But she'd never before been inside a ducal residence, and the whole place yawned over her like a huge cavern waiting to swallow her whole. It didn't cow her nearly as much as the master.

Alex stood when he saw her enter the room. Then he scowled, as if remembering that she didn't deserve the honor of him standing, and he seated himself quickly. He picked up his correspondence, deliberately not looking at her. "Morning," he said gruffly.

"Good morning," she answered, like she was some ordinary houseguest, for Christ's sake.

Everything was a powder keg, on the verge of exploding. Why had she come to him for help? Enmity sparked in the air.

Brazen it out. Showing fear only meant revealing weakness, and she couldn't have him exploit—or know—her weaknesses.

She moved to the sideboard, where a host of dishes waited. Eggs, streaky bacon, toast, cheese, fruit. A massive amount of food for just one man. The rest would likely go to the servants after Alex was finished with his meal. Cassandra took a modest amount of eggs and bacon.

She planned on sitting at the opposite end of the large table, but a footman stepped forward and pulled out a chair for her, right next to Alex. Cassandra tried to calm her racing heartbeat enough to eat. *Push away fear and sadness. Think of something else.*

By God, he was something fine to look upon. His nose might be considered a little large, but it suited the proportions of his face, and those full lips . . .

She shook herself. Now wasn't the time to think of kissing him. But he'd kissed her with such hunger, such desire. She'd be long cold in her grave before she forgot the way his lips felt against hers.

Or the heat they'd created together in bed. Or the way he'd once looked at her, as if she was something rare and wondrous.

He'd never look at her that way again.

She sighed.

Alex glanced at her, then waved over a footman. "Tea for Mrs.—I mean—Miss Blake."

She nodded her gratitude as the servant filled a cup and brought her a sugar bowl. Such a heap of small luxuries, almost hidden, like diamonds sewn on the inside of one's glove.

He eyed her plate, seemingly unhappy that she'd taken so little, but said nothing about it, thank God.

"I trust you slept well," he said as she ate.

"Well enough," she answered. "And yourself?" She chose her words with care, trying to be scrupulously polite.

His mouth curled into a wry smile. "Hardly ever."

She put a forkful of eggs into her mouth and had to keep from sighing. They were pillowy and light. Perfect. Next, she took a placid sip of tea. But she couldn't stop the exhale of pleasure curling up from the back of her throat at the taste. It was floral and rich, the best tea she'd ever had.

Opening her eyes, she caught him staring at her with naked hunger in his gaze. But the heat of their past connection disappeared into the murkiness of their current circumstance, and he looked away.

"I . . . Thank you again for helping yesterday," she said in the silence. "They would've drawn and quartered me otherwise."

"You'll pay me back," he answered.

She had no answer to that. "Last night went as well as I could've hoped," she went on after taking a bite of bacon. "Considering that half of London thinks I'm a liar and a thief."

"Part of that is true," he said pointedly.

She felt her lips twist. "I've never before been caught in a lie, so my record is spotless."

"Until yesterday," he noted.

"True."

They were quiet for a time, with her eating her luxurious but minimal breakfast, and him reading the newspaper.

It felt almost domestic. Except she sat on the blade of a sword, waiting to be cut in two.

"What are your plans for finding Hamish?" he asked, breaking the silence. "You said you'll want me for protection—I assume that means we'll be traveling to less savory venues in search of him."

"It's Hughes, not Hamish." She gave a bitter little laugh. "He's as Scottish as Ceylon tea."

"I don't know the world of the underground like you do," Alex said. "We should go to the constabulary. Or hire a Bow Street Runner."

"Most likely, I'd wind up in irons," she said. She went over her options. She was going to have to do something she truly didn't want to. "The place we need to go is also where I'm least welcome."

"The House of Lords?"

She decided it was best not to dignify that with a response. "It's a secret spot in London," she explained, "hidden and unknown to the rest of the city—a haunt just for people like me and Martin."

"Criminals."

"Swindlers," she corrected. "My hope is they'll give us what we're after."

"You won't have any cachet with them," he pointed out bluntly. "They won't talk."

"You don't know that," she returned.

He looked at her acidly. "If you've treated half the swindlers in London the way you've treated me, they'll want nothing to do with you."

"I know."

Cassandra stared down at her half-eaten breakfast, no longer hungry. What would it be like to have someone, anyone, believe in her? Impossible. There was only one person on her side, the same as it had been her whole life. She once thought she had a champion in Alex, but that had been based on a lie. Now that he knew the truth, he was at best a reluctant guardian. He would give her the protection of his body and his title. But his heart would never be hers.

Chapter 8

The carriage rolled through the city streets, heading—via Cassandra's directions—to one of London's less reputable corners. Alex had never been to this dusty, crowded section of the city. It was very clearly not his territory of club, parliament, or ballroom. He grew less certain of himself the deeper they traveled, which was an unusual feeling for him. Yet he made certain he outwardly kept his composure and air of self-assurance, if only for the sake of his admittedly battered pride.

Surely none of his other female acquaintances even knew of the place. Cassandra, however, told his driver precisely where to turn and what landmarks to use. It was obvious she knew this grim area well. It unnerved him to contemplate her at the mercy of London's most vicious elements. A desire to protect her and shelter her rose up whenever he thought about her vulnerability.

He had to push that desire away, or at least hide from her that he felt any softness toward her. Most likely, she'd take advantage of his compassion, and he couldn't allow that to happen again.

She gripped the seat cushion tightly with ungloved hands, her knuckles forming white circles. Staring out the window, her face was pale, her lips a tight line.

Cassandra was taking a risk coming here—that much was certain. It had to be a measure of how desperate she was to hazard showing her face in this thieves' neighborhood. Yet she didn't turn back. Was it fear of Alex's threat or her own valor that impelled her forward?

With her attention fixed on the alleys and byways outside the vehicle, he covertly studied her. Blonde and delicate of feature, she was still one of the loveliest people he'd ever seen. His chest squeezed hard whenever he looked at her, filling him with resentment and longing and sadness.

Other than her outward beauty, nothing about her was real. He would be damned if he let her see how much she affected him, even now, knowing who and what she was.

She'd faced the staff of the gaming hell with exceptional bravery, even knowing that they would be out for blood. What kind of courage did it take to live so uncertainly, existing from one swindle to the next?

He reminded himself that she used him, and men like him, to get what she wanted. But at the thought of countless other men smiling at her, pining for her, *loving* her, barbed jealousy rose up, choking him.

"What is this Martin Hughes to you?" he asked, breaking the silence. "A lover?"

She stared at him, aghast. "The thought of going to bed with Martin makes my gorge rise." She pressed a hand to her throat, as if forcing down bile. "He's the closest thing I've ever had to a father." Glancing to one side, as though looking into the past, she murmured, "My real father was thrown into the Marshalsea for debt. It was just him and me after my mother left. I couldn't have been more than three when she packed and hared off to God knows where." She said this flatly, accustomed to the betrayal.

Alex's hands tightened on his walking stick as he absorbed this, appalled that a woman could leave not only her husband, but her child, as well.

He had no memory of his mother tucking him in at night. Nor reading him stories. Those tasks, and countless others relating to Alex and his two younger sisters, had been left to nursemaids. As an adult, he saw his mother only at Christmas, when his sisters and their husbands and children also gathered in Norfolk. The Dowager Duchess offered her papery cheek for kisses and gave out oranges and books on etiquette, observing the antics of her grandchildren with a fond but faintly bemused eye.

She had never been very demonstrative. Yet, at the least, she had been there every day, a stately and beautiful presence at the other end of the dining table. He hadn't felt loved, but he had felt wanted.

"I was just a tyke," Cassandra went on, "so I stayed with Da in prison. I kept busy, though. Ran errands, smuggled things in for the prisoners. For pennies. It was enough to keep us in coal and bread. But Da just wasted away. Missing my mother, stuck behind the walls of the Marshalsea. He died there, covered with a thin blanket. The other prisoners cleaned us out while his body cooled."

Shock and sorrow struck him with equal force. What miserable memories, and how awful that she'd had to endure such suffering.

Yet he wondered . . . Was she telling the truth? Or were these more of her embellishments? The almost-mechanical way she recited her history—without inflection, without emotion—made him think this was the truth. She had to distance herself from the misery or else let it drag her down to drown.

He made sure to keep his face impassive, almost distant, as he listened to her relate her history. It was either that, or show her how much her past torment affected him.

"I was nine. Didn't have any living family," she continued, "so when they tossed me out of the Marshalsea, I had nowhere to go. The streets became my home."

Rough consonants and vowels altered her voice, so different from the round, soft tones she'd used in Cheltenham. But that had been a disguise. This was truly the first time she spoke to him as herself.

Mistrust hovered like a stinging wasp between

them, yet to hear her talk now as Cassandra Blake, the woman from Southwark, was nearly a gift. This was real. This was true. A hot gladness wove through him, treasuring this small prize.

She gazed back at him, but her sight was still far away. "Learned how to pick pockets. What men to stay away from because they wanted to use my body. I slept four to a pile of straw in a Southwark flash house."

Alex's nursery had been enormous, with a mother-of-pearl inlaid rosewood cradle and whole armies of toy soldiers. When he'd been naughty, his nursemaid might not have given him a second helping of pudding.

Guilt swamped him. He'd been given everything in life, and she'd had nothing. No home. No food. No stability. He swallowed hard and glanced out the window, struggling for composure.

"What of Hughes?" he asked.

A faint smile tilted the corners of her mouth. "I was fifteen, grubby as a pebble, with a robust trade in silk handkerchiefs and lace torn from ladies' cuffs. He'd been in the swindling game for decades, but his latest scheme needed a girl to pose as his daughter. I had *potential*."

Alex frowned. "Potential for what?"

"Dishonesty. Nobody cried better tears or pulled on heartstrings with greater ability." She said this almost proudly. "So he cleaned me up, got me tutors to speak like a lady, and seamstresses to dress me fine. Some people go to dame schools, but Martin Hughes taught me to read, write, and lie."

"A criminal's education," Alex noted, though he couldn't muster much heat in his words.

"A useful one." She smoothed a hand down her skirts. "We were together for almost ten years, traveling as father and daughter, running swindles in coaching inns across England. I had plenty to eat, my own bed, and clean clothing. It was a good life." She spoke fondly, her eyes bright.

The things she spoke of were the bare minimum for happiness, and yet it seemed that to her, it was as though she'd been given all the treasure in the kingdom.

Remorse haunted him. Why hadn't he known? He donated to charities, but he should do more. He should have *known*, somehow, of her suffering—though it would have been impossible for a duke's heir to know about one particular vagrant girl—and helped. But he'd done nothing, secure of his place in the world.

Her eyes dimmed and the lightness in her voice faded. "I thought Martin was happy, too. But seven years ago he left me at a coaching inn, telling me I was on my own. It was the first time I'd been alone in a long while. Didn't know what I was going to do."

He tried to protect himself against the picture that made. It pulled on him too deeply, demanding that he feel things that frightened him. The stony ramparts he'd built around himself cracked, making him vulnerable. Making him *care*. "You were frightened?"

"I . . ." She closed her eyes briefly, then opened them. "I was. I'd already seen how nasty London was for a young girl. Nothing could be worse. But I learned new ways to survive."

"The widow story." Alex fought against his impulse to comfort her, though it hounded him. *She betrayed me,* he reminded himself over and over, like a chant protecting him from a curse. "The same you used to gull me."

She glanced at him. He only stared back, refusing to let her see the hurt that still throbbed, and taking shelter in his stoicism. "I made a life for myself."

He reached for the righteous anger that kept him safe from further hurt. "Preying on others. Telling falsehoods for the prospect of money. Seducing men to line your pockets. Not much of a life."

"Better than what Southwark had to offer," she answered.

He couldn't dispute that.

"I don't know how Martin found me, but he did. I got a letter from him two months ago, summoning me to London." She gave a bitter laugh. "Like a long-lost daughter, I came running back. I didn't think he'd abandon me again." Her hands curled into knots. "I should have known. I should have expected it. Swindlers are loyal only to themselves."

"Including you."

"*Especially* me." She tilted her chin up defiantly. This was said without a trace of self-pity. It was stated as fact. She was alone in the world, with nothing and no one to make certain she was safe and well.

Their paths could not have been more different. "You

are the heir to a dukedom," his father had said to him when he couldn't have been more than nine. "You want for nothing. But never forget, privilege comes with responsibility. The livelihood and welfare of hundreds of people will depend on you. Your votes in parliament will shape many more lives. You must be dependable, trustworthy, and virtuous. Secure."

"Yes, Father," Alex had answered, awed by the weight he would have to shoulder.

She'd had no one guiding her. No concerned parent. Only Martin Hughes, shaping her to be a pawn in his game.

"What of work," he pressed Cassandra now. "*Honest* work?"

She shook her head. "There aren't many routes open to girls from South London. I could have been a seamstress, going blind as I labored over hems. Or I could have traveled north, to work at a cotton mill— and contracted lung sicknesses from breathing in the fluff. Even then, I'd be making a pittance. Starvation is noble," she concluded, "but I'm not ready to die."

She hadn't given in to despair. She had not allowed herself to be ground up by the machine of the world. There was a kind of bravery there. An audacity that was almost admirable. He didn't know how to feel— respect for her warred with his need to be virtuously angry. The net of emotion between them grew more complex, more tangled.

The fortifications of justifiable outrage weakened the

longer he was in her company and the more he knew of her history. He had always worked hard in parliament for the rights and welfare of the poor. But never before had he come face-to-face with someone's lived experience.

They sat opposite each other in his beautifully sprung, magnificently appointed carriage. It was the kind of vehicle hardly anyone could afford. How many mouths could be fed on the cost of this carriage alone? How many girls and women clinging to life on the margins could find safety for a fraction of the vehicle's price?

He wondered what he would have done, had he been in Cassandra's place, or how he'd find a means of survival.

He honestly didn't know. Could he continue to armor himself in disdain, when she'd had the courage to survive in brutal circumstances? Was it possible to heap contempt upon her, when it was very likely he would have done the same to stay alive?

"What is this place we're going to now?" he asked.

"We call it the Union Hall," she explained. "A place where fellow swindlers meet. If someone's setting up a scheme and needs people to help, they come here. We share stories and strategy. We brag and sympathize."

"Sounds like a club for gentlemen," he noted.

"Except women are allowed in our place," she countered. "A bit more equal—like America."

"Filled with braggarts and schemers," he said, "like America."

Something that resembled a genuine smile flitted

across her face. "Now there's a thought. If this comes out all right, when it's over, I can go to America. It's the right place for someone like me."

"Leave England?" he asked with surprise.

"Why not? There's nothing here for me. Only reminders of bad times."

A hard and dark knot pressed down on his chest. He hadn't thought she would leave. Not for somewhere so faraway. He told himself he didn't want her in his life—she'd caused too much hurt and anger. But did he want her sailing halfway around the world? It shouldn't make a difference to him where she went, so long as she was gone.

Yet it mattered. Against his better judgment, he cared what happened to her.

"Boston's full of lawless people like you," he said.

She shook her head. "New York is better—bigger and noisier and wilder. Could be perfect."

"You're getting ahead of yourself," he reminded her. "Hughes is still out there with the money."

She sat back and scowled. "Hell. I should know better than to dream of what might be."

A stab of remorse pierced him. He shouldn't have been so cold, so blunt. "We all dream," he offered.

"Dreams kill," she said flatly. "Especially when you believe in them and they never come to pass. Dreams took my mother, who wanted more for herself than a baby and a penniless husband. Dreams murdered my father, wasting away in debtors' prison." Her jaw tightened. "I dreamed about a new life for myself, thought it was mine, and look where it got me—betrayed, hunted by brutes like George Lacey." Her mouth twisted. "Dreams. I can't swallow their poison anymore."

He'd spoken to veterans, talked with elderly, impoverished tenants. But never had he experienced so viscerally what it meant to be poor, and a woman, in a country that didn't give a damn about either.

Alex struggled once more against empathy. She'd used and betrayed him. *No excuse for that.*

Except that she was trying to keep herself alive. And no one had ever shown her a dram of compassion, not even her own parents.

He wanted to drag his hands through his hair, or rub at his face, or curse aloud, or anything at all to release the pressure building up inside of him. It pressed at the seams, threatening to burst.

But he didn't. Instead, he sat perfectly still as proper behavior dictated. He had to be in control. Always.

He needed to be right about her. Dukes were always right.

Weren't they? Wasn't *he*?

She rapped against the roof of the carriage with her knuckles, and it came to a stop. After drawing a breath, she announced with the air of someone about to leap into the Thames, "This is it. The Union Hall."

From the outside, the Union Hall looked like any of the dusty, sprawling warehouses that popped up like sores in this part of the city. Alex was too well-bred to show his disgust, but she saw the very corners of his eyes pleat into tiny lines, and his jaw firm. He didn't like it here. And why should he? This wasn't his world.

"There's nothing but cheats and swindlers inside," Cassandra said, tilting her head toward the building. "A virtuous man like you keeps esteemed company— nothing like this."

"I'm certain my friends Ellingsworth and Langdon don't pay their tailors' bills on time," he answered.

"Not the same thing."

His grip tightened on his walking stick. "Wish I'd brought a pistol."

"There's a pecking order with us unsavory lot," she explained. She held her hand out low. "At the bottom, cutthroats and murderers." She raised her hand twelve inches. "In the middle, that's the pickpockets, house-breakers, thieves. Way up here"—she lifted her hand high—"are the swindlers."

"The royalty of lawbreakers," he said drily.

"We get blunt without having to kill or hurt anyone. We don't get dirty making our fortunes. That makes us almost respectable."

Not all of their class held to the rules. Lacey would have her blood if she didn't come up with the money. Even if she survived that, she had to live with Alex's hatred. The threat of his vengeance still hung over her head, as well. Every step she took was a step into nothingness, as if she kept throwing herself off a cliff over and over again.

"Your Grace?" the driver called down. "Shall I drive on?" He sounded nervous, with good cause. Sharp-eyed urchins massed around the carriage, ready to pry off the ducal crest on the door or strip the vehicle of its fine brass fittings.

"No," Alex answered. "Find a safe place for the carriage. Wait half an hour, then come back for us."

"Yes, Your Grace." The driver wasn't happy about any of this—that much was clear.

Before a footman could get down and open the door, Alex did it himself. Cassandra realized he did it to save the servant the real possibility of having the gold braid from his livery cut off, or the lace at his cuffs torn away.

Alex stepped down. The urchins stared at him with awe, but none of them advanced, too terrified by his imposing presence.

He turned and offered his hand to her. It had to be pure force of breeding that made him so polite. But his fingers tightened around hers when she slid her hand into his. The skin of her hand felt directly connected to her heart, because it jumped at the contact. She tried to smother the sensation.

His thumb brushed over her wrist, and his gaze flew to hers.

"Scared?" he said quietly. "Your pulse is hammering."

"Fear means I'm smart," she replied. "No one can slip close and stick me with a blade."

"I said no harm would come to you while we're together. I meant it." His gaze held hers, and that jolt skittered through her again. Nobody had ever promised to keep her safe before. Not her father, not Martin. No one.

And she believed Alex. He'd keep her safe—in order to get his money back. For now, for these few moments, she could be comforted having him close.

The handful of dirty children seemed to break free from their fear, and scurried forward to surround her and Alex. She batted their hands away from Alex's pockets and her reticule. But then she reached into the small embroidered bag and pulled out a few pennies.

"Take them," she said to the children, "and go away."

In an instant, the coins vanished, and so did the tiny gang.

"You didn't have to give them money," Alex said.

"What will they eat tonight if I don't?" she asked, then shrugged. "This way, I can pretend that I'm helping someone."

"How much money do you have left?"

She weighed her reticule with her hand. "Almost all gone."

His gaze was enigmatic as he guided her toward the Union Hall. He drawled, "Let me guess—let you do the talking."

"This isn't your world," she answered.

"Convenient."

She shot him a glance. "There's nothing convenient

about me coming here. We're the gazelles leaping in front of a pride of lions."

The loading doors to the warehouse sported a giant rusted lock. But no one and nothing entered that way. Instead, Cassandra led Alex to a narrow yet heavy door with a small peephole.

After drawing a deep breath, she knocked. The peephole opened, and a pair of red-rimmed eyes glared at her.

"You're not wanted here," the owner of the eyes growled.

"Just let me see her, Sam," she pressed. "I wouldn't come unless I wanted to make it right."

The peephole closed, and her heart sank. Failure. This was her one good lead in finding Martin. She started to turn away—then the bolt slid back and the door creaked open.

"I ain't helping if they rip off your hide," Sam spat, stepping back from the door. He was craggy-faced and stoop-shouldered, and utterly uninterested in her welfare.

Cassandra didn't answer, but took a step inside. Alex immediately followed. He exhaled in surprise.

"Weren't anticipating this, were you?" she couldn't resist asking.

"I'm learning more and more how appearances are deceiving."

She snorted at both the unspoken insult as well as its understatement. Nothing in this world was what it seemed. Everything was a surprise and a disappointment.

Cassandra used to love coming here. She loved the contrast between the outside and the inside, and reveled in this private place reserved only for people like her— professional liars and frauds. There wasn't anything better than coming to the hall and trading stories with her fellow swindlers. It was a place she could be herself.

The Union Hall was, for newcomers, unexpected. In contrast to the shabby neighborhood and the run-down look of the warehouse from the outside, no expense had been spared to create a luxurious retreat inside. Fine mahogany chairs and sofas boasting silk damask cushions dotted the huge space. Mother-of-pearl and ebony-inlaid cabinets served as dividers, creating "rooms" within the cavernous warehouse. Plush carpets from the Orient covered the warped floorboards, and pieces of marble statuary and china vases served as decoration. To combat the gloom, gilded candelabras bore lit beeswax candles, and someone had hung chandeliers from the ceiling beams. A large orange tabby cat slept on a velvet pillow on a sofa.

But as she walked slowly forward, Alex beside her, conversation between the men and women filling the hall stuttered to a stop. Outright hostile glares greeted her, along with oppressive silence.

"Old friends?" Alex asked lowly, glancing toward one couple. The woman stared directly at Cassandra and spat on the ground.

"Once, we were comrades of a sort. Some of these people even invested in the gaming hell. But word's out about Martin, and me. We broke the swindlers' code to be on the level with each other." She looked at an adolescent boy, who flung an obscene gesture in her direction.

A man with pockmarked cheeks stepped in her path and scowled at her. People nearby craned their necks, intrigued.

"Sutcliffe," she said warily.

"Never trusted either of you," Sutcliffe sneered. "Not Hughes. Not you."

"*He* took the money," she answered tightly. "I knew nothing until yesterday."

Sutcliffe made a rude noise. "That's shit and you know it." He took a step toward her. "Where's the goddamn blunt, bitch?" He raised his hand, threatening.

Then, suddenly, Sutcliffe was on the ground, cradling his jaw. Alex stood with his hand knotted in a fist, his expression cold and brutal. Everyone nearby sprang to their feet, their faces glazed with shock.

Cassandra looked from Alex to Sutcliffe and back again, disbelieving. The reserved duke had actually hit someone—to protect her.

"No one touches her," Alex said in a voice loud enough to be heard throughout the hall.

Shocked murmurs drifted up from everyone. A few asked, "Who's the tall toff?" but most were agreeing to keep their distance.

Cassandra walked around Sutcliffe, still lying on the ground. Her heart thudded. She'd asked him to lend her the protection of his highborn presence, but she didn't think he'd physically hurt someone when fulfilling his duties. It was so un-ducal.

Alex remained a steady, large presence beside her as she picked her way through the hall. At last, they came to one corner of the space, where a burly man stood guard, arms folded across his huge chest. He bore a shock of black hair that stood at odd angles from his head.

"It's alright, Dabbs," came a woman's voice. "Let her and the pretty aristo by."

Though Dabbs looked unhappy with the order, he didn't argue. Instead, he stepped to one side, allowing Cassandra and Alex to come forward.

This part of the hall was decorated like a lady's sitting room, with pretty chintz cushions on the delicate furniture, and porcelain shepherdesses lined up atop tables.

Cassandra had seen the pretty gewgaws many times. Now, she focused on the gilded chaise that took up most of the area, and the older woman in smuggled French silk reclining upon the chaise.

"Mrs. Donovan," Cassandra said, nodding toward her. The swindling Queen.

"Only my children call me that," Rose replied with a curl of her lip.

Cassandra waved toward Alex, "This is—"

"The Duke of Greyland. I know." Rose surveyed a stiff-shouldered Alex with an appreciative eye. He *did* look damned handsome, despite—or because of—the fact that he'd recently punched someone.

"Madam," Alex said coolly.

Rose smiled without warmth. "Keeping rarified company these days, Cassandra. But you're still a thieving harlot."

"I'll tell you what I tell everyone," Cassandra said, careful to keep her tone mild. "Martin Hughes ran off with the money, not me."

"With *my* money," Rose corrected her. "And George Lacey's. And a dozen others."

"He took my blunt, too," Cassandra answered.

"I don't care." Rose picked at embroidery on her cuff. "You're the one here now. And I want my money back."

"When I find it, you will have it," Cassandra answered.

"I want it *now*." Rose's eyes were sharp as tacks.

"What if Cassandra can't come up with the cash?" Alex asked.

"Her life will become extremely unpleasant." Rose's smile grew into something truly brutal, her gaze flicking to Dabbs. "Trust me on that."

Chapter 9

❧

$\mathcal{A}$lex loosened his stance, preparing for more violence. He gazed warily at the matronly looking woman lying back on the chaise. She appeared more like a doting grandmother than a criminal mastermind, but the cold, hard glitter of her eyes and the cruel set of her mouth left no doubt that she would make good on the threats she leveled at Cassandra.

He'd had no idea that this world existed. It was a city that lived beneath the surface of the London he knew, one where lawlessness and brutality ruled. To think that he and his fellow aristocrats danced and dined and laughed without realizing that less than a mile away, swindlers gathered to plan their next scheme, thieves organized like armies, and women and men like Mrs. Donavan could easily destroy lives on a whim.

He felt oddly young and green here, entirely out of his element.

But he'd be damned if anyone threatened Cassandra, not when he'd sworn to protect her. That need grew stronger each moment he spent in her presence, confusing him and obscuring his anger.

He opened his mouth to speak, but caught Cassandra's unspoken warning. This topsy-turvy realm wasn't the place to wave around his ducal authority. He smoothed his ruffled feathers. There were times for discretion—like now.

"I'll pay everyone back," Cassandra said to Mrs. Donovan. "All I want to do is find Martin and get everyone their money. But he's disappeared. Gone underground."

Briefly, he considered paying Mrs. Donavan and all the other investors what was owed. But he rejected that idea almost the same moment it formed in his mind. If he did offer financial recompense, Cassandra would owe him so much more. Thousands of pounds, instead of hundreds. She was far more motivated to find Martin Hughes with the thieves and swindlers of London breathing down her neck. If they were paid with his money, she could flee without their pursuit.

He wouldn't be played for a fool again. Yet he wondered . . . Would she do that to him *now*?

"So you aren't here to pay me back," Mrs. Donovan said in a bored voice. "What *are* you doing at the Union Hall?"

"Unless we find Hughes," Alex noted, "no one gets a ha'penny."

"Surely you or someone here has seen him within the past two days," Cassandra continued.

Mrs. Donovan was obstinately silent, appearing conspicuously disinterested as she traced patterns on the cushions.

Cassandra took a step toward her. "I'm trying to start over, Mrs. Donovan. No more swindles. No more schemes. Just a clean life, free of tricking and cheating people."

Alex glanced sharply at Cassandra. This was the first he'd heard of this plan. Was she being sincere, or was it more of her fraudulence? From the urgency of her expression, it seemed she meant what she said.

He didn't know what to make of that. The path of his anger grew more and more disordered.

The older woman scoured her with a knowing look. "Sounds dull," she drawled.

"I don't want to have to hurt people to survive anymore," Cassandra insisted.

His thoughts clashed against each other like rocks, tumbling in jagged confusion around him. Was she truly repentant? Did she regret what she had done to him, or to others? That didn't take away from the harm she'd already caused.

A corner of the older woman's mouth lifted as she eyed Alex, then Cassandra. "That's where this fancy piece comes in, I'd wager."

"I'm nobody's *piece*," Alex growled, his attention snapping back into place.

Mrs. Donovan laughed. "As you wish, *Your Grace*." She tapped her finger against her chin as she considered Cassandra with a long, thorough appraisal. To Cassandra's credit, she didn't fidget or squirm beneath Mrs. Donovan's scrutiny.

Finally, Mrs. Donovan said on an exhale, "Haven't seen Hughes."

Cassandra appeared momentarily crestfallen, then rallied. "Someone has."

"Nobody's said a word to me," the older woman admitted.

Alex pondered for a few moments. "I knew a third son whose father and two older brothers were killed in a carriage accident. As soon as he learned he'd become a viscount, he ran straight to a brothel to spend his new fortune."

Mrs. Donovan snorted. "Typical—a man thinks first of his wallet, then his cock."

Cassandra looked uncertain. "Martin never went in for paying for his . . . company. If he kept a woman on the side, he never spoke about her."

"So, besides a brothel, where would a swindler go if he suddenly acquired a considerable amount of liquid cash?" Alex wondered.

A dawning comprehension crossed Cassandra's face. "The racetrack," she said.

"Swindlers earn their coin cheating people," Alex refuted. "Why would they throw their money away on something as risky as gambling?"

"That's precisely who can't resist the track and the tables," she asserted. "Always looking to beat the odds."

"And you?" He lifted an eyebrow. "Are you a gambler?"

She gave him an arch look. "Depends on the wager." Before he could respond, she asked Mrs. Donovan, "Does Will Parsons still work the track at Hampton?"

The other woman snapped her fingers. The large man who'd been guarding her loomed closer. "Get Parsons."

Without a word, the hired muscle went off in search of the aforementioned Will Parsons. They waited in silence, until a young, sallow man came stumbling forward.

"I'm sorry, Mrs. D!" he cried.

"For what?" Mrs. Donovan asked with amusement.

"For whatever I did wrong," he answered nervously.

Cassandra took his arm. "Have you seen Martin Hughes? *Think*, Will." She gave him a small shake.

"I don't . . . I mean . . . I think . . ." The young man glanced anxiously at the people watching him, including a panicked look in Alex's direction. "I might have?"

"When?" Cassandra demanded.

"Yesterday?" It seemed Parsons couldn't state anything definitively, phrasing everything like a question. "I didn't know. This was before we knew he'd gone off with the blunt, so I didn't think to tell anyone. I'm so sorry!" He gave Mrs. Donovan a pleading stare, a man begging for his life.

"Go on, Will," Mrs. Donovan said with cheery exasperation.

Cassandra released his arm.

Seemingly relieved that nothing more was required of him, Parsons groveled and scurried off, bowing over and over again as he backed away.

"A possible sighting of Hughes in Hampton isn't much of a lead," Mrs. Donovan said to Cassandra.

Cassandra eyed Alex, who stared right back. "At this point, I'll use a twig for a boat."

"If you sink without bringing me my blunt," Mrs. Donovan said with cheerful menace, "I'll be there to watch you drown."

THE clock chimed one in the morning. Alex braced his arms on the mantel in his room, frustration sizzling through him. His hand ached from the punch he'd thrown earlier.

He'd accompanied Cassandra merely to insure his investment was repaid—but he'd moved without thinking when that pocked bastard had insulted her.

The last time he'd punched someone outside of his pugilism academy, he'd been at Eton, protecting a younger boy from being bullied. He'd stood up to Hartsfield, the class tyrant, who loved nothing more than to make the smaller boys cry. Alex had thrown one punch into Hartsfield's nose, bruising his hand but making the other lad scream and run, blood dripping onto the pavement. After that, Hartsfield had been sullen and meek.

Alex stared at his hand now. He was no better than a child, *punching* someone in anger. His actions baffled him. It shouldn't matter who said what to Cassandra. He flexed his fingers, letting the pain there serve as a remonstrance not to get involved.

The day had been a long and tiring one, with his awareness of Cassandra growing by the moment. He should be splayed in his bed, dead to the world, immersed in the realm of dreams.

Shaking out his hand, he pushed away from the mantel. At this stage in his life, he ought to be acclimated to and accepting of his insomnia. Sleepless nights had been his frequent companion since childhood. Why should it surprise him now that he was thirty-eight years old?

He rose and paced the length of his bedchamber. He was still partially dressed, wearing a shirt, breeches, and boots. His neckcloth, waistcoat and jacket had long ago been discarded, yet he had somehow recognized how foolish it would be to attempt sleep when his mind and body churned.

He couldn't put aside the revelations and experiences of the day as easily as extinguishing a candle. They burned brightly, throwing shadows over things he once believed to be true.

How much easier would things be if he could simply hate Cassandra? It had been a mercy to think of her as a grasping adventuress, impelled by avarice to cheat and swindle aristocratic men, loyal only to her own greed. Now . . . He couldn't readily cast her in the role of villain. Not completely.

She was cold. Callous. Mercenary. Courageous. A survivor trying to make her way through an unfeeling, pitiless landscape. Everyone on whom she had relied had abandoned or betrayed her. She had done what she needed in order to endure. A woman had limited choices, and few of them were good. She'd been forced into a corner, but fought her way out through intelligence and determination.

Should he condemn her, or admire her? Both?

Damn it—he didn't know. The easy categories of right and wrong that had been his previous existence were blurring, becoming indistinct. He barely recognized himself anymore. Threatening a woman with revenge, rubbing elbows with criminals, *hitting* strangers. He didn't do these things. Except now, he did.

It felt strangely freeing. More than a little daunting. He wasn't the man he'd thought he was for thirty-eight years. But there was liberation in this new identity. He didn't have to hold to someone else's ideal. Instead he allowed his own desires and feelings to guide him.

She'd given him that—perhaps unknowingly, but she'd been the instrument of this revelation.

Cassandra had confessed her desire to live a life without swindles. One free of deceit. If that was true, it made his feelings for her more complicated. Because she wanted to do right, to correct her misdeeds and move forward into a future without lies. That was something to be respected.

But there was one thing in his life that wasn't complicated. It was primal and simple. His body shouted its need. It—*he*—still wanted Cassandra. Desire hit him like a physical blow. He hungered for her. Touch, taste, feel, scent. The low music of her voice. The direct and unapologetic way she kissed him, as a woman in full knowledge of her own desires.

Her room was just down the hall, on the right. Not very far away at all.

He ought to be repelled by her. Most likely her caresses and kisses were rehearsed and artificial. But they didn't *feel* like it. Despite all her lies, that part of her felt genuine, like the heat that rose up whenever they touched. That couldn't be manufactured. Even the most practiced courtesan had a hint of disinterested professionalism in her lips, in her sighs. Not so with Cassandra.

Alex cursed aloud. Goddamn them both. She was driving him mad.

He tugged open his bedroom door. The magnetic pull of her drew on him, urging him.

In an instant, he stood outside her door. He placed his hand on the wood that separated them.

She was his guest. She was also his prisoner. There were ancient rules of hospitality that needed to be respected. He would never force himself on her.

Yet . . . He wanted her.

He turned away sharply and strode downstairs. Bypassing the library and its thousands of distracting volumes, he headed outside. His garden in the cool of night should provide him some relief from his blistering thoughts and urges.

He walked quickly down the main path leading between neatly trimmed hedges and carefully manicured flower beds. His long legs ate up the distance easily, and he paid little attention to the pruned trees and burbling fountains, or the hazy ink-colored sky arching above him. He would pace until sunrise, if need be, and then venture out with Cassandra to Hampton after breakfast.

A sound ahead brought him up short. Footsteps on the gravel. It couldn't be a gardener, since all the staff was asleep, and it wasn't common practice to work in the middle of the night.

He headed toward the gazebo, the source of the footsteps. Whoever was making noise must have heard him, because the sound abruptly stopped.

"Who's there?"

Cassandra's voice. And she sounded angry, not frightened.

"The master of the house can walk his own property whenever he likes," he answered, stepping forward. He recalled himself standing outside her door, torn between desire and the imperatives of hospitality. But she hadn't been in her room.

Instead, she stood in the middle of the gazebo, its frame covered with twining vines and fragrant, night-blooming flowers. In the darkness, he could just make out that she was fully dressed. So she hadn't searched out her bed, either.

"I'll leave," she said when he appeared.

"Don't," he said without thinking. "There's room enough for both of us." He tested himself and the draw of attraction. Easing closer, more details of her appearance revealed themselves. Her hair had come loose from its pins, strands of gold curling around her face, giving her an unearthly look. She'd reminded him of a fairy queen long ago in Cheltenham, and now she seemed a wild elf, a creature of nature.

Those curls had spread in a golden wave across the pillow when they'd gone to bed together, perfumed with vanilla and roses. Did it still carry the same scent? He could reach out and wrap it around his finger.

Stop it. He wouldn't go down that path with her again. In truth, he was almost appalled at himself that he could still hunger for her after all her duplicity.

Yet he did. Damn it, he did.

He sought a neutral topic. "Your bed isn't comfortable?" Hell. Why did he have to mention bed?

She made a scoffing sound. "Softest mattress I've ever felt. Like resting on kittens."

"Do you often sleep on cats?"

"They're usually opposed to the idea." The wry humor left her voice. "It wouldn't matter if I lay on clouds or clumps of dirt. Nothing's going to coax me to sleep tonight." She looked at him questioningly. "Who knew dukes kept such odd hours? Doesn't the nation depend on you, et cetera?"

"If that was the case, then I sorely disappoint Britain on a regular basis."

She eyed him, folding her arms across her chest. "No sleep of the just."

"It's eluded me for some time now." He could feel her edgy energy, radiating out in invisible, yet tangible pulses. "It's Hughes, isn't it? Thoughts of him keep you from your rest."

She swung away, presenting him with her back. At first, he thought she wouldn't answer, but then she spoke lowly. "I *trusted* him. I believed what he said to me, and that cuts deeper than any blade." Raw hurt reverberated through her words. "But no amount of blood I shed cleans the cut. It'll fester and rot."

"Until it eats you alive from the inside out."

Frowning, she turned back to Alex. "I . . . understand now." She pressed her hand to her mouth. "When someone you care about betrays you—this is how it hurts."

"I can't know what you're feeling," he allowed. "I've got a good idea, though."

"It's . . . hurt and anger and sorrow and helplessness," she said, "wrapped up in paper and tied with twine. A neat bundle of treachery."

"Nothing neat about it." He stalked around the periphery of the gazebo, circling her. "It's messy as hell. Throws everything into chaos."

"God, Alex." She rubbed at her face. "I'm . . . sorry."

He stopped in his pacing and stared at her.

"No one should feel this way," she went on. "And the fact that you do at my hands . . . I understand your hatred of me."

The flare of righteousness never materialized. All he felt was sadness. He walked to a planter beside the gazebo. Reaching into it, he pulled out a flask, stashed here for sleepless nights like this one. He uncapped it and drew a long drink of brandy.

He held the flask out to her and she came forward to take it. Her eyes never leaving his face, she drank, then she returned the container to him before retreating several steps.

His heart thudded thickly, and his tongue was loosened by the brandy. "I don't hate you."

"Don't you?"

"I did," he allowed. "Now . . ." He searched within himself, rooting out the hot embers of fury and pain. "It's more complicated."

She chuckled without humor. "*Complicated* is a good word for it." She walked to one of the flowers and plucked it, twirling the blossom absently between her fingers. The sight fascinated him—the contrast between her slim fingers and the petals, both glowing softly in the moonlight.

"Martin was more of a father to me than my own blood," she murmured. "Cared about me. Or so I thought," she added bitterly. She crushed the flower in her hand, then let the crumpled petals fall to the ground where they lay like abandoned hope. "There's no one I can trust," she said without self-pity. It was a fact, as straightforward as the movement of the tides. The only one looking out for Cassandra was Cassandra.

"You don't trust me?"

She lifted an eyebrow. "Surely, you see the irony of that question."

He shook his head ruefully. "It's not easy for me to absolve a wrong."

"Why should you, when I've given you no reason to forgive me?" She raised and lowered her shoulders in a half shrug. "I wouldn't, were our situations reversed."

"If you're looking for assurances I won't gain my retribution . . ." He stared up at the dark sky, smeared with clouds and smoke. He was on new footing, learning himself with each movement forward. Nothing felt certain—including his identity. "I can't give them."

"I wouldn't believe you if you did," she answered wryly.

"I don't lie." He sounded hurt, even to his own ears.

"That wasn't what I said." She took a step toward him, the fallen flower pressed flat beneath her foot. "In my line of work, it's about knowing people. That's how you turn a profit. By understanding their hearts, even if they can't understand them themselves. I didn't go to Eton or Oxford. Didn't learn to read until I turned sixteen. But I've been studying people for decades." She narrowed her eyes. "And what I've learned about you,

Your Grace, is that you're not the placid lake you think you are. You're a stormy sea. More complex than even you realize."

His breath caught. These had been his private thoughts, and yet she'd seen right into him, as if all his efforts to protect himself had been for nothing.

Only Cassandra could do this to him. Of all the people he'd encountered in his life, only *she* had the insight, the sharpness of mind and feeling, to gain entrance to the center of his labyrinth.

She narrowed the space between them further. He didn't move away or avoid her. Instead, he stood still.

Her hand came to rest flat on his chest.

Surely she could feel his rapid pulse. But she didn't tease or chide him. Instead, she stared up into his eyes.

"There's a shadow in you," she whispered. "A hunger, a darkness. You didn't believe that part of you existed."

"I was raised to believe in the innate goodness of myself," he breathed.

"You *are* good." She smiled a little, a very little. "Don't doubt that. But you're not perfect."

"No one is."

"You believed I was." She fired this bullet gently. "That's why you're hot as a boiling kettle with me. I wasn't the flawless woman you thought me to be. And," she added, even more softly, "I made you feel things. Rough, frightening things. About me. About yourself. I cut up your orderly map of the world and set fire to the pieces. That's unforgivable," she whispered.

His throat was raw, aching. "You rip me apart." He gripped her hand where it lay on his chest. It was soft but not delicate. It belonged to a woman who knew how to pull herself up from a precipice. It was a weapon. "I have no ammunition against you."

"That's not true." Her eyes were large and dark. "You could do me a great deal of damage."

"I know," he rasped. He burned with the conflicting needs to cause her pain and to protect her.

Her smile flashed. "In your hand, you hold my very life."

"Is that all?"

"What else is there?"

"This." He pulled her closer, until her chest was pressed tightly against his own. He brought up his arms, enfolding her. Cassandra was curved and lush and warm, and she stared up at him with her eyes huge and her lips slightly parted. She clutched at his shoulders. She was strong and vulnerable, and he was drawn to both parts of her.

For a moment, they only looked at each other, but their breaths mingled, both coming quickly and in short gulps as if preparing to dive beneath the surface of the sea.

He brought his lips down against hers. She opened for him at once.

They had not kissed since he'd learned of her deception. Before, he'd been almost reverential, treating her like a flawless, precious creature. He knew better now.

She was *real*. And he didn't know who he was anymore. But a furious hunger released in him now, and he wanted . . . He wanted everything.

He took possession of her, claiming her lips with his own. And she fought back. Not by pushing him away, but by pulling him even closer, through her own burning demands. Their mouths tugged and bit and snapped. They were feral together, their tongues swirling and hot. She held fast to his shoulders. Her nails dug through the fabric of his shirt, biting into his flesh. The tiny needles of pain sent lightning through his body, stiffening his cock.

She moaned into his mouth, and he swallowed the sound whole, taking it into himself. Devouring her. Losing himself.

He spun out of control, holding her so tightly it had to be painful, yet she made no sound of protest. The tighter he gripped her, the more frenzied her kisses became.

Everywhere he was on fire for her.

"I need inside you," he rumbled. He was torn in different directions, each need pushing him further and further away from his conceptions of himself. "I want to hurt you, but I also want to worship you. I want to fuck you." He couldn't believe he spoke such thoughts aloud. She should pull back. Slap him. Run away.

She moaned again, louder. She was *excited* by his crude words.

"Yes," she breathed. "Yes."

He went still. Then shoved her away.

For several minutes, they stared at each other. The air was thick with the sound of their labored breathing. He dragged his hands through his hair, took a step, stopped. He didn't know what to do with himself.

"Punishing me?" Her voice was breathless and low. "Teasing me with what I can't have?"

"I'm your torment and your succor." His jaw felt made of stone, while his cock was hard as iron. "We're both in hell."

She stood straighter. "I disgust you."

"No." He stalked the length of the gazebo. "Yes."

"Which is it?" she asked acidly.

"I want you," he confessed, "and I don't know how to feel about you." He didn't understand. He was bred to be nobler than this. He *was* better than this. Wasn't he?

"You think you're a true gentleman," she said cuttingly. "Honest, noble. England's pinnacle. But at your heart, *Your Grace*, you're just a man."

She stalked off into the darkness.

Chapter 10

A horse's alarmed whinny rose above hundreds of human voices. The noise and confusion of the Hampton races suited Cassandra just fine. She wanted to lose herself in the crowds and chaos, and break apart like a dandelion on the wind, carried by currents of people, not air. As she and Alex threaded their way through the gaily dressed masses, she tried to focus on the task at hand—finding Martin—and not on what had happened last night.

The racetrack was situated a small distance from the Town itself. A fence marked the track's perimeter, and crowds gathered there, dozens deep. The judges sat in a hastily assembled booth set up high, permitting them to watch the races unimpeded. Standing several hundred yards from the track were the stables and a small ring where jockeys in silks exercised and warmed up their horses. The rowdy gathering of people resembled a carnival, with the crowd dressed in a motley assortment of clothing, performers vying for coins, sellers of pies and oranges, men shouting the odds of the different horses, and everywhere noise and color. Raffishly dressed blokes took bets from the onlookers, their hands bulging with cash.

Cassandra and Alex had left their carriage in favor of searching the crowd on foot—the better to look for one man amid thousands. It was a hazy day, faintly cool. Perfect for a race.

She now dodged a curricle bearing two women, and collided with the solid wall of Alex's body.

"Sorry," she muttered, though her voice was lost in the din. He didn't answer, but his look was dark and rich with meaning.

Want to hurt you, but I also want to worship you. I want to fuck you.

For the rest of her life, she'd remember what he'd said to her in the gazebo, looking like an animal trying to free itself from a cage. His rude, raw words had been a powerful drug, making her drunk, heating her body, rendering her feverish and needy. She couldn't believe that Alex—the dignified, proper duke—could think, let alone speak, so shamelessly. And she couldn't believe how potently she'd sparked from his words alone. Combined with the passion of their kiss, she had been a breath away from begging him to be inside her.

She would've dragged him down to the ground and demanded just that, except he'd pulled back. Confusion and desire had warred in both of them.

Her body craved him. Taking him to bed would assuage the ferocious hunger that was a permanent part of her now. He wanted her, as well—so the power wasn't completely in his hands. She could make him say filthy things and lose control of himself. She had sway over him, too, and Cassandra craved that balance.

But was it enough? She craved his heat, but she also wanted him to look at her with caring and tenderness and respect. Could he give her those things after all that had happened? She feared that would never come to pass.

Alex carved a path through the milling throng waiting for the race to begin. As always, people stepped out of his way, naturally yielding to the authority that radiated from him like heat from a fire. He'd dressed down for the day, dimming his ducal radiance, yet there was an inherent confidence in him that couldn't be disguised.

His hand engulfed hers as he led them. "To keep from losing you," he said above the racket.

She wasn't going anywhere. Not when her breath came fast from the feel of his gloved fingers weaving with hers, and his eyes were warm and focused on her alone. She had to stay fixed on their goal—finding Martin—but when it came to Alex, she was at sea. Things like right and wrong never meant much to her, yet it was wrong that she desired and cared for a man who didn't even *like* her.

His hate gave way to a more strange, more tangled relationship.

If only she could fit them back in their tidy boxes. Swindler and mark. Betrayer and the betrayed. The world had more shades than black and white, however.

They continued to weave through the crowds milling beside the racetrack, when a voice called out.

"Mrs. Blair?"

Oh, God.

She turned to see a familiar handsome blond man approach. He wore perfectly tailored bespoke clothing, from his hat to his gleaming boots. He looked at her with a mixture of surprise and suspicion.

"Lord Keene," she said with a wan smile. She tried to move on, but he maneuvered his body so that going forward was impossible.

Alex stopped. He swiveled to look between her and the newcomer, his expression hardening. "You know him?"

"This is Lord Keene," she explained, wishing one of the horses would get free and trample her to death.

"Tunbridge Wells, wasn't it?" Lord Keene asked. His look darkened. "Where did you go? I searched for you, but you'd vanished. Nary a trace of you."

Out of the corner of her eye, she observed Alex. From the narrowing of his eyes, she saw the moment he realized who and what Lord Keene was to her. A former dupe, on whom she'd run a very similar swindle to the one she had with Alex. The widow cheated out of her portion by a cruel relative. Lord Keene had given her a hundred pounds after she'd toyed with him for several days at an elegant hotel in Tunbridge Wells.

"I had no choice." She fell back on one of her usual tales. "Creditors were dunning me, and if I didn't flee, they would have thrown me into the Fleet. I was heart-broken to leave you without a word."

Lord Keene didn't seem to hear her. Instead, he glared at Alex. "She's yours, then?" He looked mean-ingfully at their joined hands.

Though she tried to pull away, Alex held her fast.

"Not your damned business," he growled to Lord Keene.

Again, the young buck tried to make up in swag-ger what he lacked in true courage. "Well done, Your Grace," he attempted to sneer. "Locked up tighter than a Spanish prison, that one. Wouldn't yield, no matter how I begged her."

Alex looked briefly stunned, before his expression turned harsh, his nostrils flared while his brow lowered.

"Pistols? Swords?" Alex asked lowly.

"I beg your pardon?" Lord Keene looked ashen.

"Keep nattering on," Alex explained, "and you'll have to pick either pistols or swords for our duel. I'm bloody good at both." Absolute confidence firmed his words.

Lord Keene gulped. "As silent as a library, that's me." In an instant, he vanished into the crowd.

A tiny bloom of relief flowered when Lord Keene

finally disappeared. But Alex stared at her for so long that she shifted nervously from foot to foot. He didn't seem to notice the crowds massing and swirling around them.

"You had me believe"—it was an accusation—"that you took all your victims to bed."

"I don't care for people touching me," she replied. "Especially if I don't like them."

"You let *me*."

She said nothing. Then, "You were different from them." In Cheltenham, he'd looked at her as though she was worth respect, as though she meant something more than a pretty damsel in distress. Her other dupes had seen in her an opportunity to play the hero, but they never cared about *her*. Alex had.

"Why?" he demanded angrily. "Why not tell me the truth?"

"My words mean nothing to you," she answered. "You said as much."

He couldn't answer. Yet emotion gleamed deep in his eyes. A man jostled him, and Alex glared back. The man shrank away, but the mob grew thicker and thicker as the beginning of the race continued. People shouted their bets or the odds, and vendors worked the crowds, selling pamphlets describing the horses, as well as ices and pies and sweets. Everything was noise and disorder. Including her heart.

"We'll speak of this again," Alex vowed.

Secrets had been her life's companions. Now they

were all coming out in the hot light of day, to shrivel in the sun.

THE crowd was a mix of high and low, not unlike Cassandra and Alex.

She scanned the masses of people, looking for Martin. Craggy, working faces mingled with smooth, pale leisured faces, and the quality of clothing varied from threadbare castoffs to custom gowns and coats from Bond Street. The air smelled of perfume, dust, and horse manure. It would be so easy to slip her hand into an unguarded reticule, or a gentleman's pocket. A few coins here, a timepiece there.

But that wasn't her life anymore. That wasn't her.

Alex had been all too ready to cast her as the thieving villainess, yet he didn't seem to think of her that way anymore. He kept defending her when he'd had no reason to come to her aid.

He clearly struggled with their constantly shifting roles. Yet, as they continued to look through the spectators, he kept glancing back at her, as if making sure she was safe.

There was a goodness in him that went beyond duty. It was innate, even as he continued to mistrust her.

Was it merely desire that pulled Alex to her, or had they progressed to something even more complicated— two people, free of pretense, seeing each other as they were for the first time? Her chest ached with the desire for him to want *her*, all of her. Perhaps that was impossible. Perhaps she wished for foolish dreams—and she already knew what happened to those who dreamed.

Her head throbbed. Little made sense anymore, and it seemed that this lead in tracking Martin came to nothing. They'd been combing the spectators with no sign of her former mentor. Where else could they look for him? Maybe searching London's brothels would yield some results. Or the theaters, or pleasure gardens, or any of a hundred places a swindler might go to spend his blunt before slipping out of town forever.

Cassandra was about to suggest to Alex that they pack it in, when the crowd shifted slightly, revealing a man in a checked coat. Nobody gently born would ever wear such a thing. Yet it seemed familiar.

The man wearing the coat turned to watch the horses at the starting line, revealing his face.

"Alex," she hissed, tugging on his hand. "It's him." She nodded in the checked coat's direction. "Look slowly."

Alex did as she commanded, casually glancing over his shoulder. But she felt his hand stiffen as he recognized Martin.

"Approach him cautiously," he said between his teeth.

"We should split up," Cassandra suggested. "You take him from one side, I'll get the other."

He eyed her warily.

"Why would I run?" she demanded. "If we don't move on him now, we could lose him."

His look softened, and Alex nodded.

They broke apart, and she swiftly but stealthily made her way past the spectators in her path, carefully keeping her face averted so Martin couldn't see her. She drew on her experience as a pickpocket to slip through the crowd without causing a disturbance.

She espied Alex coming from the other direction, slowly but determinedly approaching Martin.

There was a cry, and the first race began. The crowd surged toward the track, jostling her. The movement caused enough of a disturbance that Martin looked right at her.

She prayed he would look at her with misery and an apology in his expression. That he'd rush toward her with open arms, insisting it was just a stupid, horrible misunderstanding.

The moment his gaze met hers, he looked aghast, then panicked. Not ashamed or apologetic. Fearful. Of her, because he knew he'd done wrong and had no desire to make things right.

Her heart shattered. She'd gulled herself.

She wondered why he'd stayed in London—but some part of him must crave the excitement of knowing he was a wanted man, of staying a step ahead of everyone.

Her resolve hardened. If Martin didn't have the money, she'd drag him in front of Rose and Lacey and let *them* deal with him. He'd chosen his fate, and she would treat him with the same heartlessness with which he'd treated her.

She took a step toward him.

Seconds before Alex reached out to grab hold of his arm, Martin darted away. He slipped between bystanders.

She gave chase. Both she and Alex pursued Martin as he wove and careened through the crowd. A man cursed Martin as he rammed into him, causing the man to spill his ale. But Martin didn't slow. He led them away from the turf, where the race thundered past.

The crowd moved to keep up with the progress of the racing horses, blocking Martin before she or Alex could reach him. When the crowd broke up, Martin had disappeared. There was no sign of his checked coat.

"Where is he?" she asked Alex, spinning around in a circle.

"Can't see him in this bedlam," Alex said, frustration in his voice. He craned his neck to scan the area. "He's close. Nobody can just vanish."

She'd seen bag snatchers do exactly that. There'd been a time when she could lose a tail as easily as snapping her fingers. Despite Martin's age, he still had a whiff of the streets about him.

Her heart sank. They'd come so close, but for nothing. They'd have to find some other lead, if any existed.

Then her breath caught. "There!" She pointed toward the stables.

Martin hurried past the stalls, away from them. Cassandra's pulse thundered, fearful that he would slip through their fingers.

Before she could move, Alex took off, outpacing her. He ran full speed toward Martin, but she was close at his heels. Anger pushed her forward, urging her faster and faster.

Alex reached Martin first. Grabbing his shoulder, he spun Martin around, and pushed him into the side of a stall. The horse inside nickered in surprise, and a distant part of Cassandra winced at the force of Alex's shove. Even after everything, she still feared hurting Martin.

But the person who gaped at Alex wasn't Martin.

A younger man stared at Alex, his face turning chalky with fear. Cassandra saw now that he wore Martin's checked coat.

As for Martin, himself, he was nowhere to be found.

"How did you get that coat?" Alex demanded as Cassandra reached them.

The young man gulped. "A bloke bought mine and gave me his."

"A switch," she muttered angrily. An easy dodge, and she'd fallen for it. "What does your coat look like?"

"It's brown," he answered.

That wouldn't be much help, since half the men in attendance wore brown coats.

Alex released the stranger and pulled out several pound notes. "I'll purchase *that* one from you."

Befuddled but intrigued, the young man stammered, "Done." He slipped off the coat and handed it to Alex, who exchanged it for the pound notes.

"Odd day at the races, but profitable," the stranger muttered before hurrying off.

Cassandra turned to Alex. "Why'd you buy that?"

"It might hold some indicators as to where Hughes might be." He held it up and studied the garment. As he did, a horse poked its head out of the stall and nuzzled Alex's shoulder. He gave it a distracted pat.

"Let's go somewhere quiet." She stepped quickly behind the stables, and he followed.

They stopped by one of the stalls. She waited tensely while Alex rifled through the pockets. He found a pencil, a stub of a cheroot, and a sheet with the horse race odds listed. A few of the horses had been circled, marking them as possible bets.

"Nothing here that's worth a ha'penny," Alex muttered.

"I'll have a go." She took the coat from him. "Secret pockets are my specialty." She ran her hands up and down the garment, sensing slight variations in the fabric. A little lump caught her attention. "I need a knife."

A small gleaming blade appeared in Alex's hand. It was a beautiful little silver folding knife engraved with his ducal crest. He handed it to her without a word.

She slid the blade between the coat's lining and outer fabric. A bright circle flashed before it fell into the dust.

He bent down and picked it up, then handed it to Cassandra. She held it aloft so both she and Alex could study it.

The object was a circular token of stamped brass. One side of the coin bore an inscription she couldn't translate. *Amici secreta tuentur.*

"Friends keep secrets," Alex said.

Naturally, he knew Latin. She turned the token over, where the image of a masquerade mask had been stamped.

"It's not currency," she murmured. "There's no amount on it."

Alex plucked the token from her and examined it. "Looks familiar somehow."

"How?"

"Secret societies often use things like this to gain entrance to their gatherings." He held it up to the light. "I know I've seen this before." Alex slipped the coin into a pocket inside his coat. "There are some people I can ask."

"I'll go with you."

He shook his head. "Not this time."

She raised a brow. "You won't let me out of your sight, but you can stomp off to make inquiries on your own?"

A corner of his mouth turned up in a disarming half smile. "There's no fairness in life." He glanced around. "There's also no need for us to stay around. Unless you'd like to watch the race."

She didn't want to run into Lord Keene again, or risk the possibility of encountering another of her marks and having more secrets about herself exposed. "I've had enough chases for one day."

$\mathcal{I}$N the carriage heading back to Alex's home, Cassandra's attention kept dancing between the passing scenery and watching Alex. He sat in a brooding silence, his hands cupping the head of his walking stick, his chin lowered in thought.

They hadn't spoken since leaving Hampton. But if she could read him—and she could—he was mulling over the day's events.

"You didn't expect to see Hughes at the races," Alex said, relieving the silence.

She sighed. "Part of me wished he'd be there. The other part . . ." She rubbed at a spot between her eyebrows. "It makes it all the more real. His running out on me."

"And when he saw you today, and fled . . ." Alex frowned. "That made it real, too."

"I suppose I thought he'd tell me it was all a mistake, that there was a decent explanation for everything." Her mouth twisted. "You must think me a fool to keep holding on to hope."

He exhaled. "I think you cared for him. Trusted him. And it's a hard thing to lose that trust."

"Speaking from your own experience," she said wryly.

He shrugged. "It's different, what happened between you and I."

"Is it?" she wondered.

He gazed directly into her eyes, and it felt both alarming and exciting. He saw too deeply inside of her, touching places she wanted left alone. "I don't believe I was the only one with my heart involved." His eyes, dark and warm, searched her face. "I wish I'd known . . . that you thought I was different."

"Does it matter?"

"It does." He reached across the carriage and ran a finger down her cheek. "I believed I was one of hundreds. Another fat purse to be plucked. But I think . . . I think I meant something to you." The tenderness in his gaze made her ache with longing. "And you meant something to me."

Her heart leapt. "Did I?"

"I've been a title, not a man, for so long. You were the only one who believed I was so much more, even when I didn't see it myself. When I'd learned that you were a swindler, I thought everything had been a lie. I see now, that wasn't true." He leaned closer, and she felt overwhelmed by him. "You were far more honest than I knew."

She'd wanted to hear this from him for so long that it physically hurt to listen to him now. She felt raw and exposed and so full of yearning, she felt herself being torn into pieces.

"I'm sorry," he said, his words a rasp. He gazed at her, his eyes burning, his features sharp. He'd never looked more handsome, and it devastated her. Need and want filled every part of her.

It was too much. She'd drown in her own desires, her own hopes.

"We're past apologies," she managed.

"But that doesn't mean we don't need to hear them," he answered. The distance between them continued to shrink as he leaned closer and she was drawn helplessly toward him. His lips were close. Close enough to kiss.

She turned her head to the side. "Please," she gasped. "Let us talk of other things. I can't . . . I can't bear this."

He seemed to understand, and moved back a little, giving her room to breathe. She pressed herself into the upholstered seats as if she could lose herself in the cushioning and find some safety from the temptation he offered.

"Who will you ask about the coin?" she asked after a long while.

"My friends Ellingsworth and Langdon."

"The two handsome blokes with you at the gaming hell?"

He seemed to bristle at her use of *handsome* to describe his companions. "I have a memory of one of them showing me the token with the mask, yet I can't recall specifics."

"When will you see your friends?"

"Tonight. I can't let the sun rise again without having a bead on Hughes."

"Do you hunt foxes with such determination?"

He was silent, then, "I don't hunt. No honor in killing vulnerable creatures."

It made sense that he'd refuse hurting something that had no means of protecting itself.

"I thought all aristos hunt," she said.

He gave her his half smile, the one that made her heart somersault. "You're going to have to learn that us *aristos* aren't all the same."

"I'm realizing it." They'd been one thing to her before: targets. Not people with individual hopes and wishes and vulnerabilities. Oh, she knew they had weak spots, but those soft areas had been perfect for exploiting for her own benefit. Now she realized the gentry were all too human. And she'd willingly hurt them.

To survive, she reminded herself.

Her choices had been made. The past remained unchangeable. She could wish, but couldn't turn back the clock and become someone else. Someone good and honorable. All that was left was moving forward, and taking responsibility for her choices now.

She and Alex fell into silence, ripe with things unspoken. He'd apologized to her—something she had never expected to hear from him. The air between them was thick with a new understanding.

But the long day and the swaying of the carriage took their toll, and soon she found her head snapping up. She'd nodded off.

"Here." Alex edged over. He patted the seat beside him. "You can put your head on my shoulder."

"I'm fine," she said automatically.

"I've tried sleeping in here." He spoke in a matter-of-fact tone, one that brooked no argument. "The carriage is expensive but it makes a poor bed. You'll rest easier with someplace to put your head."

She hesitated. Weariness swamped her, dragging her eyelids down and demanding she rest.

He sighed, exasperated. "As you like. I'll come over there so you can continue to face forward."

Before she could argue, he maneuvered his body across the space between the seats, then lowered beside her. She had just enough time to scoot over before being crushed by his bulk.

The carriage became much smaller with him sitting next to her. The side of his solid, warm body pressed against hers, making her feel little and delicate.

He shifted, and she sensed the movement of his muscles beneath his clothing. His scent wove closely around them, hot and masculine and intimate.

Alex glanced at his shoulder. "Go on then. Make a pillow for yourself."

Gingerly, she pressed her fingertips to his firm shoulder. "Like sleeping on boulders," she muttered.

He shot her a dry look. "You're determined to refuse my consideration."

Which would make her the most ungrateful—and stupid—woman in England. After untying the ribbons of her bonnet and setting the hat down on the opposite cushion, she carefully tilted her neck until her head rested on the round cap of his shoulder. It wasn't a perfect resting place. He was tight with muscle and there wasn't much padding in his coat. But it was comforting, just the same.

"I've never done this before," she admitted.

"Can't say I have much experience with it, myself," he confessed.

"It's . . . nice," she allowed.

"Good," he said gruffly. "Now be quiet. And sleep."

"So commanding," she murmured with a little smile.

"Can't fight my nature." He brought up his gloved hand and lightly cradled the side of her face. Heat and awareness stole through her at his touch. "Hush."

Warmth stole through her body at his touch, gentle and masculine at the same time. Soon, her lids lowered. She felt her breathing grow slow and even.

Then . . .

Her eyes flicked open. The carriage had stopped.

She lay curled up, partially in Alex's lap. His arms circled her, holding her gently but firmly, keeping her from rolling onto the floor. He looked down at her, unsmiling, but with warmth in his eyes.

No one had ever held her this way.

She shot upright. "What happened? Where are we?"

"We're home." He kept one arm around her shoulders. "We've been home for half an hour."

"And you let me just lie there?" she cried.

"It would be rude to wake you."

"I—" Her heart thudded painfully. That night in Cheltenham, she'd kept from falling asleep beside him. Instead, she'd waited until he'd dozed off before sliding out of bed and throwing on her clothes. She'd known what it would do to her to fall asleep next to him, how it would tie them closer together, creating an intimacy stronger and more potent than sex.

But she hadn't been so wise this time. Closeness wove thickly through the interior of the carriage. Shards of emotion buried deep in her chest, wounding her. She couldn't allow herself to give in to the feelings she had for him. A swindler could *not* love a duke. It was awful to even entertain such an idea. It was a certain formula for heartbreak.

Yet she was falling, falling—even deeper than she had in Cheltenham. And the longer she stayed close to Alex, the greater the danger became.

Without saying another word, she lunged for the door. She almost fell to the pavement, but managed to right herself before bolting past the butler, who held open the front door, and raced up the stairs to seek the safety of her room.

Curse her for a fool and an idiot. She'd tried to stop it from happening again, but it didn't matter. She was losing her heart to the duke.

Chapter 11

Alex strode into White's. Men gathered in groups, or sat with the newspapers near the fireplace, or took their supper in solitude. The air was heavy with the scents of brandy and tobacco and beefsteak. Male voices murmured or laughed, free to do exactly as they pleased without the burden of female company.

It was a peculiarity of his class, he realized, that it looked for excuses to separate men and women. After dinner, the ladies had to retreat to the drawing room while men were given the liberty to smoke and swear. As far as Alex knew, there were no clubs that only permitted women. But genteel men thought it necessary to hide themselves away, as if they sheltered delicate feminine sensibilities from men's brutish, coarse nature.

He'd once thought Cassandra one of those women who couldn't bear to hear of raw, earthy topics. Society widows needed protecting. But he'd been very wrong. She knew every aspect of the world, from the high to the low. Nothing disturbed or shocked her.

But *he* was still shocked. He'd believed that she'd slept with all of her marks. That she'd used her body to line her pockets. Yet that hadn't been the case at all. He had been the exception.

And, now that he thought of it, she'd only gone to his bed *after* he'd given her money. Nothing but her own desires had motivated her.

His axis had shifted, realigning entire hemispheres. The apology he'd given had been entirely sincere. He saw now that she wasn't the cold mercenary he'd believed. He had meant something to her besides another source of money. Guilt and relief filled him now, a strange alloy of emotions he wasn't certain how to address. He winced when he thought about how he'd made her suffer, and said such cruel things to her.

Neither of us are innocent in this, he told himself as he moved farther into the club. They'd both hurt each other, and acted from self-interest and self-protection. Now, they had to move forward—wiser, wary, but clear-eyed.

He'd always been so sure of himself, smugly discharging his responsibilities as the Duke of Greyland, confident that he acted precisely in the way he was supposed to. Yet ever since Cassandra had returned, he'd been forced to face the realization that he was not the infallible creature everyone believed him to be. He'd ventured off his narrow route into realms unknown to him. And he liked it.

He didn't want to be the staid, stolid duke any

longer. She'd shown him there was much more to life than going through the motions by rote. In Cheltenham she'd reached the man buried beneath the title. Now she showed him a world much wider, more dangerous, more thrilling, than anything he'd known.

A footman approached him. "May I get you something, Your Grace?"

"Whiskey, and the location of Lord Langdon and Mr. Christopher Ellingsworth."

"Of course, Your Grace. And the gentlemen are in the billiards room." The footman bowed before heading off to fetch Alex a drink.

Alex meandered back toward the room set aside for billiards. He needed to speak with his friends—yet his body urged him to return home. To Cassandra.

In this unlikely place, hours after the event had occurred, his arms still felt the warmth of her body as she'd lain within them, sleeping peacefully. He'd never seen her so unguarded, yet despite the softness of her expression, a small line formed between her brows, as if even in sleep, anxiety managed to find her. Would she ever discover a way to fully let go, or would her troubles haunt her always? He wanted to smooth that line away. He wanted to hold her until the strength of his arms gave out. His heart throbbed to see her in his embrace, and a painful yearning thrummed through his body to repeat the experience.

Every step led them into murky waters that showed no sign of clearing.

Conflicting feelings clashed against each other in his heart, his mind, and his body. No denying that he desired her—powerfully—but that hunger didn't exist alone. It kept company with something warmer, more expansive.

He couldn't consider this now. The situation with Hughes had to be resolved, and soon. Cassandra was in desperate straits. Ruthless underworld figures demanded money—or her hide.

Following the click of billiard balls striking each other, Alex made his way toward the back.

"Your whiskey, Your Grace," the footman said, appearing with a glass on a tray.

Alex took the drink and swallowed it in one gulp, then returned the glass to its tray. The alcohol didn't dull the edges of his emotions, however.

He paused in the doorway of the billiards room, where tables were arrayed, all of them surrounded by small groups of men. In the middle stood the distinctive figures of Langdon and Ellingsworth. Langdon was setting up a shot, but he glanced up and saw Alex hovering in the entryway.

"My God," Langdon exclaimed after taking his shot. He neatly sank a ball in the pocket. "The great beast awakens."

Ellingsworth came forward, holding his cue. "Where the hell have you been?" He stuck out his hand and Alex obligingly shook it.

"Been busy," Alex said tersely.

"Doing what?" asked Ellingsworth.

"Or whom?" Langdon added with a leer.

"Neither of you are named in my will," Alex noted, "so I fail to see how any of my activities are your business."

"You haven't solicited our congratulations," Ellingsworth said drily. "Clearly, then, you aren't engaged."

Alex had forgotten that the last time he'd spoken to Ellingsworth, he'd been on the verge of asking Cassandra to marry him. It felt like several lifetimes had passed since then. He now held the wisdom of a much-older man. Yet he felt more liberated than he ever had in his life.

"Not engaged," Ellingsworth continued, peering closely at him, "but definitely engrossed."

"The widow from the gaming hell?" Langdon demanded. Evidently, Ellingsworth had apprised him of some of the particulars. "Did she refuse you?"

Alex stepped forward and ran his hand along the baize covering the table. He'd always enjoyed the feel of the fabric's nap against his fingers. Why didn't he play billiards more? He was always too busy with a thousand different responsibilities.

He also couldn't ignore his friends' questions.

"She's not exactly wife material," he allowed.

"Then she's mistress material," Langdon declared.

"She's complicated," Alex growled.

"Apparently," Ellingsworth answered. "Since she's not a wife and not a mistress."

"What is she then?" Langdon pressed, leaning against his cue. Their game was forgotten in the wake of this unwanted interrogation.

Alex answered in a low voice, "Some women don't fit into categories." Cassandra especially defied all definitions. "I'm not here to discuss her."

Ellingsworth and Langdon groaned in frustration. "You are the least accommodating person in England," Langdon said sulkily. "How are we to amuse ourselves if not at your expense?"

"I've heard the cure for boredom is work." Alex folded his arms across his chest and couldn't resist a smile when his friends both made sounds of horror.

"Sirrah, you will recant those words immediately," Ellingsworth declared hotly.

"I cannot accept blame if you find the cure worse than the disease." He looked pointedly at Langdon. "Aren't you going to inherit a dukedom one day? Surely *that* will entail you dredging up a speck of dependability."

"My father is a hale and healthy man," Langdon answered. "May all the gods of debauchery protect him for many more years."

"Not me," Ellingsworth said cheerfully. "I'm a third son. No one gives a rat's arse what I do with myself."

Alex shook his head.

"You can't go quiet on us," Ellingsworth insisted. "Not now, when it's patently obvious that this Cheltenham chit has got you in a spin."

Langdon seemed to remember that they were in the middle of a game. He lined up another shot and called it, but came up scratch. "Damn." He straightened.

Alex sighed. They were determined to rile him. He grabbed one of the billiard balls and rapped it like a gavel on the side of the table. "This inquest is closed. We will now move on to other topics."

"You ruined our game." Ellingsworth pouted. "That's fifty pounds to both of us."

"Bring it up with my man of business." Alex straightened. "I'm here because I need your help—despite the fact that you're London's most irresponsible bachelors."

"Don't flatter us," Ellingsworth said.

Alex produced the coin and set it on the side of the billiards table.

Both Ellingsworth and Langdon came forward and studied it. After a moment, smiles wreathed their faces.

"Never knew you had it in you," Langdon said, his eyes bright.

"Bloody sly dog, that's what you are." Ellingsworth grinned. "Keeping more secrets from us. You had us fooled, I admit it. Years, we've known you. And all this time . . ." He wagged a finger at Alex.

"I've no idea what either of you are blathering about," Alex growled.

Langdon took the coin and held it up between two fingers. "It's a token given to people who visit the Orchid Club more than three times."

"Never heard of this Orchid Club."

Ellingsworth raised his brow. "Never? You're the sodding Duke of Greyland, and you don't know about this?"

"Clearly, I don't," Alex ground out, "or else I wouldn't be here with you two hyenas."

"The Orchid Club," Langdon said, stepping closer and lowering his voice, "happens every few weeks. It's a place where people of all walks go to fulfill their erotic desires."

Alex blinked. This was not what he was expecting.

"Everyone wears masks." Ellingsworth continued the thread, his voice also lowered. "No one is allowed to reveal their identity."

"And," Langdon added with a widening smile, "within the confines of the club's walls, you can indulge your every sexual fantasy."

"A club for masked, anonymous sex," Alex concluded.

"I cannot believe you've never heard of it." Langdon sounded appalled.

"It's a secret club, isn't it?" Alex snapped. "And I've been too busy running the country to spend time wearing masks and having sex with random strangers."

Ellingsworth smirked. "That's precisely why you need to go."

"Have *you* gone?" Alex demanded.

Both of his friends smiled, but neither answered.

"I will tell you this," Ellingsworth said after a long pause. "Young buck Langdon here goes to see a particular woman. He's holding a *tendre* for the club's manager, Amina."

A wistful look came over Langdon's face. "I'll allow that I wouldn't return to the club as often as I do, if it wasn't for Amina." Even the way he spoke the woman's name sounded reverential. The fact that Langdon could prefer one lady over another stunned Alex. His friend was hardly ever without female company, always a new woman. But clearly, Alex didn't know everything about Langdon.

"She's not on the menu," Ellingsworth added. "Much to Langdon's dismay."

Indeed, the man in question appeared crestfallen that this Amina would never yield to his seductions. What a novel experience it must be for Langdon, to want a woman and not be able to have her.

"When is the next time the club meets?" Alex asked.

Langdon brightened. "You're in luck, because it's tomorrow night. I can give you the direction, if you want. And the password. If you want to go."

A union hall for swindlers? Secret masked sex clubs that required passwords? London was a far more varied place than Alex had ever given it credit for.

"I do," said Alex. It was the best clue toward finding Hughes.

"What about the widow?" Langdon wondered.

"It's because of her that I'm going," he answered.

His friends exchanged baffled looks, but he wasn't about to explain what he meant.

"Don't forget," Langdon cautioned, "wear a mask. Tell no one your real name."

"And tell us *everything* that happens," added Ellingsworth.

"I'll wear a mask and keep my identity a secret," Alex said. "But I'm not telling either of you a thing. I thought that was the object of the club—secrecy."

Ellingsworth laughed. "Point to Greyland."

Alex laughed in acknowledgment. He had a feeling his friends kept him around just to tease him and rile his sense of decorum—but they were there when he needed counsel and attention, so surely they had some genuine fondness for him.

Langdon gave him the address and password, which he scribbled down on a slip of paper and tucked away with the coin in his pocket.

With his mission completed, Alex started for the door. "Already taking your leave?" Ellingsworth asked with a puzzled frown. "The night's barely started."

"I've no taste tonight for the theater or another gaming hell," he answered. Impatience gnawed on him.

"At least join us in another round of billiards," Langdon protested. "Before you ruined our game, I was two-thirds of the way to beating Ellingsworth, and I need someone else to play."

"More like three-fifths toward besting me," grumbled Ellingsworth.

"No need to rush away," Langdon concluded. "Unless . . ." His look turned speculative. "You're scurrying off to see the Cheltenham widow."

"I don't scurry," Alex answered at once. He paused.

Was that what he was doing? Running home so he could be near Cassandra?

He was.

Alex was balanced precariously on a sword's tip. He could fall in either direction. He could stay and try to prove to himself through sheer obstinacy that he did *not* still have feelings for Cassandra. Or he could follow his heart's demands and go home.

Langdon and Ellingsworth gazed at him expectantly. A film of sweat coated Alex's back. He looked at his friends and wondered what the hell was happening to him.

CASSANDRA slowly walked along the length of bookshelves lining Alex's library. She ran her fingers over the spines, enjoying the feel of the smooth leather and the scent of quality paper. She wasn't much in the mood for a book—despite her fifteen years of literacy, reading still didn't come easily. She could peruse a book for its meaning, but the process was slow and difficult. The theater suited her much better, and she'd heard that Lady Marwood had penned a new burletta for the Imperial Theater. Yet she hadn't the funds or desire to venture out of the safety of Alex's home. No one could threaten or hurt her here. That also meant she'd have to find some way of amusing herself for the length of the evening.

The library felt strongly of Alex, as if he somehow lived within the rows and rows of books and knowledge and privilege—a private library was an expensive luxury reserved for very few. The scents of smoke and leather also reminded her of him. She could picture him here, soberly perusing book after book, filling his mind with information and facts. There were few novels here, mostly treatises on history, science, and politics. She smiled to herself. None of the tart, sentimental works of Miss Austen for the duke.

She pulled a large volume down from the shelf. *The Fauna and Flora of North America.* This might prove interesting, considering the fact that she might be emigrating soon.

Settling down in an armchair by the fire, she opened the book and propped her chin in one hand. Leisurely, she turned the pages, enjoying the sounds of crinkling paper and the bright colors of birds and flowers. She didn't bother reading the small descriptive paragraphs about each specimen. Her mind was too much at war with itself to hold on to anything of worth.

She hadn't left her room until she'd been certain Alex had gone for the night, off to seek the counsel of his friends. Her body still felt the heat and strength of his arms enfolding her, keeping her safe. Holding her as if she mattered.

The tip of her finger traced the outline of a creature called the golden eagle. The bird's sharp profile and powerful gaze—as well as its dangerous talons—evoked Alex. They were so alike in looks and character. Both were striking and commanding, lethal and regal. An illustration of a mother eagle on her nest accompanied the image. She looked protective yet caring for her defenseless young. Even that recalled Alex, and the way in which he'd cared for and sheltered her.

She exhaled in frustration. Her feelings for him grew more knotted by the moment. She dreaded the emotions he stirred within her whenever he was near, yet she couldn't hide from them. There was no running from the fact that part of her heart already belonged to him. It had, ever since Cheltenham. Moment by moment, she sensed herself tumbling further down a dangerous slope, linking her closer and closer to Alex, yet knowing there was nothing she could do about her desires.

Quick, heavy footsteps sounded in the hallway. She glanced up. The servants were almost silent as they went about their work. It couldn't be a footman. Then who . . . ?

Alex appeared in the doorway of the library. Her breath caught at the sight of him, slightly windblown and gravely handsome.

She found her voice. "You're back early." It had only been an hour. She'd fully expected not to see him again until the morning.

He strode into the room and went to the bookshelves, his hands clasped behind his back. He didn't look at her as he spoke. "My business wrapped up quickly. Besides," he added, "I can go wherever I please without facing a barrage of questions."

Her brows lifted. Clearly, this was a point of contention for him. It would be the wiser course of action to let the subject go.

"Were your friends helpful?" She shut her book and set it on a nearby table. "Did they tell you the meaning of the coin?"

He turned to face her, then leaned against the bookshelves with his arms crossed over his chest. "It's for someplace called the Orchid Club."

She frowned. "Never heard of it."

"It's a secret society," he said. "The guests wear masks to keep their identities hidden. But that's where the discretion ends."

"I don't understand," she said. "Speak plainly."

"The guests have sex with each other," he said quickly. "That's the point of the club. A location where they can indulge in their carnal fantasies."

No glib reply came from her lips. This news actually surprised her, and she'd thought nothing could shock her anymore. She knew brothels existed, particularly those that catered to clients' specific desires, but what the Orchid Club offered was new to her.

"Martin goes *there*?" she wondered aloud, vaguely appalled. "That's . . . not like him."

"You know his sexual preferences?"

She made a face. "God, no." Thinking about his erotic appetites made her dimly nauseated. "It doesn't seem like him, though. He kept that part of his life private."

"A man has needs," Alex said lowly.

They gazed at each other, heat gathering between her legs. No mistaking the hunger in his look, or how her own body responded at once with its own demands, warming her, making her both languid and alert. Craving his touch.

But he didn't cross the library to come to her. Instead, he kept himself rooted in place, as if shackled.

A thought struck her with the force of a blow. "This means we have to go to this Orchid Club." It was outrageous. Appalling. Intriguing. "Wear masks and search for Martin while people have sex all around us."

"Appears so." His voice was no more than a guttural growl.

Oh, God. How in the bloody hell was she supposed to attend a secret sex club with Alex? On her own, she could easily stay on task. But with him beside her . . . that changed the equation significantly.

She could do this. She could stay focused, despite the fire between her and Alex, and her growing attachment to him. They'd go to the club, perform their reconnaissance, and move forward. She wouldn't throw herself at him. She wouldn't get lost in the maze of desire and yearning.

Keep telling yourself that.

Whatever she felt for Alex, she'd have to set it aside while they hunted Martin. Yet that was easier said than accomplished. Words and deeds were two very different things, and she knew from personal experience that one often had nothing to do with the other.

"Are you ready to face the Orchid Club?" he asked.

She fought a hysterical laugh. *Ready?* Ready to be surrounded by people giving in to their hungers as she struggled against her own? Ready to hide behind a mask while her heart was open and exposed to him?

Never, she thought.

"Of course," she said brightly.

Chapter 12

From its exterior, the three-story house in Bloomsbury looked to Alex like any other affluent home, with
its tidy plantings and neat, columned portico. Heavy
curtains shielded all the windows from prying eyes—
like his own—and as he stood with Cassandra on the
curb outside, he could very faintly hear a pianoforte
and violin above the night's quiet.

"Doesn't look like a place where people go to roger
each other," Cassandra murmured, echoing his thoughts.

"The value of concealment should be well-known to
you," he answered.

She ran a finger over the beaded edge of her violet
silk mask. It matched her cloak and gown, which he'd
ordered from a dressmaker that morning. He'd paid a
goodly sum to ensure the disguise's timely delivery, despite Cassandra's vehement protests over the expense.
She'd only calmed herself when he had assured her the
cost wouldn't go to the already-substantial tally she
owed him.

"But it's new to you," she noted, lightly tugging on the cord that affixed his own mask in place. Alex's tailor had readily provided the gray silk mask, most likely happy to attend the needs of one of his best customers. The dark evening clothes Alex sported had already been in his closet—though his valet had looked slightly bemused by Alex's request for an anonymous-looking ensemble.

"This is unknown territory for both of us." He nodded toward the building, where, supposedly inside, people indulged in their every sexual desire.

He'd fallen into an upside-down world, where nothing was as it seemed. Alex barely recognized his own razor or the shape of his face as he'd shaved in preparation for the night's excursion. He was doing things he'd never done before, journeying off the map. The most shocking thing of all was that he enjoyed it.

He *liked* not knowing where he was heading from one moment to the next. He reveled in living in the shadows, rather than the harsh light of day. Respectable noblemen didn't don masks and venture to secret erotic societies. Yet he was doing precisely that, and it gave him a giddy sense of freedom. He could be anyone, do anything.

It was intoxicating.

"Martin used to say that the best way to try something new was to brazen it out," she said wryly. "Pretend that you know what you're doing, and everyone will believe you're an expert."

He exhaled. "Not unlike the first time I stepped into the House of Lords."

Her smile flashed before disappearing quickly. "That's the first time you've equated yourself with someone like me. What new wonder is next? Maybe the capital of England will relocate to Siam."

Every moment in her company, he grew less and less certain of his fundamental beliefs. He'd known himself so thoroughly until he met Cassandra. Or so he had believed. Yet each step forward revealed aspects of himself he'd never realized.

"It's nearly midnight," he noted, checking his pocket watch. "Surely if Hughes was here, he'd be inside by now."

"Time to breach the den of iniquity." She straightened her shoulders. "Lead on, Macduff. And no," she added, her eyes glinting behind her mask, "I haven't read *Macbeth*. Or any Shakespeare."

"You know the lines."

"Seen the plays performed by strolling companies," she said pragmatically. "Didn't care for them, but I know your kind can't get enough of Billy W's flowery words."

The audacity of this woman. Shaking his head at her name for Shakespeare, he led them through the gate and up the front steps. His pulse was a steady, hard throb. He knew logically what was behind the door of this Bloomsbury house, but that didn't take away his trepidation and excitement about seeing it in the flesh.

Recalling Langdon's and Ellingsworth's instructions, he knocked on the door. *Tap. Tap tap. Tap.*

A moment later, a woman in a ruby-red mask opened the door. She wore her dark hair loose, and her black eyes were guarded but curious as she surveyed him and Cassandra.

"I've come for the plums," he said.

The masked woman answered, "We haven't any."

"Peaches will suffice," he replied.

She smiled in welcome and held the door open wider, permitting them to enter. They walked into an elegant, dimly lit foyer. "Welcome, friends. Is this your first time joining us?"

"It is," Cassandra answered.

The woman's smile widened. "You are most heartily received here. As my gift to you, your first time at the Orchid Club costs nothing. A fee is required for each additional visit. But for now, please accept my compliments along with your admission."

Alex bowed and Cassandra executed a flawless curtsy. He'd almost forgotten that she easily moved within elite social circles, but seeing her so politely thank the masked woman, he recalled how effortlessly she could inhabit the role of Society widow.

"I am Amina," the woman continued.

Intriguing. This was the woman who ran the club—and who had captured Langdon's interest. Her age was impossible to tell, but she was slim and richly dressed. The slightly darker hue of her skin evinced that somewhere in the mysterious Amina's history, there had been a mixed union. She had a sleek, regal appearance and held herself with elegant reserve.

How unlike Langdon's usual tastes for lushly curved, bold actresses and dancers who made no secret of their interest in a man.

"Before you proceed," Amina went on, "I must advise you of the rules of the house." She held up a finger. "I am the only person within these walls permitted a name. Everyone else must keep their identities to themselves. Further," she added, "no guest can do anything to anyone else without consent. Nothing is forced. Participation is always optional. This is a place of freedom and safety."

"Of course, madam," Alex answered as Cassandra said, "Yes, Amina."

The manager's face grew serious. "Those who violate the rules are told to leave and can never return again. Will you comply?"

Alex and Cassandra exchanged a quick look. "We will," he replied for them both.

Amina's smile returned. "Then I bid you enter. Please, indulge yourselves. No one is judged here." She smoothed a hand down her gown. "If you will excuse me, I have business to attend to." She disappeared down a hallway, melting into the shadows.

Alex glanced at Cassandra in silent question. *Shall we go forward?*

We shall, she said wordlessly, tilting her head.

With her still on his arm, they walked down the corridor, following the sounds of voices and music. The hallway opened up to a large chamber, not unlike a grand parlor, where guests in a wide variety of clothing gathered in small groups. There were women and men wearing the height of fashion and others less expensively dressed. Regardless of the cost of their garments, everyone wore masks, and they mingled freely amongst themselves, heedless of the difference in their social rank.

"Not quite the usual soiree," Cassandra murmured.

"A little of the ordinary," he noted, glancing toward the servants circulating with trays of wine and cake. Music continued to swirl, flowing through an open door that led to what appeared to be a ballroom, where guests danced. He'd been to wilder gatherings, particularly when thrown by Ellingsworth or Langdon.

"There's more to this party than polite conversation and piquet." She looked pointedly at a nearby couple. The woman openly stroked the man's chest as his hand slipped inside the neckline of her bodice. More of the guests overtly touched each other: faces, bodies, as well as beneath their clothing.

In one of the corners, a woman gasped as she reclined on a sofa. A man's head and shoulders disappeared beneath her skirts as he knelt before her.

Against the wall, three men stroked the front of each other's breeches.

Groups of two or more were everywhere, kissing, touching. Blatantly. Unashamedly.

Now he could smell it—the mingled scents of wine,

sweat, and sex. It hung thickly in the air, along with moans and whispers. He had been to small gatherings that consisted of wealthy men and courtesans, where ribald talk and unconcealed touches were encouraged. But nothing on this scale. No place where people of both sexes permitted themselves any and all pleasures.

Cassandra's hand tightened on his arm. He tore his eyes from the scenes around him to watch her. Her mask concealed part of her face, but her nostrils flared, her lips parted. One of her hands fluttered at her throat.

She was aroused. And so was he.

His body was on fire, and his heartbeat pounded hard and steady.

What had he been thinking, bringing her here?

Pulling his gaze from Cassandra, he saw Amina across the chamber. She spoke with a tall, dark-haired man. Was it Langdon? The stranger had his friend's height and ranginess. The unknown man also angled his body toward Amina, as if she absorbed his full attention and he wanted to shield her from other prospective suitors.

The man said something to Amina, causing her to tip her head back and laugh. It was a low, rich sound, full of sensual knowledge. One of the servants eased up beside Amina and whispered in her ear. She spoke quickly with the servant, then curtsied to the man and hurried off. An almost-palpable longing radiated out from her would-be swain as his shoulders sagged and his hands curled into frustrated fists.

It had to be Langdon. When Amina disappeared, he stared after her for a few moments before slowly ambling off. He hardly seemed to pay attention to his surroundings. A barely dressed woman intercepted him and smiled in invitation. He merely bowed before going on his way. Alone.

Curious. Very curious indeed, to see a duke's heir so smitten by a woman who managed a place for clandestine erotic encounters. She was clearly of mixed blood, as well. The *ton* wasn't precisely known for its tolerance. Alex wished he could console Langdon, but he couldn't speak of what he'd seen here tonight. He had to respect the Orchid Club's tenets, as well as his friend's privacy.

"We should keep moving," he said. "Seems suspicious if we're just standing here."

"Here *looking* is just as popular as *doing*," she remarked breathlessly. She nodded toward a lady standing not two feet from two other women lying on a chaise. The lady peered through a lorgnette, watching the women kissing and fondling each other as if she was attending the Royal Opera. The kissing women paid her no attention—an arrangement which seemed to suit both parties.

"But we should explore the rest of the club," Cassandra added. "It's always key to get a sense of the place before taking action."

"Spoken like a strategist," he observed. How was it that they could carry on a rational conversation, when not ten yards away, a woman sank to her knees in front of a man dressed like a shopkeeper?

He guided Cassandra into the next chamber, where guests danced the waltz with their bodies pressed tightly against one another. The music continued as if this was a typical assembly, and not one where a man fucked a woman up against a wall in full view of everyone.

"Difficult to think of strategy with . . . *this*," Cassandra remarked, her gaze fixed on the couple having sex. She shook her head. "What a marvelous place London is—anything and everything is there for the taking." She touched her lips.

The urge to put his fingers on her lips, to taste her mouth—to taste every part of her—roared through him. He'd crowd her against the wall, pin her wrists, savage her mouth. Run his hands up the long lines of her legs. Touch her.

None of this was part of the plan.

"We're here to look for Hughes." He needed to remind himself.

"I'm grateful for the masks." She glanced around. "But they make it hard to identify anyone."

"Even the servants are masked." He tipped his head toward a pretty, redheaded woman carrying a tray of wineglasses. When her tray was empty, she tucked it beneath her arm and took a man's hand, then led him to a woman standing on her own. Through a few words and gestures, the servant made introductions, and within moments, the two strangers were locked in a passionate embrace. The serving woman moved away, satisfied by a job well done.

"Did you notice?" Cassandra murmured. "Around the servant's throat . . ."

"A necklace."

"An expensive bauble for someone who serves wine and acts as a go-between."

Alex looked closer as the servant picked up empty glasses. Indeed, the necklace appeared a good deal more elaborate than a woman on servants' wages might be able to afford. Triple strands of pearls formed swags between gleaming sapphires, with pearl drops hanging from each precious stone. Even from a distance, the quality was clear. Nothing was paste. There was something vulgar about the display—a well-bred woman would eschew elaborate adornment.

"A present from a grateful guest?" Alex suggested.

"Looks familiar . . ." Cassandra mused. The woman moved to another room, and Alex and Cassandra discreetly followed, observing her from the doorway.

"I don't see how it can," Alex noted. "It appears one of a kind."

Cassandra swore softly under her breath. "Before the gaming hell opened, Martin and I went shopping for furnishings. We passed a jewelry shop. He stopped and admired a necklace. It looked almost identical to the one that woman's wearing."

"The connection might be there," Alex said, considering. "She works for Hughes?"

"Or she's his mistress," Cassandra answered grimly.

"Makes sense." Alex rubbed at his chin as he watched the woman move through the guests. "He'd give her something as a token of affection after he ran off with the money. If she lives in London, he might stay in town for her." He glanced at the redhead, who was pouring glasses of wine. "We can follow her."

"She'll be here all night," Cassandra pointed out. "We'll need to wait her out, and follow her home once she gets off of work."

Realization seemed to hit Alex and Cassandra at the same time. They stared at each other. Most likely, the club ran until the early hours of the morning. They were going to have to stay here—together—all night. Surrounded by blatant displays of carnality.

It was torture. It was heaven.

"Wine, friends?" The redhead approached them with two full glasses.

Alex wanted to snap, "Did Martin Hughes give you that necklace?" Instead, he said, "No, thank you."

"None for me," Cassandra added. The redhead smiled and moved on, heading into another room.

Wine would only fog Alex's brain, and he needed to be perfectly in control tonight. This club was dangerous. More perilous than a room full of gunpowder and lit candles. He needed to be sharp and smart to make it through the night with his sanity intact.

"Shall we dance?" The words left his mouth before he could consider their wisdom.

She glanced toward the dance floor where couples waltzed. You couldn't fit a leaf between their bodies. Some barely danced, merely swaying in place as they kissed or caressed their partners.

It was the absolute last thing they should do. He prayed she'd refuse.

"Yes," she said after a moment. "Let's dance."

He took her hand in his. Neither wore gloves, their skin sliding against each other, absorbing heat. With deliberate, formal steps, he led her to where the others danced. They took up their positions, her hand on his shoulder, his at her waist, with their other hands clasped. But they didn't allot the usual distance between their bodies. Her chest grazed his. They weren't intimately entangled, yet each brush of her breasts against him sent molten heat through him, pooling in his cock.

She gazed up at him. Her face in the candlelight was a luminous thing, flushed and dewy. Beneath her mask, her pupils had grown large, dark and fathomless. Her lips were parted, and the tip of her tongue grazed her bottom lip, making it glisten.

They waited a heartbeat, then began to move with the music. Both of them knew the steps, moving in unison across the floor. They spun together. The room was a whirl of color and heat, substantial yet growing distant as he focused only on her. On the feel of her. The life and breath and flesh and warmth of her in his arms. She was lithe and supple, fragrant with roses and sweetness, and her own scent rising up from her skin in an invisible, intoxicating mist.

Nothing mattered more than this *now*. Her. Him. The press of her hips against his. The sway of them aligned and perfect, needing no words, boundaries dissolving. It no longer signified who had cheated whom, who had lied, who demanded more than the other could give. They were elemental. Man and woman in a timeless dance.

He couldn't resist any longer.

Without stopping their turns, he lowered his head and kissed her. She opened to him at once, eager and ravenous for more. The kiss sank deeper, tongues stroking velvet sleek depths. Her hands gripped his shoulders. Through the tissue of her cloak and the silk of her dress, he cupped her arse, bringing her tight against him. She moaned into his mouth at the feel of his cock, hard and demanding as it rose between them.

They stopped the movements of the dance, too enraptured by the kiss to do anything more. He pulled away enough to growl in her ear. "Yes. Open for me. Give me everything." He nuzzled against her throat. "I'll take it. I'll take everything you offer. Over your clothes. Beneath your gown." Lightly, he stroked his fingertips across her collarbone. "You're wet for me. I know you are. I want to feel your flesh all around me. You're hot. So goddamn hot. A flame. Burn me up." He pressed his lips to the spot where her neck curved into her shoulder. "Take me into you and burn me to ashes."

Words poured from him between kisses. Words he couldn't—wouldn't—stop. They were a tribute and a command. He was hers and she belonged to him. And they were lashed together by their kisses and his words.

The more he spoke, the more fevered her lips became. The more urgent the feel of her body against his. Higher and higher, to heights that couldn't be measured, they rose together.

The room around them fell away. He noticed nothing but her as she broke the kiss, leading him toward a chaise in the corner.

She lay down on the chaise and pulled him atop her. She was alive and hot beneath him, writhing in demand. "Alex," she said, low and husky. Her arms wrapped around him. She pulled him down for another long, scorching kiss. "Touch me. Now."

He didn't care about where he was or who might see him. He glanced to one side and saw a trio of women watching him and Cassandra.

It didn't matter. All that signified was her. After pushing her cloak out of the way, his hand found the round swell of her breast rising up against the fabric of her bodice. He dipped his fingers beneath the neckline, finding her tight nipple. She gasped against his mouth as he rubbed and lightly pinched the firm point of her breast. Answering pleasure tore through him to hear her respond so readily to his touch.

With his other hand, he gathered up the fabric of her skirts. He glided up her leg, testing the feel of silk-covered flesh beneath his palm. She had smooth, sleek legs, and they moved restlessly under his hand. His fingers brushed the ribbons of her garter. Then he found the creamy flesh of her thigh. She wore no drawers.

He groaned at this revelation, but didn't stop the progress of his hand. He cupped the silk and satin of her mound. She arched up with a cry the moment his fingers dipped between her folds, finding her as wet as he'd hoped, eager and ready for him. Delving deeper, he stroked her—around her opening, circling her clit. She was wild beneath him as he teased and caressed, and when he sank two fingers inside her, she came with a long, low moan.

But he wasn't satisfied—continued to stroke and caress her until he made her come again, and once more. Finally, her body splayed limp against the chaise. He brought his fingers into his mouth, and she blushed deeply, gorgeously, as he licked her up.

He felt the press of her hand against his urgent cock. She wanted to give him the same satisfaction.

Carefully, he removed her hand from him.

"But you haven't . . ." she murmured.

"When we're alone, you'll cry my name, and I'll shout yours. This is a place for namelessness." When it was time for her to touch him, for him to be truly seated within her, he desired nothing and no one around them. Just the pleasure and experience of her body and his.

If he wanted mere sexual gratification, he could have let her touch him. Yet he desired more than the brief release of orgasm. He hungered for *her*. All of her. Body and heart.

They sat side by side on the chaise. After resetting her skirts, smoothing them down, a rush of tenderness threatened to overwhelm him. He'd done everything he could to protect himself, but for naught. He had crossed a bridge. The battlements had been breached.

There was no going back. They were bound to each other now.

His hand settled possessively on her thigh. The night would be a long one, and all too brief.

Chapter 13

With Alex's hand on her thigh, Cassandra felt every nerve alight. Normally, she would grow sleepy after achieving release. Not with Alex. Never had she felt more aware of every sight, every sensation.

She wanted so much more. This had merely been a prelude. Her body glowed with need and wanting him. A fuse had been lit, and she was ready to explode.

They sat side by side as though they were guests at an afternoon soiree. Cassandra couldn't believe she'd just allowed Alex to touch her quim and bring her to orgasm in front of an audience. She was certain they'd had watchers, but couldn't care. She'd wanted him too much to worry about making a spectacle of herself, lost utterly in the web of need they'd woven.

A woman strolled past and gave Cassandra a wink. Clearly, they'd drawn some attention to themselves.

There was no greater danger for a swindler than to let their emotions take command. But she'd been out of control ever since she'd seen him at the gaming hell.

What had been a mere promise in Cheltenham had fully flowered in London. There was no protecting herself from it any longer.

She was his, and would be until fate tore them apart. And it would separate them—it was only a matter of when.

Her chest squeezed at thoughts of future doom. Yet it was unavoidable, like the sunrise.

"We've hours until dawn," she said lowly. "How can we fill our time?"

"I don't see anyone playing cards." He craned his neck, looking into another adjoining chamber. But people didn't come to the Orchid Club for games of loo or whist. Strange that they were conversing so normally, when just a few minutes ago, he'd brought her to ecstasy. Several times.

He turned to her, sharp and handsome in the low light. "Tell me what you'd do with yourself if you didn't earn your coin from swindling."

"I've got little half-formed ideas tumbling around my mind, but nothing solid," she admitted. "All I've really concerned myself with is keeping my head above water. This can't last forever, but what happens after?"

"There's nothing at all you want to do?"

"Maybe own a shop," she finally admitted. "Or learn to draw, or play an instrument. The kind of things ladies do to fill their time." She gave a strained laugh. "Been pretending to be a lady for so long, but to really *be* one . . . I'll never know what that's like."

"I can't tell you," he said with a self-deprecating shrug. "Since I'm not a lady." His mouth quirked. "Lady Emmeline was fond of dancing, pianoforte, and. . . . I can't think of anything else."

"Surely she had passions," Cassandra objected. A tiny jolt of jealousy coursed through her, thinking of the woman he'd almost married.

"Either she didn't voice them," he allowed, "or I'd been too concerned with myself and my need for a suitable bride to ask her." He shook his head. "Thinking on it now, I'm not proud of how I behaved toward her. Even if *she* jilted *me*."

"Powerful dukes probably don't receive much education in empathy," she pointed out.

He took two glasses of wine from a passing servant, while she took a few iced cakes for sustenance. They sat quietly, sipping wine and nibbling very good, sugary cakes, as they watched more couples spin around the dance floor. His thigh pressed against hers, reminding her of the intimacy they'd shared—and how much more they had to explore.

"And if you weren't a duke," she continued, "what would *you* do with yourself? Indulge me."

He was silent a long while, but then said, "I've always been the heir. From the cradle, they told me, 'This will be yours someday.' It's all I've known."

"You can dream now," she suggested, lightly knocking her shoulder against his. "The Orchid Club doesn't have to only be about sexual fancies. Give in to your other fantasies now. If you could be anything in the world, other than a duke, what would you be?"

He fell into another pensive silence. They were, she realized, part of what made Alex who he was. He didn't blurt out answers. He thought, he pondered and brooded, choosing words and thoughts carefully like a man picking through a coffer full of gems.

"A ship's captain," he finally said. "Exploring unknown worlds. Sailing beyond the horizon in search of adventure."

She raised her brows. "I would have thought you'd want to be an architect or mathematician—using numbers and rules to make order out of chaos."

"I would have agreed with you only a few weeks ago."

"And now?"

A corner of his mouth tilted up as he gazed at her. "I'm discovering that I like chaos."

"That can't be on my account!"

"It surely is." He smiled, then sobered. "Truth be told, I'm glad I'm a duke."

"All that wealth and power," she said, nodding.

"Well, yes," he allowed. "But when you've got the ear of the Prime Minister, when you can argue a law in front of Parliament . . . it means you can truly do something. You can effect real change in the world." He glanced toward the curtained window. "The Greyland name has always tried to help the poor. We build schools, try to institute more lenient policies toward impoverished people, give subsidies to farmers."

"Noble endeavors." She'd never known this about him or his family. Always, she'd believed the wealthy and influential sought only to keep themselves in power, never to change anything in case they should lose their authority.

"You've given me an education," he went on.

"Me?" She sat up straighter.

"I thought there wasn't a difference between being a poor man and a poor woman. But you've shown me. Being a woman makes life a hundred times more challenging. It's another world. A greater struggle. There has to be more that I can do to help. Small ways, or bigger ways. Anything at all."

Unease crept over Cassandra. "The only person I help is myself."

"People change," he said gently. "You do, too."

The redheaded woman walked past them, her attention fixed on several guests at the other end of the room.

"I'm no different than I'd been in Southwark." She watched the woman handing out more glasses of wine. "Only differences are my clothes aren't patched and I don't sleep on dirty straw."

"There's more, and you know it," he insisted. "Yet it's easier to think of yourself as just a pickpocket."

Was it? She didn't have to believe herself capable of anything more than survival. She could rest comfortably thinking that she didn't have to worry or think about others, not when her own neck was on the line.

"You could take a portion of your earnings from the

club and give it to a charity," he suggested. "Start a school for girls to learn trades. Anything."

Her mouth curved wryly. "I'm not ready to become entirely altruistic. Nobody's going to look out for *me* if I do."

"Maybe you have more friends than you realize." He gazed deeply into her eyes, and warmth stole through her.

She had no answer. Nothing clever or quick to keep that burst of light from filling her. So she said nothing.

Looking across the room, she noticed a tall, dark-haired man with the stubble of a pirate talking to the club's manager, Amina. The manager leaned against the wall, her hands behind her back as her chin tilted up, her chest on prominent display. The pirate gent braced one hand high above Amina's head, his body angling toward hers. As they talked, the pirate grinned in true buccaneer fashion, while Amina's smile was smaller but frequent. Even without hearing what they spoke about, it was clear that both were captivated by each other's company.

"Didn't think our fine club proprietress would spend time making eyes at one of the guests," Cassandra noted to Alex, glancing at the flirting couple.

Alex followed her gaze and guardedly nodded.

"You know him," she deduced.

"Hard to know anyone's identity in here." He tapped his mask.

"But you *do* know him."

He shrugged.

"Whoever he is, he's made his intentions clear." The pirate dipped his head lower, as if to steal a kiss, but Amina turned her head away, so the pirate's lips grazed her cheek. At his disappointed look, Amina laughed.

The pirate must have sensed that the power wasn't in his favor, because he stood back, bowed at Amina, and quickly strode from the chamber. Amina straightened, but rather than return to her duties, she watched the doorway through which the pirate had exited, as if her gaze could draw him back.

"I feel sorry for the both of them," Cassandra murmured. "Neither can get what they want."

Alex gazed at Amina. "It's in her control as to whether or not they'll get their desires."

"If she yields," Cassandra explained, "she gives up everything. Her power. Taking a guest to bed would make her fully human, and vulnerable. She'd give herself what she wants, but she'd lose a piece of herself in the process."

Alex turned his attention from Amina to Cassandra. He said nothing, but his look spoke eloquently. *Who is it you speak of?*

"Let's play our own game," Cassandra suddenly announced.

"Cards and dice are in short supply," he noted.

"There are other games to play." She nodded toward a man standing alone in a corner. "Tell me his story."

"I don't know anyone here," Alex insisted.

"But you can *guess,* can't you? Come now," she chided, "surely someone so influential can judge a person from their outward appearance. How else can you manipulate others so effectively?"

"Through the strength of my character," he said.

"And . . . ?" She looked at him encouragingly.

"And through assessing them and using their hidden strengths and weaknesses to my own benefit."

"Aha! You admit being human, at last." She downed the last of her wine. "I'll drink to that."

"I never said I wasn't human," Alex grumbled. "I'm only a man."

There was nothing *only* about him as he leaned against the arm of the chaise, large and shadowy in his evening clothes, guarded by his mask. He was her opposite in so many ways. Dark where she was fair. Sharp where she was soft. Decidedly masculine in contrast to her femininity. He radiated with potency, made all the more compelling by the fact that he'd pleasured her so thoroughly. There was so much more pleasure to explore with him.

And he listened to her. He cared what she thought, what she felt.

My heart is his.

"But a perceptive man," she added.

"Who doesn't respond to flattery." Still, he smiled a little at her compliment. He sat up straighter and studied the man. "Dresses like a banker or a brewer. He's made his money in trade. Not a gentleman, but financially comfortable. The cut of his clothes shows that he pays considerable attention to appearances. He's unmarried but hopes to wed a daughter of the aristocracy to gain the prestige of the connection."

All of Alex's observations were similar to those that Cassandra had made when first sizing up the bloke. "What else?"

Alex considered the man. "He likes to be spanked."

She lifted a brow. "Oh?"

"He stares at women's hands. And if he has power but not influence, he'd enjoy having a woman govern his passions. He'd like submitting himself to her will, especially if there's some pain involved."

Cassandra nodded. "You'd make an excellent sharper. Reading people like a fisherman can read the ocean."

He smirked, but it was an endearing expression on his usually sober face. "Now you. What about that woman coming into the room? The one in yellow."

Cassandra studied her target. The woman retrieved a glass of wine and watched the dancing—and fornicating. "Married."

He looked dubious. "I see no betrothal ring."

"She removed it, but she keeps stroking that finger with her thumb. Feeling its absence." Cassandra continued to watch the woman in yellow. "Her husband is frequently unfaithful, but she's only now deciding to get her revenge by coming here. See how she keeps glancing toward the front door? She's not certain she can do this, but she feels like she's got no choice. He's forced her hand."

The woman looked both intrigued by the proceedings as well as frightened.

"But no," Cassandra continued, "she can't do this. She's going to leave."

The woman in yellow put her wine down on a table and hurried away, her head down.

"Excellent prognostication," Alex said.

"It's not prophecy," Cassandra corrected. "Fortune tellers at fairs can't look at a palm and know a person's past and future."

"Perhaps you should turn your attention to becoming a Bow Street Runner."

"If they allowed women," she returned, "maybe I would." Then she shook her head. "I couldn't go after the people I once considered my friends. That'd make me the worst kind of traitor."

He tilted his head in consideration. "Even after the way they treated you at Mrs. Donovan's, you wouldn't turn against them."

"No," she answered simply. "I couldn't hurt them."

He exhaled. "There's integrity in you. You keep denying it, but I see it."

Vehemently, she shook her head. "Don't mistake stupidity for honor."

"Most people do," he noted.

"But we're not discussing me," she said, turning the conversation to safer topics. "We're reading the people in the room. Tell me about the gentleman who's currently sucking another gentleman's . . . *honor*."

Hours passed this way, as she and Alex watched the redheaded woman and spun stories about the other guests at the Orchid Club. His nimble mind continued to astonish her with its perceptiveness. He wasn't a simple, spoiled nobleman. He might have been born into his role as one of England's leaders, but he earned it through his intelligence and thoughtfulness.

This was like Cheltenham again. It was easy to talk to him, to speak of things important and inconsequential. He was an attentive listener, engrossed and focused, and when she spoke, he looked at her as though she was the only person in England. It felt almost more intimate than the pleasure he'd given her earlier. Bodies were simple. Hearts and minds were far more complex.

Several hours later, the club had grown less and less populated. People staggered off to their homes, exhausted by their excess.

Alex glanced at his pocket watch. "An hour until sunrise. I'd wager they'll close up shop soon, so the remaining guests can get home while still in disguise."

True to his prediction, Amina came into the room and rang a small silver bell. "My friends, it is time for us to part ways. Please collect everything you came with, and find your paths safely home."

Servants made their way through the chambers, picking up empty glasses, sweeping up crumbs. A maid stood ready with a mop.

The redhead with the necklace joined the other servants in straightening the rooms. She helped a female guest to her feet and guided her toward the front door. On her way back, she stopped in front of the chaise where Alex and Cassandra sat.

"Amina has spoken," the redhead said gently. "Time to search out your own beds. But we'll be open next week, should you desire to return."

Alex stood, and assisted Cassandra as she got to her feet. He bowed at the redhead. "Our thanks."

Placing her hand on his arm, Cassandra accompanied Alex as he walked to the exit. Outside was bitingly cold, but they couldn't seek shelter just yet.

"There's an alley just across the street," she pointed out.

"I see it." He led her to the narrow span, only as wide as two men standing abreast. The paving stones were slick with morning dew, and the brick walls glistened. A faint smell of rotten apples rose from the alley's recesses.

Cassandra rubbed her hands together to keep them warm. She hadn't worn gloves, and her cloak was too thin to offer much protection from the icy air.

"Come here." Before Cassandra could speak, Alex brought her close to his body, his front pressing to her back as he wrapped his arms around her. Heat from his body seeped into hers, chasing away the chill.

This could turn into a habit. Having his warmth. His protection.

She couldn't remember the last time he'd spoken of his revenge against her. Should she say something? That wouldn't be wise, reminding a man of his need for vengeance. Maybe he was still planning something.

The way he touched her, though, made her wonder exactly what it was he intended.

Perhaps he schemed to make her care about him. Then, when her heart was lost, he'd cruelly cut her from his life. Leave her to scrabble in the dust for pieces of happiness. Just as she had done in Cheltenham.

Too late.

Chapter 14

❧

As they waited for the woman with the necklace to emerge, Alex tried to keep his attention on the house across the street. But he could not avoid the thought that nipped at him, over and over again.

Cassandra belongs in my arms.

Each time he'd held her, she fit seamlessly in his embrace. His body ached with the rightness of it, as though he'd been frozen before and now life returned, wakening his dead limbs, stirring his blood. Though *he* was the one keeping her warm now, he drew heat from her and took her into his body, his breath.

He pulsed with the need for release—and the desire to give her pleasure again and again. The logic and reserve that he'd held so dear had sailed away on a voyage of unknown length, perhaps never to return. He could only watch from the shore as the ship grew smaller, until it disappeared over the horizon, leaving him alone with only his instinct and hungers to accompany him.

She'd been molten to touch, silken and responsive. And her taste . . . He'd savor it forever.

He drew Cassandra closer as a shiver worked its way through her body.

"We'll get you warm when we're home," he said, then realized he'd used the word *home* without putting *my* in front of it. As if it was *their* home.

If she noticed his grammatical slip, she made no sign. Instead, she nodded, and continued to watch the club. Dawn was still some time away, and shadows cloaked the houses and streets.

She stood up straighter. "They're leaving now."

Servants exited the club, some alone, some in groups. They laughed or talked quietly, their voices too low to be heard from across the street. Many slumped in exhaustion from a long night's work, hunched against the cold, hurrying toward home and sleep, or waiting families.

It didn't seem to matter whether one worked at a secret sex club or a tavern or hat shop—work was work, and it took its toll on the employees.

"There she is," Alex murmured.

The woman with the necklace emerged from the back of the house alone, fastening the buttons of her coat. She'd removed her mask, as the other servants had, but it was impossible to tell her age or anything noteworthy about her face with the darkness so heavy. Her head was bent as she focused on the pavement.

Once the woman was a block away, Cassandra pulled

out of his arms and quickly followed. Alex kept pace, trying to walk as lightly as he could so that the rap of his boot heels on the pavement didn't echo loudly and alert the target to his presence. He'd never shadowed anyone before. A small thrill of the hunt worked through him as the woman hastened down the dark streets, turning corners, finding small passageways through the avenues that grew more and more disreputable.

At last, she crossed a street and made her way to one of the only open businesses: a gin house. The door to the establishment stood wide, spilling sulfurous light onto the pavement. Windows revealed men and women stooped over their glasses at tables, hardly speaking to one another. The alcohol took the majority of their attention.

The woman entered the gin house and someone inside called out to her. Clearly, she was a regular patron.

Alex and Cassandra exchanged looks. "Do we?" she asked softly.

"At the least, let's get out of the cold."

She took his arm, and together they walked into the gin house. As they went in, a few bleary pairs of eyes watched them, but most of the clientele was too intent on staring at their cups to give them notice. A tatty bar stood at one end of the room, with long tables and mismatched chairs serving as furniture. One woman stood behind the bar, wearily wiping down its battered wooden top. She grunted in acknowledgment when Alex and Cassandra appeared.

He'd never been inside a gin house before. It was sobering.

The woman in the necklace sat alone in the corner, her hands cradling her cup, her eyes on the level of alcohol in that cup. She had unfastened her coat, revealing her necklace. In the dull light, she appeared attractive but older than Alex had first surmised. This woman had seen much of life, and now drank to ease her burdens.

"Two," Alex ordered the barkeep. The woman poured two cups of clear liquid and slid them across the bar. He paid, then picked up his cup. He'd no desire to drink here, but it would look suspicious if he and Cassandra were empty-handed.

"What now?" he whispered to her as they stood at the bar. This was a realm with which he was unfamiliar, but Cassandra didn't display any horror at her surroundings. Given what he knew of her early life, she was well familiar with places like this.

Cassandra studied the woman. "She's not looking toward the door, so she's not expecting company. So we approach. Carefully."

Slowly, Cassandra made her way toward the woman in the corner. Alex followed. The woman didn't look up when they stood beside her.

"Pretty bauble around your neck," Cassandra noted. Her accent had dropped, becoming rougher, less polished.

The woman's hand went to her necklace, fingering the pearls and stones, as she glanced up at Cassandra.

Her eyes quickly flicked to Alex, standing at Cassandra's back. She tugged up the neckline of her coat, trying to cover the necklace.

"Thank ye," she answered warily. The genteel accent she'd used in the Orchid Club was gone now, taken off like a mask. Her weary blue eyes sized them up, widening slightly at the fine cut and fabric of their clothes. "You look familiar . . ."

"The colors suit your complexion," Alex said quickly.

A tiny smile appeared on the woman's lips, softening the lines lightly creasing her face. "Thank ye," she said again, warmer this time.

"I'm Alex," he offered. "And this is Cassandra."

Cassandra nodded in greeting.

"Becky," the woman said. "Becky Morton." Her gaze sharpened. "I ain't for hire, if you two are looking for fun."

"Nothing of the sort," Alex quickly assured her. "May we sit?" He glanced at the chairs opposite Becky.

She shrugged and took a drink.

After seating themselves, they sat in silence for a few moments. Alex lifted his cup, then set it back down without having a sip. He'd wait until he was home before permitting himself a healthy swig of whiskey.

"You and me," Cassandra said to Becky. "We got someone in common. A mutual friend."

"Doubt it," Becky answered.

"Known him most of my life," Cassandra continued. "Martin Hughes."

Becky immediately straightened, her expression frosty. "Don't know any Martin Hughes." Yet her fingers played with the necklace.

"Ah, but you do, Becky," Cassandra answered. "He gave you that fine bauble."

"How would you know?" Becky fired back.

"I was with him when he saw and admired it." Cassandra placed her hands on the table and leaned in. "Sure he's spoken of me."

Becky's lips pressed together tightly. She eyed Cassandra suspiciously. But she didn't speak.

"What's he promised you?" Alex asked gently.

"Ain't promised me nothing," Becky spat. "If I knew him. Which I don't."

"Not a good one for holding to his word, Hughes." Alex gave a rueful smile. "He broke his promise to Cassandra."

"He's never shown loyalty to anyone other than himself," Cassandra said flatly. "You a gambler? Because the odds are right strong that he's going to leave town without taking you with him."

Again, Becky worried the pearls of her necklace.

"That pretty trinket, the one he gave you with many promises," Alex noted. "He gave it to you to placate his own conscience. Gifting it to you makes him feel better about abandoning you."

"Shut your toff mouth," Becky snapped. Then she realized she'd already given away too much, and slammed her lips shut.

"We need to find him," Cassandra said urgently. "He wronged people. Loads of people—me included. And if I don't find him, I'm as good as dead. But if you help us find him," she continued, her tone softening, "I'll make sure you get something for your trouble."

Becky shoved back from the table and got to her feet. Fury and fear waged war in her expression. "Don't got to listen to either of you." She started for the door, then swung around, pointing her finger. "You follow me, I'll lose you. These streets is my home. I grew up here. I can take care of myself, mind."

Alex stood. "I'm the Duke of Greyland." Before Becky could speak in surprise at his rank, he went on. "You can find me in Mayfair, Portman Square. When you're ready to talk."

Becky opened her mouth, then shut it. She left the gin house quickly, her steps rapid and urgent on the pavement.

Alex turned back to Cassandra, who had risen to her feet.

"What if she doesn't come to us?" she asked. "Martin's got a slick way about him. He can talk his way out of a tiger trap."

"There are more leads to follow."

She lifted her empty hands. "I'm tapped out of ideas."

"Something will come to us." He stepped closer. "We've run all over this damn city, chasing information, hunting hints. Looking for Hughes and the money.

Now," he said lowly, "I take you home. This time is ours. Dawn is almost here, and I want you in my bed before sunrise."

Her eyes widened. Yet she didn't object. She crossed to him and took his hand in hers. Their gazes locked, and even the grim gin house fell away as he fell deeper under her spell.

In the waning hours of the night, she would be his. Truly his. And he would be hers.

Without speaking, they exited the gin house to hasten back to Mayfair.

$\mathcal{D}$ESPITE the shabbiness of the neighborhood, it didn't take long for Alex to hail a cab. The world bent and shifted to his will. He simply wanted something, and it was his.

Including me.

This thought turned itself over and over in Cassandra's head until it became like a stone worn smooth by handling. They rode back to the Orchid Club, where they retrieved his carriage, and then on to Portman Square.

Neither of them spoke on the journey to Mayfair—but intent was thick and heady in the cab's interior. His fingers wove with hers. His thumb stroked her wrist, ensuring her pulse never slowed. It was almost as if they couldn't speak of what was to come—as though looking too long at it would blind them. So they left it alone out of a sense of self-preservation.

In Cheltenham, when they had gone to bed together,

she hadn't truly known what she was getting into. Cassandra had told herself it was merely the pursuit of pleasure, but she'd never truly believed that. And in the intervening years, when she chose not to take other lovers, she saw more and more that Alex had branded himself upon her body and her heart. She only wanted *him*.

Heading toward his home, toward his bed, she knew exactly what she was doing. There would be no going back once they'd made love again. Her soul would ache for the feel of him and to watch Alex lose himself to desire. In the solitary years that inevitably followed, she might curse herself for having a taste of what could never be. Yet she couldn't stop. For this moment, she'd yield to the demands of her heart. She would suffer the consequences—later.

Unlike in Cheltenham, this time she was more purposeful and deliberate. But that didn't make her heart stop pounding, or stem the heat that gathered between her legs and tightened her breasts. If anything, she felt all these sensations even stronger than before. Because she knew what was to come. Because she'd looked into the void and decided, against better judgment, to jump.

Dawn was minutes away when the carriage pulled up outside Alex's home. After they exited the vehicle, he walked her up the front steps and inside, his hand at her back. Was he afraid she'd change her mind and run? She couldn't speak just yet, but if she'd been able to, she would've told him his concern was unfounded.

There was nothing she wanted more than to feel him inside her. She wanted it . . . and she was afraid. Afraid of the pain of isolation she would feel in the months and years ahead.

They stood together in the foyer. He dismissed the footman. Acting the role of servant, he helped her take off her cloak and set it aside solemnly. For several moments, they did nothing but gaze at each other as the sky outside began to turn ashen and pale.

"A drink?" he suggested.

She considered it. A nice, soothing dram of whiskey could chase away the nerves that stretched her taut.

But that was hiding behind another disguise. This time, she would be fully herself with him.

She shook her head. "Upstairs."

His chest filled and broadened at her words. Then he took her hand and led the way up the curving stairs. Each step resounded low in her belly. There would be no going back from this. Even she couldn't pretend that once she and Alex went to bed together without the disguises they'd once worn, life would go forward as it always had.

Turn back. Turn back now.

But she couldn't. She let herself be guided past her own room and down the hallway, until they came to Alex's bedchamber. He pushed open the door, revealing a room centered around a massive canopied bed. The fire was already lit, filling the room with warmth and golden light.

She didn't pay attention to the landscapes and por-traits hanging on the walls, or the Chinese vases on the mantel. Her gaze caught on the mahogany table and its collection of silver grooming tools: comb, brush, razor, bottles of lotions and tonics, a pair of scissors. She swallowed hard.

"Cassandra?"

She hadn't realized she'd shut her eyes until his voice called her back again.

"Maybe I'll have that drink after all," she said, and attempted a laugh.

He walked to a cabinet and produced a decanter and two glasses. After pouring them both two fingers of what she hoped was whiskey, he handed her one of the glasses.

"We'll sit by the fire," he said.

She smiled to herself. He was in command, as al-ways.

They sat down in two wingback chairs placed near the fire. For a while, they simply drank in silence, lis-tening to the pops of the flames. White light edged the heavy curtains, heralding the approach of day. Most of the servants would be awake by now, going about their tasks. They'd know that Cassandra wasn't in her bed, but the master's door was closed.

Sod them. She didn't get this far in life by worrying over others' opinions of her.

But *his* mattered. It always had.

"Why didn't you tell me the truth?" he asked softly.

She frowned. "I've told you everything."

He shook his head. "But you could have said sooner, about that night in Cheltenham—you already had the money, but you came to my bed anyway."

Ah. That. She stood and paced around the room. "I hadn't had a lover in a long while," she answered.

He rose to his feet. "Still, you don't speak honestly."

"I'm slow to trust."

He smiled without humor. "I don't even have faith in myself anymore." He exhaled, then took a drink. "Trust. It's a wall we keep running up against."

"I doubt we can ever climb it." She stopped in her pacing and stared at the bottom of her glass, watching the whiskey glow in the firelight. Hunger pushed at her, demanding him, but she clutched hard at control.

"Not on our own," he acknowledged. He took a step toward her. "Together, perchance. I boost you up, then you hold out a hand so I can scale the rest of the impediment."

"What do we do once we're at the top?" she wondered. "The jump down could break our necks."

"We can't stay on top of the wall forever. Sooner or later, we'll have to risk it and make the descent."

She resumed pacing the chamber. Everywhere, tiny luxuries winked and gleamed in the firelight. Silver combs, gold and pearl-inlaid boxes. All around them were expensive trinkets that in years past would have tempted her, but now she wanted one thing only—him. "I'd rather just go around the wall."

He smiled wryly. "Impossible. It's either forward or backward, and we both know there's no going back."

Tightness clutched her chest. "I wish we could."

"I don't."

She stared at him.

"I'd rather be here with you now, knowing everything, than live in some misguided paradise." He drained the last of his drink and set the glass on a table. He took two more steps toward her. A hunter steadily approaching.

His chest rose and fell quickly. She wasn't alone in her nervousness and excitement. For all his steadiness and attitude of being in command, he didn't know what was to follow, either.

"As a child," she said suddenly, picking up a little ebony notions box, "I never had a toy or a doll. Well, I did, but then my Da was put in the Marshalsea, and all my toys were stolen by other children. I'd go hunt them down and grab them back, but the others just kept taking them away. It was the same when I lived in Southwark. Couldn't get attached to something—a piece of ribbon, a shiny bead—because somebody else would snatch it away and I'd cry, but it didn't matter. Nothing mattered."

She gazed steadily at him. "I went to bed with you in Cheltenham because I wanted something for *myself*. And no one could take that away from me. I wanted *you*. My own handsome, honorable hero. A man who, in less than a fortnight, gave me more than anyone else ever did. The memory of you would be mine for always."

He was solemn, profound. "Yet you left before I woke."

"I had to." She set the box down and stood before the fire, her gaze fixed on the changing, always-moving flames. "My life is made up of lies. If I had stayed, I would have started believing them. But eventually, the truth would come out. And then . . ." She followed a spark rising up from the burning wood, until it vanished. "I'm used to loss. Yet to give away a piece of myself, and then have it thrown back in my face . . . I can survive a great deal, but not that."

She felt his warmth and solidness at her back. She hadn't heard him move to her—he'd been silent as a cat. His hands curved over her shoulders. He trailed hot kisses along the exposed flesh at her throat and neck, and she leaned back into him.

"I will never force you," he whispered against her skin. His hands stroked up and down her bare arms. "But I want you so much. It makes me strong and it makes me weak. I could tear down the city with how much I want you. From the moment I saw you in Cheltenham to now. All I've ever needed is the feel of you, the taste of you."

Acute hunger gripped her, wringing her like a rag. Her legs shook, and she had to rest against him to keep herself standing. Surely, her heart would break free from its cage if he kept talking, kept touching her.

She turned to face him. He cupped the back of her head, holding her in place, as he continued to kiss her throat. She held fast to his biceps, feeling them flex and tighten beneath her touch.

Morning continued to press against the curtains. The day moved forward. Everything moved forward, no matter how she might wish the world to stand still.

Yet tomorrow didn't matter. All that signified was now. This moment. She should have known from her rough life that she had to grab what she wanted with both hands and hold tight. There was a very good chance that whatever it was she cherished would be ripped away. But wasn't it better, so much better, to have felt pleasure than to have known nothing but absence? There was time enough for loneliness and loss. It came regardless of what she did. These moments had to be seized and treasured, especially because they were so brief.

No more denial. No more chases. This belonged to her.

She released her grasp on his arms. Bringing up her hands, she threaded her fingers through his hair and pulled his head up to have her gaze meet his. Alex's eyes glittered darkly, like an animal on the night of a full moon. His breath came fast and labored.

"Don't tell me to stop," he rasped.

"I want more," she answered, and pulled his head down for a kiss.

Chapter 15

❦

*H*er lips pressed to his, and he opened his mouth to let her in. Her tongue swept in, finding his, and they stroked and lapped at each other, tasting, discovering, claiming. A low growl of approval sounded deep in his chest at her boldness. She felt no shame, only want and fierce, uncompromising demand. Desire was fast and devastating.

She released his head to claw at his clothing, wanting him naked beneath her touch.

"Not yet," he murmured. "Not yet."

"*Now*," she insisted.

"There's something I want first."

"Anything," she said, uncaring what his stipulation might be.

He pulled back, and at once she missed the feel of his hard, lean body against hers. But he took her hands, and with a wicked, promising look, led her to one of the chairs by the fire. She frowned as he gently sat her down in the chair.

"What—"

But he raised a finger to his lips. "I'm going to take care of you."

"I can—"

He held up a hand, asking for her silence and compliance. "Prepare yourself."

She didn't see how that could be possible, with her every nerve alight and her body smoldering for his touch. Yet she leaned back and watched with puzzled amusement as he knelt at her feet.

He reached down and removed one of her shoes, setting it aside before moving to the other shoe. A smile played about his lips as his hands slid up the curve of her stocking-clad calf. She bit back a moan at the feel of him on her legs, but couldn't hold back her sounds of pleasure as his hands went higher, over her thigh, until he found her garter. His fingers trembled slightly, growing clumsy as he undid the ribbons. Then the garter fell away. He peeled away the stocking, revealing her bare leg. With a mixture of confidence and reverence, he stroked her leg from thigh to ankle, then set her foot down on the carpet.

He repeated the process for her other leg with agonizing, delicious slowness. His hands shook, however. He was a man on the edge of control. She gripped the arms of the chair tightly, her breath quick as a flush stole into her cheeks.

His own labored breathing rose above the sound of the fire in the grate. His gaze flicked to hers and she was seared by the intensity and heat of his look.

This is mine, his gaze said. *This is ours.*

Her breath held as he gathered up her skirts, uncovering her legs inch by inch. Calf, knee, thigh. Warm air stroked her skin. Until her skirts gathered at her waist, and she was completely exposed to his gaze. He couldn't look away from her quim, like one entranced. His hands came up, but instead of touching her directly, he gripped the naked curve of her bottom as he pulled her forward, until she sat on the very edge of the chair. He hooked her legs over the chair's arms, exposing her more fully.

She knew what he meant to do. And she couldn't breathe. Couldn't think. Not when he licked his lips, and not when he lowered his head to give her one thick, glossy stroke of his tongue against her folds.

Arching up, she couldn't stop the cry that rose from deep within her. She pressed her head into the chair's cushions as Alex bent to his task. He ran his tongue up and down her flesh, teasing her entrance, making tight rotations around her clit. He savored her. He devoured her, taking her into himself like a man who wanted no other sustenance. And when he thrust two fingers into her passage, she spun away from the world and lost herself in sensation.

She couldn't stop watching this proud man, this stately duke lick and adore her in an act so primal, so intimate, she felt nothing but his caresses. He gripped her thighs tightly, holding her open for his ravishing.

Pleasure built in hot, clutching waves. Higher and

higher it rose with every touch of his tongue and stroke of his fingers. She lifted her arms to grip the top of the chair, surrendering herself to his demanding worship.

He found a spot deep within her, swollen and needy, and pressed against it. Sensation built higher, higher, but then he eased off the spot. Was this to be his revenge? Keeping her at the edge of release?

But then he stroked her again and sucked at her. Release came in a crash, ripping through her unrelentingly. She cried out in a long, low wail as her body surrendered. Heat expanded outward, bright and consuming, holding her fast until she collapsed against the cushions.

Yet that wasn't enough for him. He continued to suck and lick, teasing and tormenting and pleasuring her so that she came again. And once more.

Finally, he let go of her thighs and lifted his head. He licked his lips slowly.

"You'll kill me," she managed to slur.

"I'll give you everything," he said.

She pushed herself up and stroked his face, tracing the hard planes that had only grown sharper with unmet hunger. "Take me to bed."

She tried to stand, but the world tilted. He'd gathered her up in his arms. He carried her over to the bed and set her on her feet. Though she swayed bonelessly, she managed to stay upright long enough to work at the folds of his cravat and the buttons of his waistcoat.

A small pile of discarded clothing heaped beside

them as they bared his broad, thickly muscled torso. Dark hair curled in the center of his chest and trailed down to a line that disappeared into the waistband of his breeches. She stroked this hair, testing its crisp texture against her palm, and went lower still, down the twitching contours of his abdomen. Until she rested her hand over the long, pronounced ridge of his cock, straining against his breeches.

He groaned when she cupped him, and made animal sounds as she stroked him through the fabric. Arching into her touch, he tilted his neck back and growled.

The buttons of his breeches yielded to her, and she pulled open the placket. His cock pushed against the thin cotton of his drawers. She reached through the opening and took him in her hand. He exhaled jaggedly at the feel of her grasping him.

She stroked him, loving the sensation of his hardness, and the velvet softness of his skin. The head of his cock was round and full. Already, a gleam of moisture shone at the tip, and her heart climbed into her throat at the sight.

More.

She sank to her knees, still holding him.

He gazed down at her with a piercing, feral look. Waiting. Needing.

"Tell me what you want," she demanded.

Muscles in his jaw clenched and loosened. "Take me in your mouth. Lick me all over. Suck me."

Her eyes closed as she soaked in his filthy, wonderful words. He freed himself just with her. This was a secret language saved only for themselves.

She lowered her mouth and took the plump head between her lips. Running her tongue around the rim, she tasted musk and salt. Then she dipped farther, and his shaft slid into her mouth. His hand cradled the back of her head, holding her, but giving her freedom to do as she pleased.

"*Yes,*" he growled as she sucked him. Heat and slickness grew between her legs, and her arousal climbed higher the more she tasted him. What she couldn't take into her mouth, she stroked with her hand. A steady stream of curses passed through his lips, and she rejoiced in his abandon.

She chanced a look at him, and he watched her through slitted eyes, focused and lost. Very gently, she scratched her nails down his shaft, and he hissed with pleasure.

Alex pulled back suddenly, then hauled her to standing. In moments, he stripped her to nakedness. They discarded the last of his clothing, until they were both nude and panting beside the bed.

He gripped her arms as he pulled her against him, kissing her savagely, deeply.

They separated, long enough for her to lie back on the bed. He positioned her so that her hips were at the edge of the mattress, and he held her legs. Her breath caught as he stood between her legs, positioning himself at her entrance.

He thrust into her.

She gasped, flinging her arms wide to clutch at the counterpane. Much as she wanted to lose herself in sensation, she kept her eyes open as he moved, stroking in and out of her. The firelight shone on his chest and the flexing muscles of his arms, highlighting the movement of his shoulders as he drove into her. At first, he went slow, taking each plunge with deliberation. Then his movements grew faster.

Primed already, the need for release rose within her. She moaned in demand.

He moved quickly, manipulating her so that she lay fully on the bed. Like a beast, he crawled over her, and like an animal claiming her mate, she wrapped her legs around his waist. He braced himself on his elbows as he slid into her waiting, willing body. They cried out in unison.

"Now you tell me what you want," he ground out. "Tell me you want me to fuck you."

"Fuck me, Alex." She could barely speak.

"Like this?" He thrust hard into her.

"Yes." She moaned.

"You want my cock?" He thrust again.

"God, please!"

"As my lady wishes." He began to fuck her, just as she'd demanded. Steadily and fiercely. Each thick stroke was felt everywhere. There was no part of her untouched.

Yet it wasn't enough. She needed everything. Her release danced just out of reach. She made a small sound of frustration.

"You need more," he rumbled.

And then he spun them around so he was on his back and she straddled him. He gripped her hips and stared up at her, the tendons in his neck standing out, his jaw sharp.

"Take what you want." He thrust up and heat spiraled through her.

She braced her hands on his chest and began to ride him. Her clit rubbed against the base of his cock, he was deep within her, and she never knew anything this perfect. It was consuming and humbling and miraculous, and she threw herself into the completion of her pleasure.

Release came like a thunderclap, reverberating deeply. She cried out as she arched her back. Smaller climaxes echoed as she continued to move, until there was nothing left.

Alex groaned and pushed his hips up. A few more pushes, and then he pulled away just enough to slide free from her body. His seed jetted out, hot, and he growled with satisfaction.

Spent, she rolled off Alex, and lay beside him, their bodies cooling. She rested her hand on his chest, feeling it slow from its frantic pounding. He gripped her hand and brought it to his lips.

How could she have known? She and Alex had gone to bed before, but it wasn't like this, where they were fully themselves, free of disguise and subterfuge. Though she'd had lovers in the past, never had she known the connection she shared with Alex. They were open and honest, at this moment. Because he was stubborn and true and proud, and her body and heart craved him with an intensity that stole thought, robbed her of breath.

She'd willingly discarded her armor. Now, unprotected, Cassandra realized that she'd sealed her fate. And one day, soon, she would have to leave him.

CONSCIOUSNESS gripped Alex in a sudden rush. His eyes flew open and he inhaled sharply, like a man surfacing from deep water. The sight of his own bed's canopy greeted him. A thought pressed at the back of his mind—he needed to learn something, to settle his concern over something . . . But what? His heart pounded.

Turning his head to the side, he saw Cassandra asleep beside him, curled gently into herself. His heartbeat slowed, assuaged.

She didn't leave.

Clear, bright pleasure rose within him. He'd expected her to flee again, but she hadn't. She'd slept beside him the whole of the morning, into . . . What time was it?

The clock on the mantel revealed the hour to be close to four in the afternoon. Shards of yellow sunlight scattered across the floor, sneaking through narrow gaps in the curtains to glimmer on the carpets.

Alex let his head fall back onto his pillow. Good

God, he hadn't slept so long or soundly in weeks, possibly even months or years. But after making love with Cassandra, he'd fallen into an enchanted sleep. Alex had never known such a well-deserved exhaustion, having given the whole of his energy to pleasuring her.

The need to give her even *more* burned hotly in his chest. He had a small box which he kept in a drawer of his desk, and in that box he kept small treasures that had no value to anyone but him. A rock from a pond near his country estate. A chapbook given to him by his favorite tutor. The paper that had enclosed a cake he'd eaten as a student in Windsor one bright Sunday afternoon.

He wanted to give her all of those small tokens, all the things that carried the weight of his heart.

Instead, he stayed where he sprawled in bed, affixing invisible shackles to his wrists and ankles so that he didn't hurry off to make a fool of himself. *It was only sex*, he reminded himself. Yet it felt like so much more than that, with Cassandra gently breathing as she slept beside him, her hands curled in front of her face as if to shield herself from a blow.

His chest contracted. She'd known such hardship, and to persevere as she had was nothing short of miraculous. The qualities he'd admired so much in Mrs. Blair had been in Cassandra Blake all along. Courage, intelligence, determination—they were all within her. She had played the part of the wronged widow, but her true self had been there the whole time.

Cassandra's survival had come at a heavy price. She had been, and was, a criminal. He could never allow himself to forget that or gloss over that fact in his haste to exonerate her from wrongdoing.

But her past or who she had become didn't make a damn difference to his heart. With her clever thief fingers, she'd picked the lock that kept him safe and protected, and stolen away with his soul. It belonged to her now, to keep or to sell as she pleased.

How could he have shielded himself from this fate? The answer was that he couldn't have. The moment he saw her in Cheltenham and again at the gaming hell in London, his lot had been set. They belonged to each other now.

Pain clawed at him to think of their parting, essential and unavoidable as it was. It wouldn't—couldn't—last. No matter what happened with Martin Hughes, there would come a time when he and Cassandra must journey down their separate paths, likely never to see each other again.

Need for her was a tidal wave, flooding him. He'd let himself drown. Because soon, too soon, she would go. He surrendered now to the deluge.

Rolling over onto his side, he gathered up Cassandra's drowsy form, feeling the silken drape of her limbs over his, the warmth of her breath against his chest. His body stirred to life. By the time her eyes slowly opened, he was already half-hard.

She smiled languidly at him, and he pressed a kiss

to her curved mouth. Her wakefulness grew in increments as she responded, her fingers curling against his pectorals, and she opened both her lips and her legs to him in invitation. He hardened fully in an instant and slid into her.

In moments, they were panting and straining against each other, lost in the union of two bodies searching for release. They came within seconds of one another, collapsing together in a tangle of slick limbs.

Lying on his back, he pulled her close, soaking in the sensations of her hand moving lazily back and forth across his torso, her head resting on his chest.

What would he give to always wake like this? His dukedom? His name? Nothing seemed to have any weight. He'd lose it all and never feel the absence. She would bring him desire and affection and intimacy and a hundred other things that his title and estates never could.

Dreams, all of it. These moments were transitory. He couldn't have the fantasy, so he had to contend with reality. She would go one day. He'd no choice—only acceptance.

He asked, "Hungry?"

"I could eat the cushions off a mail coach," she said.

"Anything you want, you can have it. Pheasant pie. Roast trout. Toast and sausage."

"I'm quite sated with your sausage." She gave his thigh a squeeze. "A fine banger."

"Aye, missus, there's more where that came from," he said, mimicking an East End accent.

She grimaced. "Terrible effort. Promise me you'll only talk in your toff voice."

"You speak in both," he noted. "Surely I can, too."

"You were born and bred to the high life," she said, tracing a circle over his heart. "It's who you are. Be glad you've got a place in the world."

The gulf stretched between them, wider and deeper than any oceanic trench. Seeking to shorten that distance, he said, "Tell me what you want for breakfast. Or supper. Whatever time of day it is."

She seemed to understand his need to avoid the topic of their social divide. "Anything from your excellent kitchen will suit me perfectly."

Though he didn't want to leave the bed, he managed to drag himself from her embrace in order to rise and put on a robe. He tugged on the bellpull, and when a servant appeared at the door, he ordered as lavish a repast as could be brought to his rooms. After the servant left, Alex turned back to the bed and saw with a measure of disappointment that Cassandra had risen. To his pleasure, however, she wore only one of his shirts as she sat at his vanity table and brushed the tangles out of her hair.

"This style ought to be the height of next Season's fashion," he proclaimed, leaning against the door and folding his arms over his chest. He leered appreciatively at the lines of her legs, sleek and long. The hem of his shirt grazed just above her knees, revealing glimpses of silken thighs as she spun around on her seat to gaze at him.

"Mantua makers might go on strike," she said, running the brush through her long, golden hair.

He had the absurd idea to pluck some of those strands from the bristles of his brush and sew them into a little pouch he could carry in his breast pocket. To keep for later, when she had gone.

"And no work would ever be accomplished," he added. "Bricklayers would just watch women pass in the street, and clerks would neglect their ledgers to ogle ladies."

"We owe it to our nation to insist women wear skirts," she decided. "Which is to the betterment of men, since unencumbered females would easily run roughshod over males. Britain would belong to us within a fortnight. Come to think of it," she added, tapping a finger on her chin, "perhaps women *ought* to forgo skirts. I have a lot of ideas about how to run this country."

"Starting with . . . ?" He pushed away from the door and crossed to her. Taking the brush from her hand, he ran it slowly through her tresses.

Her eyes closed and she hummed in pleasure. "I'd rule that only handsome, strapping men could serve as ladies' maids, to start."

"Watch the birthrate soar as a result," he said drily.

"Oh, but if I was in charge, I'd make it one of my

priorities that natural philosophers must invent better means of contraception. The whole country would thank me."

"If you think no work would get accomplished when women forgo skirts," he noted, "imagine the idleness if sex didn't result in babies. We'd be vulnerable to foreign invasion because the soldiers would all be shagging themselves into unconsciousness."

"Then I'd share the secret with the world," she proclaimed loftily. "No more unwanted children and all the rogering your heart could desire."

A tap sounded at the door. "Your food, Your Grace," said a muffled voice.

Cassandra took the brush back from Alex. "That was fast."

"Never underestimate the power of a hungry duke." He strode to open the door.

Three servants entered. They kept their gazes lowered as they set up a table with numerous covered dishes, then hurried away.

After pulling up chairs, Alex and Cassandra attacked the meal. There were sweet and savory pies, slices of roast beef, hot bread, wedges of cheese, and a bowl of fruit. He and Cassandra traded bites and ate with their hands. He couldn't remember a meal ever tasting better.

She gnawed on a pheasant leg contemplatively. "I'm certain Becky won't come through with the information about Martin."

"There are always more options to be pursued," he countered.

She looked dubious. "The longer it takes to find him, the better the chances of him slipping away. And the more time runs out for me." Setting the bone aside, she exhaled. "Emigration's a possibility. Set sail for far-away shores."

Panic rose up in a cold spike. He worked to keep his words light, his manner casual. "I could hire a Bow Street Runner or someone to conduct the investigation privately."

She frowned as she contemplated this prospect. "An investigation takes time."

"If you're worried about where to stay," he said, gazing at the wine in his glass, "you needn't concern yourself. There's more than enough room here. Until Hughes is found," he added quickly.

"Protecting your investment?" she asked, an edge in her voice.

"I don't see why my motivation should concern you," he countered levelly.

"Because it does," she answered tightly.

Suddenly, their pleasant mood evaporated like so much steam. They both picked at the remainder of their food, neither meeting the other's gaze.

Despite the distance between them, he couldn't deny the gratification and pleasure it gave him to have her here, in his bedchamber, in his clothing, being fed from his kitchens. Her life had been a difficult one, and if he could give her a few moments of luxury and indulgence, he would. He'd give her anything she wanted.

All the emotions he'd felt for her in Cheltenham were back, stronger than ever. They filled him like light, warm and glowing. Everything was different. Money was immaterial, and he only needed her close. As close as she would allow for as long as she would permit.

He opened his mouth to speak, to tell her of his feelings. No words came out. Alex silently cursed himself. He should just tell her.

He'd never been at a loss for words in Parliament. Men often congratulated him after a speech, praising his eloquence and perseverance. "You could charm a lizard out of its scales," Lord Kendall once said after a particularly rousing demand for more funding for the poor.

Yet as he gazed at Cassandra, sitting opposite him with her chin down and her brow creased, he couldn't find the right words to say what he felt, and silence gripped them both.

Chapter 16

$\mathcal{F}$ighting melancholy, Alex was determined to make the rest of the day take a turn for the better. After the food had been cleared, he ordered two baths—one in each of their rooms. Half-clothed, she slipped from his bedchamber to bathe in privacy.

As he washed, he tried to push away thoughts of the immediate future and the distant future, as well. Over and over, Alex wondered what would happen if Martin Hughes wasn't found and what he would do when Cassandra disappeared from his life a second time. Would it be any easier, knowing her departure was coming? Or would it be more painful this time, seeing the inevitable and being unable to stop it from happening?

Unresolved, unanswered questions swarmed him. They mystified him by their very existence. Certainties marked his life—or they had, before she'd tumbled back into his world, full of secrets and subterfuge and that one mole on her thigh.

Clean and dressed, Alex hastened downstairs. He went to the footman watching the front door.

"Have any women come to see me while I slept?" he asked the servant. Hopefully, Becky had changed her mind and come with Hughes's whereabouts.

"No, Your Grace," the young man answered. "Only the usual associates. Business and politics and the like. I said you weren't at home and to leave their cards." He glanced toward the tray that held at least half a dozen calling cards and a stack of letters.

He'd only been asleep for a few hours, but life proceeded apace.

"Did I do right, Your Grace?" The footman looked worried.

"Of course you did," he assured the servant, who exhaled in relief.

"Has Becky Morton come by?" Cassandra asked, standing at the top of the stairs. Damp tendrils of hair curled around her ears, and she'd dressed in a pale green walking gown, looking like some Italian Renaissance ideal of Spring.

God, now Alex was thinking poetically. He really must be in a bad way.

"No ladies, madam," the footman replied. He bowed, then resumed his post.

Cassandra descended the steps, a pensive frown tightening her mouth. "The longer it takes for her to make up her mind," she said to Alex when she reached him, "the more I'm afraid she won't give him up. Martin's got a devil's gift for words. He can make anyone believe whatever he says." A shadow of regret passed over her face, as she no doubt recalled that Hughes had played her for a dupe through his application of more honeyed words.

"You've planted the seed of doubt," Alex noted, "and that's a powerful thing. It will sprout and grow and bear fruit."

"I wish I had your confidence." She sighed.

"Confidence is *your* bailiwick." He did and did not speak the truth. He had little faith in Becky—which meant they'd have to find new avenues to pursue Hughes.

But did Alex *want* to find him? So long as the investors were owed, they remained a danger to Cassandra. Yet the longer they looked for Hughes, the more Cassandra could stay close to him.

She would go, eventually. But he'd seize all the time he had with her to make certain he remained a part of her, the way she'd become a part of him.

He took her chin between his thumb and forefinger and kissed her. When he pulled back, he said, "The meal we had was fine, but I think we could both use something sweet."

"Catton's?" Her eyes brightened. "They make the best iced lemon cakes."

"Then lemon cakes you shall have."

Hats and coats and other accoutrements were brought, and in a few minutes, Alex walked with Cassandra on his arm toward the sweet shop. He declined the carriage, as the day was mild and fine, though the sun was already gliding toward the horizon. A warm breeze from the west carried green hints of approaching summer, and recent rain had washed the streets clean. An air of expectancy hovered over the city, something just about to show its face, but still in hiding.

The bustle and activity of London surrounded Alex and Cassandra as they strolled toward Catton's.

It was sweet—and temporary. He felt the pleasure of it slipping away even as he reveled in the experiences.

"I forget how much I like it in London," she said, watching a woman driving a wagon full of beer kegs shout at a tinker slowly crossing the street. "The exhilaration of the place. The possibility." She smiled ruefully as the tinker made a rude gesture toward the woman driving the wagon. "The city's not afraid of itself."

"You don't have to stay away." Alex guided her around a suspicious puddle.

She shook her head. "There are enough sharpers and swindlers in this town."

"Once Hughes is found," he noted, "you won't be part of their number anymore."

"I wish I could stay," she said wistfully. Her eyes glided upward, toward the sky, where dreams lived. "But it's better I start over fresh. Argentina's supposed to be a place rich with potential."

"It's very far," he said darkly. "The journey's long and dangerous."

She glanced at him. "I'm able to meet the challenge."

"That's never in doubt." What he did doubt was how much time he and Cassandra had left together. If Hughes was found, she would leave. If Hughes remained hidden, she would leave. Either way, he'd be here, and she'd be gone.

A thick miasma of sorrow spread through him at the thought. The weeks and months and years without her seemed to stretch on in a blank void, empty of happiness and pleasure.

They turned onto an elegant street lined with shops, the sidewalks filled with men and women of fashion who were busy with the weighty task of seeing and being seen.

"It's a living edition of *La Belle Assemblé*," Cassandra murmured with a smile. She glanced down at her indigo pelisse. "And I'm two Seasons out of date." She frowned at him as he looked at her meaningfully. "No. Absolutely not."

He held up his hands. "I've said nothing."

"But I saw the look in your eye. You want to buy me a new pelisse."

"There's no harm in purchasing one garment. It could even be ready-made."

Yet she was intractable. "The harm is that I'll owe you even more for its cost, and I've got nothing to spare."

"Consider it a gift," he offered.

"How do I know it won't be added to my tally?" she asked with suspicion.

"It won't," he assured her. "Trust me."

He'd said the words without thinking, but once they'd left his lips, he realized what they truly meant.

As did she. She gazed at him for a long moment, then slowly nodded. "If it will please you."

"It would. Very much." She had reluctantly accepted everything he'd grudgingly given her. But this would be the first item that he'd willingly, happily granted for the pleasure of itself, not toward a goal. Even more important, she agreed to take what he offered.

And she trusted him. That alone was his profit.

He guided her toward one dressmaker's with a fetching yellow dress in its window. "This way, madam."

But as they approached the shop, a man and a woman stepped in their path. They were both of middle age and prosperous looking in their walking ensembles. The man sported an old-fashioned wig, and the woman wore the style of an earlier decade, though everything they wore was immaculate and expensive.

"Lord Greyland," the man exclaimed with pleasure. "I'm heartily glad to see you, Your Grace. You're looking quite fit and well."

"Lord Massey," Alex said with a bow. "Lady Massey."

The woman curtsied and smiled. "It's so rare for us to see you in such frivolous pursuits, Your Grace."

"I have learned that small amounts of frivolity can be most beneficial to the constitution," he answered.

"Well said, well said," Lord Massey said genially. He glanced with expectancy and interest at Cassandra, clearly waiting for an introduction.

His mind blanked for a moment. Who was Cassandra? He had no idea what to say to these two pillars of high Society.

"This is Mrs. . . . ." He scrabbled to come up with the appropriate name.

"Blair," Cassandra smoothly filled in for him. "Cassandra Blair, of Northumberland."

"Indeed?" Lady Massey asked with curiosity. "Where in Northumberland?"

"Mostly Tynedale, though I have spent time in Alnwick."

"Lovely," Lord Massey exclaimed.

Alex had no idea she knew anything about Northumberland, but knowledge of the place rolled readily off her tongue. Damn, but she was good at her work.

He couldn't believe he actually *admired* her swindling ability, but he saw it now for what it was: the steadfast desire to survive. And she did it splendidly.

"I confess I do miss it," Cassandra said with a confiding tone, "though Lord Greyland has been most gracious in showing me the town. He was a childhood friend of my late husband, you know. I shut myself away in the country for too long, Lord Greyland said, and must come for the Season."

"It's not to be missed," the older woman agreed.

"I most energetically concur, Lady Massey." Cassandra nodded enthusiastically. "Nowhere presents itself as well as London in the spring. The most notable personages gather here." She smiled, as if to say, *Including yourselves.*

Both Lord and Lady Massey grinned and chuckled.

Again, Alex could only marvel at her ease with the couple. He wasn't nearly as deft when talking with strangers.

"Have you been to Astley's?" Lord Massey asked. "And there's the theater, of course. One can't miss the theater."

"I'm especially fond of the works of Lady Marwood," Cassandra said. "So full of poetry and color."

"She's my favorite, too!" Lady Massey exclaimed. She clasped Cassandra's hand in hers. "Oh, do say you'll accompany us to the Imperial while you are in town."

Alex quickly began thinking of excuses, but before he could, Cassandra spoke.

"Much as I would adore the opportunity, I'm afraid that my time in London is very limited."

She looked rueful, and the couple appeared crestfallen.

"But I will see if I can find the time in my schedule for an outing," Cassandra amended.

"Excellent," Lord Massey said, beaming. He wagged a finger at Alex. "You've been remiss, Your Grace, by keeping Mrs. Blair all to yourself."

"I think he's being perfectly romantic." Lady Massey sniffed before Alex could defend himself. "He deserves it, too, after . . ." She gave Lord Massey a meaningful look.

Hell, Alex had completely forgotten about his failed suit of Lady Emmeline. But the *ton* hadn't let the memory of her slip away.

"Enjoy the rest of your evening," Alex said, guiding Cassandra away. When they were out of earshot of the couple, he said lowly, "It's a gift you have."

"What is?" she asked.

"Charming people. No one can resist you."

"I can think of one person who grew immune to my charisma." She eyed him meaningfully.

"Not so immune." He gazed at her with heat. "I've caught a fever. You're both the cause and the cure."

Though she was a master at hiding her emotions, he'd learned the subtle shifting of her expression, and saw fear warring with hope in her face. Then she was sardonic and said, "You'll recover soon enough."

"Is that your desire?" He would not let her evade him.

She glanced around at the people ebbing and flowing around them. Some looked with curiosity at the sight they presented: a couple having a serious discussion in public. Such displays weren't condoned by polite Society, and were preferred to be conducted in the security and privacy of home.

"A duke must always comport himself in public with the utmost decorum," his father once said to Alex. "It is to him that others look for guidance and instruction."

Alex didn't care. He and Cassandra had danced

around their feelings for each other, yet he demanded more than possibility and potential. He wanted certainty. What they were to each other. The parameters and constraints of their association. He needed to know when, exactly, she planned to disappear—if only to prepare himself for the inevitable pain. He believed, hoped, that if he knew precisely the time he had left with her, he could be better prepared for her absence.

She turned her face away from him, seemingly interested in the display of gowns and fripperies in the dressmaker's window. "We'll speak of my desire another time."

Alex had just begun to argue when someone slammed into him from behind. Stumbling, he avoided hitting Cassandra, who reached out to help him. Alex righted himself and turned to berate whomever had clumsily barreled into him.

He faced a thickset man in laborer's clothes. Before he could angrily rebuke the man, the stranger started yelling.

"What the bloody hell do you mean," he bawled, "banging into me like that! You think you own the damn sidewalk, do you, fancy fellow?"

"See here," Alex growled, "you ran into me."

"Ain't taking responsibility for yourself, eh? Fine, indeed."

Cassandra approached. "If you'll calm down, sir—"

"Stay out of this, missus," the man shouted, and *shoved* her toward the street.

Red fury clouded Alex's vision. He grabbed the man by his grimy neckcloth. The man's eyes bulged as Alex tightened his grip, cutting off his air. "By God, I'll beat you to pulp," Alex snarled.

He barely noticed the carriage pulling up right beside Cassandra. Without stopping, the vehicle's door slammed open. Another man appeared from inside the carriage, crouching on the floor. He reached out and seized Cassandra, then hauled her inside the still-moving vehicle.

She screamed in fury as she was pulled into the carriage.

Alex moved to grab her, but the damned laborer blocked his path and the vehicle sped away with Cassandra inside.

Alex grappled with the laborer. The other man was stronger, but Alex had speed. Alex ducked a punch, then swung his walking stick at the man's knee. When he buckled in pain, Alex threw his fist into his attacker's jaw. The laborer sprawled backward, dazed.

Alex didn't spare him another thought. Moving purely on instinct, he raced toward a boy holding a horse's reins outside a boot shop. Alex flung coins at the boy before snatching away the lead, then vaulted up into the saddle. He kicked the horse into motion, and it sprang forward.

He took off in the direction of the carriage. He sped down the street, heedless of whomever was in his way. Just ahead, he thought he could make out the vehicle's form, half-hidden by traffic. It turned a corner, and he followed.

Several carts rolled into the street, blocking his path. There were too many obstacles to vault over them.

"Get these out of the way," Alex roared.

The carts' owners took their time moving their wagons. When at last the path was clear, Alex surged forward. He galloped down the street, racing in pursuit.

But the carriage had disappeared. Cassandra was gone.

She'd been abducted.

Chapter 17

❧

Choked with fear and helpless rage, flung to the floor of the speeding carriage, Cassandra threw punches at her kidnapper crouching over her. She landed blows on his chest and shoulders and arms, but he was thick with muscle, his face impassive and showing no pain. Or compassion. He tossed her onto her stomach with the ease of a person well used to manhandling others.

A flurry of terror struck her as her arms were pinned behind her back. The bite of coarse rope ground into her wrists. She tried to move them, but it was no use. He'd tied her up like a parcel.

He rolled her onto her back. Cassandra opened her mouth to shout for help—they couldn't have gone far from the busy shopping district—and he shoved a grimy rag between her lips.

"You don't fight me," he said in a rough voice as he squatted over her, "I don't hurt you."

Bugger yourself, she tried to say, but the gag kept the words lodged in her throat.

Pulling at the rope binding her wrists proved useless. He'd secured her tightly. She tried to kick him, but he grabbed her ankle and gave it a painful twist. Agony shot up her leg.

"What did I just say?" her abductor said mildly.

She let her head fall back as tears of frustration and fear pricked her eyes. There was nothing to be done but wait out the rest of this hellish ride. When they reached their destination she'd try again. She had to fight and fight until she couldn't anymore. It was the only way to survive.

Would she ever see Alex again? Their last words together hadn't been good ones. Is this what sinners felt on their deathbeds, knowing they'd have no chance to make right their wrongs?

All she could do was lie on the floor of the rocking carriage, knowing nothing about where she was going or what fate awaited her. She examined her kidnapper for details—his boots were worn but newly soled. He'd been paid recently. His shave was uneven, so there was no woman at home to tell him to clean up stray whiskers.

She didn't know how these bits of information might help her, but anything could be of service.

The vehicle finally stopped. She had no idea where she was, and her abductor hauled her out of the carriage like a sack of wheat. He set her on her feet on a street in some shabby corner of the city, with dusty-faced town houses and tenements crowding around the narrow lane. Shadows came together in clots. No other people were out, so there was no possibility of anyone coming to her assistance.

She tried to run, but her kidnapper caught up with her before she'd taken three steps. He grabbed her arm, bringing her to a sharp stop.

"In you get," he said, dragging her up the steps leading to a town house's entrance. He pounded on the door, and an old, impassive woman answered. Her eyes were dull and uninterested and barely registered Cassandra's presence as the kidnapper crossed the threshold, shoving Cassandra ahead of him.

She stumbled through the foyer. The furnishings were abundant and gaudy, done up in bright gilt and garish fabrics. Someone with money but no taste lived here.

Her abductor hauled her up another flight of uneven stairs. She stumbled on her ankle the kidnapper had twisted, but he didn't stop pulling her behind him. They reached a landing, and he shoved open a door leading to a study. Here, more overly ornate furniture competed for space with gewgaws and bric-a-brac. Whoever owned this place wanted to impress someone with their ability to buy things. Cassandra would have smiled at such bald attempts to awe, but fear—and the gag—choked her.

She was pushed into a chair in front of a desk. The kidnapper stood behind her, keeping guard.

It was clear the man who'd knocked into Alex had merely been a diversion. Her abduction had been the goal all along. Was Alex hurt? He'd been grappling with that large man before she'd been pulled into the carriage. A double fear iced her blood, for herself, and for Alex.

Which of the investors would want to kidnap her? The room didn't give her many clues as to her abductor's identity.

Yet when a door leading to the study opened, and George Lacey sauntered into the room, Cassandra wasn't surprised. Lacey stood beside the desk, his hands in his pockets as though he was casually waiting for a mail coach.

He nodded at the man behind Cassandra, and he pulled the gag out of her mouth. She sucked in a breath, relieved to be finally free of the foul piece of cloth.

"This is pleasant," Cassandra said. Showing her fear was the worst thing she could do at the moment, since people like Lacey respected courage. The more Cassandra wept and begged, the worse her prospects would become. "Let's ring for tea."

"You're game," Lacey said with an approving nod. "I'll give you that."

"Then let's have done with trussing me." Cassandra tugged on the rope at her wrists.

"That stays," he declared.

Cassandra asked as if it didn't matter to her, "Until when?"

"Until," he replied, "I get my investment back."

"Martin's got the money," Cassandra answered. She

struggled to keep her voice level, remove all traces of fear from her words. "I'm tracking him down."

"That doesn't help my coffers now," Lacey sneered.

"Search me," Cassandra fired back. "Check under my mattress. I haven't got the money. And I can't get it to you when I'm tied up here. You'll get nothing from abducting me."

"Not so," said Lacey. "You've been keeping company with the Duke of Greyland."

Cold terror climbed up her spine. "What of him?" God, Lacey had better not threaten Alex, or she'd tear her ropes apart and unleash bloody hell upon him.

"He'll be willing to pay for your safe return," Lacey said smugly.

Cassandra stared at the person responsible for her kidnapping. What could she tell him? That she and Alex had gone to bed together, but had made no avowals of affection? She had no idea what she meant to him, other than using her as a marker for his five hundred pounds—more, with the addition of the staff's salaries. She struggled with smothering panic.

"And your plan is to do what?" she pressed.

"A note's on its way to your duke's home right now," Lacey said, proud of his machinations. "He's to meet us at midnight in the ruins of Welden Gardens."

Cassandra remembered Welden as an abandoned pleasure garden on the western border of London. It had been fashionable fifty years past, but fell into ruin and disrepair, until it was finally closed a decade ago.

No one who valued their life would venture to Welden. It was a maze of derelict buildings and dead trees.

"I'll bring you with me," Lacey went on. "Insurance, in case your duke tries to give me short shrift."

"And if he doesn't show?" Cassandra couldn't stop her voice from cracking.

Lacey smiled benevolently. "You'll be weighted and thrown into the Thames," he pronounced cheerfully, as if nothing could make him jollier.

The urge to scream clawed its way up Cassandra's throat. She had known uncertainty and fear on the streets of Southwark. Her whole life had been spent balancing on a precipice. But never had she known terror like this.

Lacey had to have a weakness. It was just a matter of finding it. She'd search and search until all her options were exhausted.

And if she failed . . . Everything depended on Alex. God help her, her salvation was in the hands of a man who had once made no secret of his hatred for her.

ALEX was on the verge of losing his mind. He'd ridden around the city like a lunatic, chasing after every vehicle that looked like the one used to take Cassandra. But all his efforts had been fruitless.

He returned home, seething, maddened. Alex slammed through the front door, only to find Bowmore waiting for him, a scrap of paper in his hand. "This arrived for Your Grace not fifteen minutes ago."

Snatching up the note, Alex read it. Then read it again. Each time he scanned the words his fury and fear grew, until it was a monstrous thing, big enough to dwarf all of London.

It was a ransom note, written in a barely legible hand and demanding an obscene amount of money in exchange for Cassandra's life.

"Who delivered this?" he demanded.

"A girl of ten, Your Grace," Bowmore answered.

"Did no one think to follow her?" Alex shouted.

"Forgive me, Your Grace." The butler bowed. "We thought she was a beggar child importuning you for charity."

Alex wanted to bellow in rage, but Bowmore had done exactly as he should have.

What to do? He needed to *think*.

Calling the authorities was absolutely impossible. The note had made it clear that any attempt to bring in the law would result in Cassandra's immediate death.

With an angry roar, Alex swept his arm across a side table, shoving porcelain vases to the ground. They shattered into shards as jagged and cutting as his thoughts.

Bowmore murmured something about cleaning up before disappearing to fetch a broom, but Alex paid the butler no mind.

He wanted to level the city, to rip up every building and corner of London to find her. The thought of Cassandra in danger drove him close to lunacy. What the bloody good was it being the Duke of Greyland when he couldn't *do* anything to help her? He raked his fingers through his hair and tugged off his cravat, flinging it to the ground.

She'd been in his bed, in his arms, not hours ago. Her heart had been in her eyes when she looked at him, and her soul had been in her lips when she'd kissed him. And now—her life hung in the balance.

There was only one thing he could do: play by the kidnapper's rules. Plunge deep into London's underworld to make certain that Cassandra came home to him—alive.

LACEY left Cassandra alone in the study for hours, and for added measure the ropes binding her wrists were secured to the chair. However, he seemed to fancy himself her host. Every hour, he'd appear, poking his head in the door and smiling like he was her favorite uncle come for Christmas. He'd been so threatening in Soho, but now, with the prospect of either money or her death on the horizon, he seemed downright cheerful.

"Hungry?" he'd ask. "Thirsty? There's a shop around the corner that makes a damned fine kidney pie. I can send someone over and have it for you in a trice."

"Seems a lot of trouble if you're only going to kill me," she answered.

He chuckled. "Come now, you'll think me remiss if I don't keep you fed. If that duke of yours holds up his end of the bargain, I should say."

"Mr. Lacey," she said, "George. You've known me

for years. Since I was a tyke running barefoot and ragged."

"Aye," he agreed, "what a pitiful sight you were back then."

"I did errands for you, remember?" She sifted through the debris of her memory, dredging up a past she wanted to forget. "You'd give me a ha'penny to deliver messages, or bring you gammon and bread when you were at the card tables late."

"What's that word the toffs use?" Lacey scratched his chin. "*Entrepreneurial*. That's what you were. Always looking for a way out of the gutter."

"With all the fond history between us," she said, attempting to smile despite the fear gnawing holes in her gut, "you can't mean to have something as petty as blunt stand between us. You wouldn't send your errand girl to the bottom of the Thames."

His own grin never wavered. "Ah, but there you're wrong. It wouldn't help me to give you a kiss on the cheek and send you toddling off. Sends a bad message."

"I'd think compassion would show you in a better light." She gave her most winning smile.

His grin faded, replaced by a look of such cold indifference it froze the blood in her veins. "Been spending too much time with the nobs, Cassie. You've forgotten how the underworld works." He took a step toward her, his thumbs hooked in the pockets of his waistcoat. "It's power what makes you king of the streets. Reward them that does right by you. Crush them that does wrong."

He held up one hand and slowly curled his fingers into a fist, and she felt the vise around her own throat tighten.

"But I didn't take your money," she choked out. "Martin did!"

Lacey shook his head mournfully. "As close as a daughter, you were to him. He'll shit himself with terror when he hears I've done you in. He'll crawl back with my blunt, and maybe I'll let him go. Maybe I won't. But he'll know—everyone will know—you don't fool George Lacey." His eyes were hard and pitiless, and there was not an ounce of mercy in the set of his jaw.

He would kill her if he didn't get what he wanted.

She tried to swallow but couldn't. A wave of nausea crashed over her.

Then he smiled again. "Sure I can't get you some food?"

"A shot of whiskey," she croaked.

He chuckled. "There's my girl." Without looking behind him, he exited the study, leaving her alone again with nothing but her churning thoughts and stomach.

She'd never felt so utterly helpless. Even on the streets, or struggling to get by through swindles, she'd always had a measure of control over her fate. But this complete powerlessness carved her hollow, leaving her guts to rot in the sun. Anger swamped her. Goddamn Martin! Goddamn George Lacey!

She'd dragged Alex deep into her world. How would he handle himself in the thick of things? A knife or bullet didn't care if he was a duke.

So many possibilities whirled through her mind, dozens of scenarios. Some of them good, some of them ghastly. She could break free from Lacey and find her way back to Portman Square. Or they could catch up with her and cut her throat.

Someone whimpered.

God—it was her.

What time was it? There were no clocks in the study, and none chimed in the house. It felt like months had passed since she'd been dragged into this pit, but surely it was only a matter of hours.

Her head sagged. Tears rolled down her cheeks and dropped into her lap, leaving little dark circles on the blue of her pelisse. Only earlier today, Alex had offered to buy her a new coat. She hoped that his generosity extended to paying her ransom. But a pelisse was a fraction of what Lacey demanded.

At last, several footsteps sounded in the corridor. The door opened, and Lacey and two thickset men entered. One was her kidnapper, the other was the man who'd barreled into Alex on Bond Street.

"Almost midnight," Lacey said as cheerfully as if they were going on a holiday outing. "Get her in the carriage," he directed the two men.

The man from Bond Street loosened her ropes to free her from the chair. Cassandra sized him up. She could jam her knee into his crotch. Then she could go after the kidnapper. Eyes and throats were delicate parts of the body. If she just rammed the heel of her hand into his nose, she could break it and disorient him. Then maybe—

"Oh, my dear, don't bother." Lacey pointed a pistol at her.

Cassandra felt the color drain from her face. "That's not necessary."

"I assure you, it is." He nodded in satisfaction as Cassandra was pulled to her feet and the ropes around her wrists were tightened. "It's for your duke. In case he doesn't play by my rules."

More terror clawed at her, combining fear for herself with dread over what might happen to Alex. Could she warn him? How?

As she tried to formulate a strategy, she was hauled out of the study and down the stairs. They led her outside. Cold and damp night lay over the street. A carriage waited, the horses pawing at the ground, and the driver looking at Cassandra with boredom.

She was hefted by one of the ruffians into the carriage. Lacey climbed in after her, holding his serpent-headed walking stick like a cudgel. Once they had taken their seats, he knocked on the roof of the carriage, and they drove away.

No one spoke on their way to Welden Gardens. Lacey rested his walking stick against his thigh and kept his fingers laced across the expanse of his stomach, smiling gently to himself, as if recalling a private joke.

The city sat dark and quiet—they passed almost no

one save for a few drunken stragglers and a dustman collecting rubbish that had been thrown into the street. Cassandra's thoughts roiled and tumbled in a fever, a hundred thousand different scenarios playing through her mind like the worst sort of melodrama. Sickness curdled in her stomach, and her mind was all sharp angles and cutting edges. Would she live to witness another dawn? Would she see Alex again? The fact that she didn't know made her agony all the more acute. Uncertainty killed her by slow degrees.

Finally, the carriage rolled through a huge, rusted gate covered in ivy. The gravel path crunched beneath the vehicle's wheels, until they stopped in what looked like a semicircular drive.

The door to the carriage opened, and Lacey shoved Cassandra into her kidnapper's arms. He didn't bother handling her gently as he set her on the ground. Her legs wobbled beneath her, but she managed to steady herself as Lacey climbed out.

The dilapidated pleasure ground rose up like ghosts of forgotten joy, its decayed and crumbling walls and colonnades stark against the stained gray sky. Though it was dark, what Cassandra could see only inspired more dread. The gardens had lost their battle with nature. Webs of vines covered most of the standing structures, while weeds grew in abundance out of cracks in the pavement and between bricks. Rustling in the scrub proved that animals had made the derelict Welden their home—most likely rats and feral dogs, and God only knew what else. A lone, faded bit of bunting hung between two columns, shining whitely in the night like a skeleton's rib.

"This way," Lacey grunted. He gestured with the pistol toward an amphitheater, though half its steps had crumbled away and only a portion of the stage remained.

Cassandra hesitated. She could run now, lose herself in the shadows and hope the single shot from the pistol missed.

Lacey jabbed the weapon between her shoulder blades. "Get on, then. This isn't a pleasant night's stroll."

"I don't know where I'm going," Cassandra said, fighting to keep a stammer out of her words.

"I'll get you there," he declared, digging his surprisingly sharp fingernails into her arm as he led her toward the amphitheater. They made up a party of four—Cassandra, Lacey, and the two men who served as Lacey's hired muscle. When they reached the top, he shoved her toward the laborer from Bond Street. "Take her to the stage. I'll wait up here. And mind," he added coldly. "I've got my barking iron trained on you."

"Difficult to forget," Cassandra muttered.

Her escort was even more brutal in his grip than Lacey. Surely he'd leave bruises on her skin—if she survived long enough. He pulled her behind him as he took the steps down to the run-down stage, and several times she nearly fell. Her ankle still hurt, making the going difficult.

Finally, they reached what remained of the stage. The wooden floorboards had partially rotted away, leaving a yawning hole in the middle. It was too dark to see how deep the hole was, or what lay at the bottom. They took up a position on one side of the chasm.

Night settled thickly, along with an uncanny silence that came from being in a ruin.

She could try breaking free and running, taking her chance that Lacey might miss if he shot at her, and also risking falling into the void in the middle of the stage. With Cassandra's hands tied behind her, her balance was off, and she didn't trust being able to make sense of this place in the dark.

But was it better than meekly waiting for Alex to come to her aid?

A blade pressed against the side of her neck.

"They said you might run," the man holding her growled. "You so much as wink and I'll give you gills."

She gulped. "Staying right here."

If she kicked him maybe . . . But she'd still have to contend with the man from Bond Street, and Lacey's pistol. There was no choice but for her to wait and to hope. Would Alex come? Or was this to be the last night of her life?

Chapter 18

$\mathcal{F}$or what felt like hours, nothing happened. Cassandra's heart shriveled and withered within her. She struggled against the tears that threatened to spill.

He's not coming.

Death by drowning in a filthy river awaited her. She didn't know how to swim. Maybe she could catch a piece of debris and float to safety. Resting her hopes on that remote possibility was all she had. Otherwise, it meant giving in to despair.

She'd started down a path long ago that led her here, to an anonymous, forgotten demise, mourned by nobody, leaving nothing of herself in the world but bitter memories.

This is it. The bad end I always knew was my fate.

She straightened, tilting up her chin. If she had to meet death, she'd do so with as much bravery as she could cobble together. It would be her only, fleeting legacy.

"Time to go," the hired muscle said flatly.

A sound rose up, faint but steady. It grew louder as something—some*one*—approached. Footsteps. Steady and rapid, they came nearer with the tread of a good-sized man. Whoever it was moved quickly and directly toward where Cassandra and her escort waited.

Her heart climbed up and up, choking her.

Alex appeared at the other side of the stage. It was too dark to see him clearly, but she recognized the width and set of his shoulders, his long legs, and the power and gravity radiating out of him. Relief struck her like a hammer, robbing her of breath.

She fought to keep from shouting out, the knife at her throat a reminder to keep still.

"Cassandra!" He took a step toward her, then stopped at the edge of the hole in the stage. He started to move around it.

"Easy . . ." She swallowed. "They're out there. With a gun."

"Button it," her guard snapped.

Alex glanced toward the back of the amphitheater. "Show yourselves."

"I'm no fool, Your Grace." Lacey's voice rang across the rows that once held seats. "Give my man the blunt, and you get the gel."

Alex reached into his coat and produced a thick wad of cash. He held it up above his head so that it could be clearly seen.

There it was. The price of her life. And he carried it in his hands.

"Place it on the ground," Lacey instructed him, "then back up. Slowly."

Cassandra could imagine how irritating it had to be for Alex to follow someone's commands. Yet he did as he was instructed, setting the money on the floorboards and taking three paces backward.

"Go get it," the man with the knife said lowly in her ear.

"My hands are bound."

A bite of something cold pressed at her wrist, then the blade sliced between the ropes, unbinding her hands. Pain shot up her arms the moment her hands were free. She rubbed carefully at her abraded wrists. The skin there had been chewed up by the rope.

"Fetch the blunt," she was instructed. "Then bring it back here. And go slow. Old Lacey, he's a crack shot. Even in the dark."

Gingerly, Cassandra made her way closer to Alex and the money. As she neared, his features became more distinct, and she could have wept to see the sharp angles of his face once more. He'd come for her. She'd dragged him into the filth of her world, and still he'd shown up to free her.

He took a step toward her, hand outstretched.

"Stay where you are, Your Grace," Lacey called out. "Who knows where my bullet might stray? In your heart, or in hers?"

Cassandra reached the bundle of money. She scooped it up, feeling its strange lightness. It felt like nothing at all in her hands, just paper, and yet men and women were willing to kill for it.

As soon as she had the money, she walked back to the man with the knife. He held out his hand. She dropped the cash into his outstretched palm, keeping herself as far from striking distance as possible.

"Count it, Foyle," Lacey's voice ordered.

Several moments passed as Foyle went through the bundle of money, his lips moving as he counted to himself. Finally, he lifted his head and shouted, "It's all here."

"Then we're done," Alex said in icy, precise tones.

"Take the wench," Lacey said. "I got the better bargain." He chortled.

"I disagree," Alex said.

Cassandra didn't wait. She sped away from Foyle to Alex. Alex ran toward her. They met at the edge of the ruined stage. He wrapped her in his arms, holding her close, his breath hot and fast against the top of her head as he cradled her tightly.

"Are you hurt?"

"My ankle's a little tender. Wrists are sore."

"Can you walk?"

"Yes." She fought to speak. "Alex—I—"

Suddenly, Foyle bellowed angrily as he charged them. Alex shoved her aside as the man leapt forward, his blade gleaming in the dull moonlight. Alex spun, his fist a blur as it crashed into Foyle's jaw. The man crumpled to the ground, his knife clattering beside him.

Alex grabbed Cassandra's arm. Together, they ran from the amphitheater.

"This isn't finished," he called to the darkness behind him. "You've made an enemy of me."

"We'll see who triumphs in the end," Lacey shouted back.

Alex and Cassandra ran quickly through the deserted gardens to where his horse was tethered to the front gates. He swung into the saddle, then pulled her up in front of him.

"I've got you," he breathed. He held the reins with one hand, with the other wrapped around her middle, holding her tightly. Nothing had ever felt as good— the smell of him, the feel of him, the movement of the horse beneath them both. She was alive. It was over.

Everything she had been holding back came flooding to the surface. The security of Alex surrounding her broke the dam and unstoppable shivers tore through her body.

Alex kicked his horse into motion. They took off into the night.

ALEX didn't stop until they'd reached Portman Square. Nothing and no one, except Cassandra herself, could convince him to halt. He needed to get her home. He needed her safe. The demand to protect her at all costs was a drumbeat in his veins. Never had he thought of her as fragile or vulnerable, yet she felt so human and delicate in his arms, he wanted to battle any and all who would do her harm.

Periodically, a shudder ran through her body, transferring from her to him. The tremors lessened over the length of their journey, but he had to take them away completely, shield her from the lasting effects of her ordeal.

Anger and fear waged war within him, obliterating rational thought. Energy sizzled along his limbs. He wanted to rip the city apart. He hungered for blood. Tonight, he had to concern himself with getting Cassandra back to safety, but later, he would track down and punish the man that had taken her. He swore it to himself with the vehemence of a holy oath.

At last, they reached Portman Square. A groom met him as he clattered to a stop outside his house. Alex dismounted, then helped Cassandra down. The groom sent Alex a curious glance as he led the horse away, but said nothing. Cassandra leaned against him, her steps faltering as she favored one leg. A fresh wave of fury choked him at the thought of anyone hurting her.

How had her ankle been injured? As she'd run from her kidnappers, and they'd thrown her roughly to the ground? Did one of the brutes actually lay hands on her, using his strength to hurt her?

Rage built upon itself the more he thought of it. He took steadying breaths. She was safe now, and he would take care of her.

After being let in by a drowsy footman, Alex guided

her upstairs and directly into his chamber. He sat her before the fire, rubbed her hands, and wrapped a blanket around her shoulders.

"I'll summon a bath," he announced, heading for the bellpull.

"No, don't." Her voice shook. "A glass of whiskey will set me right."

He poured her a goodly amount, then pressed the glass in her shaking hand. She took several healthy gulps, draining the glass, and set it at her feet. Her gaze remained fixed on the leaping fire in the grate, and its glazed vacancy alarmed him.

He crouched in front of her, taking her hands in his and trying to meet her gaze. "It was Rose Donovan, wasn't it? She took you."

"No. George Lacey." She recited this in a monotone. "Underworld king. Another investor in the gaming hell. Not a man to be crossed." She blinked, coming back to herself in slow degrees. "The money owed him, it wasn't a paltry sum. You paid it."

He frowned at the surprise in her voice. "Of course I did."

"Why?"

He couldn't fathom what she meant by that question. "What the devil do you mean, *Why*? Because it was either your life or the money."

"You didn't have to pay."

He stared at her. Then he shot to his feet, dropping her hands. "Did you honestly believe I wouldn't?"

"I . . ." She glanced away. "I didn't know."

A new kind of anger filled him. It was righteous, and resentful, and it curdled the pureness of his previous fury into something bitter.

"God," he rasped. "You think so little of me?"

She shut her eyes, then opened them. "Not you. Never you."

"And yet you say you didn't believe I would come for you. That I wouldn't pay *any sum* of money to keep you alive." Hurt, he moved away. She'd been through a terrible ordeal. He needed to remember that.

"Why did you come?" she asked softly.

"Because I care about you," he said simply.

She stared at him, eyes wide, and only then did he realize what he'd said. He felt his jaw turn to iron, while his heart pounded.

"That was . . . not how I pictured myself saying that," he finally managed.

She pushed the blanket off her shoulders, then crossed to him. Gently, cautiously, she placed her hands on his chest. Surely she felt the furious throbbing of his heart. Words could cloud the truth, but there was no denying the truth of his body.

"I shouldn't have doubted you," she whispered.

"I understand why you did," he answered softly. "I haven't given you much cause to trust me."

"Thank you. For . . . everything." Her eyes were full of gentleness and also sadness. "I've brought you nothing but misery."

"Not so." He gathered her hands in one of his and pressed a kiss to her fingertips. "Before you, I slept. Now, because of you, I'm conscious. For the first time in my life, I am fully awake." He gazed at her, his heart full. "I'd been like an automaton, going through the paces of my life mechanically, dutifully. But you've taken me from the confines of my comfortable, familiar world and introduced me to danger, and excitement, and a giddy sort of joy I never believed myself capable of feeling."

He released her hands, then pulled her snug against him, wrapping her in his arms. Cradling her head, he rubbed his lips against her hairline. Warmth and tenderness enveloped him, so much so his eyes felt hot and his throat tightened.

It was only when he felt the shaking of her shoulders and the growing damp on his shirtfront that he realized she was crying. This courageous woman—who had faced the callousness and brutality of the world all on her own without flinching—wept against him. She never showed weakness. But she revealed to him her own fragility, which was in itself an act of bravery.

"Shh," he crooned. "It's done now. It's over. I have you."

But that only made her cry harder, soft little sounds escaping her mouth that broke his heart.

She swallowed hard, gulping down air. "This can't last forever."

The thought was a hot knife in his chest. Yet he said,

"Later, love. We'll think of that later. Tonight, you are out of danger."

"There's more money added to what I owe you."

"Not a concern right now."

"Will you go after George Lacey?"

"Depend on it." He felt his gaze go cold. "A titan in the underworld he might be. I'm also the goddamn Duke of Greyland. Wrong me or someone I care about, he'll find life to be unkind, indeed."

"I believe you," she said solemnly. A quick, hard shiver ran through her.

"A hot bath will warm you right up," he suggested.

But she shook her head. "Take me to bed. Warm me from the inside out."

"I need no further convincing." With delicacy and care, he stripped off her clothes, layer by layer. The threadbare condition of her underthings didn't escape his attention, and he set these items aside carefully, vowing to himself to buy her all manner of silk and satins covered in ribbons and lace. But that would wait. Now he needed her bare.

When she was at last naked, he took her hand and led her to the bed. He pulled back the covers, and, at his silent urging, she slipped between the sheets. He quickly undressed, heedlessly tossing his garments aside.

He slid into bed beside her. In an instant, they were in each other's arms. And though his body responded immediately at the feel of all her naked flesh against his own, he held himself back from ravishing her. Instead, he drank in the sensation of her closeness, cradling her tightly as she pressed into him, her breath soft on his chest.

So close, his mind reminded him. *You were so close to losing her.*

He might never lose that fear. It would become a part of him always, like a scar. But scars meant one had survived, so he would embrace this and acknowledge its presence.

They held each other like that for a great while. Sometime in the small hours, she finally dozed off, her trembling subsiding until it stopped. He kept himself awake for a bit longer, keeping vigilant, absorbing the sensations of her in his arms, in his bed. And then, finally, he slept.

Chapter 19

$\mathcal{M}$orning broke through the curtains, and Cassandra felt something she hadn't in a long, long while—perhaps for the first time in her life. *Peace.*

She lay in Alex's arms, and all the dangers that threatened her from every side seemed to have ebbed.

But that peace was an illusion. Even if Lacey had been paid, there were still many other investors demanding their money. When they learned that he'd gotten his investment back, they'd want the same from her. Maybe they'd even resort to other kidnappings. Her life continued to hang in the balance.

"Shh," Alex murmured against the crown of her head. "I've got you."

For how long?

A tapping sounded at the door.

"Go away," Alex called.

"I'm sorry, Your Grace," came the butler's apologetic voice. "I must speak with you immediately."

Alex rose from the bed and threw on a robe as he

strode toward the door. Fortunately, he used his body to block the view of her nude in his bed. The servants clearly knew that she and Alex had been sleeping together, but she didn't fancy parading around naked in front of them. She had *some* morals, after all.

"What is it?" Alex demanded of Bowmore.

"Again, my most humble apologies, Your Grace," the butler murmured. She had to strain to hear his low voice. "I would not have awakened you, except I know that Your Grace has been waiting for a female visitor. One is downstairs now, urgently asking to see you."

"Does she have red hair?" Alex pressed.

"Yes, Your Grace."

Alex answered at once, "I'll be right down."

"Shall I send for your valet?"

"That won't be necessary. Give our guest some refreshment and let her know I'm on my way." Alex shut the door, then turned back to face Cassandra, who sat up in bed. "Becky's come calling." He strode to his clothing, scattered like so much debris around the room, threw off his robe, and began pulling on garments.

She hopped out of bed and also started dressing. Within a few short minutes, they were clothed.

"Ready?" Alex asked, pacing to the door.

Cassandra took a deep breath, then nodded.

She led the way down the stairs and followed the butler's instructions toward the parlor.

Pausing outside the parlor, she glanced at Alex, who

stood just beside her. In the morning, as yet unshaven, slightly mussed but impossibly handsome, he was everything she dared to dream of but could not allow herself to expect. He sent her a brief but devastating smile, heartbreaking in the way it encouraged her. Oh, she was so lost in him. And would be lost again when they parted. *If* she survived.

But she wouldn't think of that right now. This moment was for finding Martin and reclaiming the money he'd stolen.

Opening the door, they discovered Becky Morton perched on the edge of a sofa. An untouched cup of tea sat on the table beside her. She looked worn and fearful, dark circles under her eyes and her cheeks drawn and pale. If she wore her necklace, it was covered by the high collar of her modest pelisse. She clutched a reticule on her knees, her knuckles whitening. When Alex and Cassandra entered, she looked up at them with eyes brimming with unshed tears.

Immediately, Cassandra went to her. She sat beside Becky and wrapped one arm around her shoulders, rocking her gently.

"It's all right now," she said softly.

Becky produced a handkerchief from her reticule and dabbed at her eyes. "It isn't," she sniffed. "It isn't all right."

"Has he gone?" Cassandra asked as gently as she could, when inside she clamored for news of Martin, half in fear that he'd already fled.

"No, but's he's going," Becky choked. "I know it."

Alex and Cassandra shared a speaking look. Martin *was* in fact staying with Becky. Their instincts had been right. But there wasn't much time.

"How do you know he's leaving, Miss Morton?" Alex also spoke carefully, as if afraid of startling a bird.

"On account of me asking him about what we'd do once we left London," Becky answered, her lower lip trembling. "I wanted to know where we'd live, if we was to have a business or maybe act like gentlefolk and not work at all. He had plenty of smooth patter, saying we'd go to the south of France and we'd have plenty of sunshine for the rest of our lives. But . . . it didn't sound right to me. As if he wanted to throw me off his real track." She wiped at the tears that rolled down her cheeks. "He's going, but he's not taking me with him."

A sob escaped her, and she covered her face with her hands. "I thought he loved me. He made me so many promises."

A webwork of cracks spread through Cassandra's heart. How well she knew that pain—at Martin's hands. And now he'd gone and hurt another, goddamn him.

"I'm so sorry," she said gently. "You're not alone. I believed in him, too. And he crushed me beneath his boot heel. Without a thought for anyone but himself."

Becky wept in earnest, and Cassandra pulled her close, trying to offer as much comfort as she could. It felt strange to offer solace to someone, especially someone she didn't know at all.

She chanced a look at Alex, who watched her consoling Becky. His eyes were grave and full of sympathy. She realized what an odd picture she made, giving succor to the mistress of the man who had deceived her so grievously. Yet it was impossible to stop. Here was a person suffering, and if she had some small way of relieving that suffering, she wanted to give it. Through Alex, she saw now that people were more than things to be exploited for her own gain, and she had to make right the wrongs she'd done in her life.

"Miss Morton," Alex said softly, "if I may, I advise you to sell the necklace Hughes gave you and start over somewhere new. Away from London and painful memories."

"My mam lives in Grimsby," Becky said between hiccups. "My sister, too, and her babes. They've been leaning on me to come home."

"A good plan," Alex said, patting her on the shoulder.

"It's by the sea, isn't it?" Cassandra asked. "Salt air is good for curing heartbreak."

Becky gave a wobbly smile. "Aye, I hear that, too." She wiped her nose. "I've come . . . to take you to him." Her eyes welled. "I don't want to, but . . . it's what's right."

"Just give us your address," Alex counseled. "You can be on the next mail coach to Grimsby, well away from Hughes when we find him."

"Are you going to hurt him?" Despite Martin's dishonesty, it was clear that Becky still cared about the blighter.

"Only talk," Cassandra assured her. "And get back what's owed to so many."

"All right," Becky finally said. "You'll find him at Hope Street, in Whitechapel. Above a chandler's. It's the third door on the left."

Once more, Alex and Cassandra shared a look. They were nearing the end of their hunt. Her safety would be secured. And when everything finally fell into place, their time together would be over. How could she want something so badly, but fear it at the same time?

AFTER a quick consultation with each other, they decided to approach Becky Morton's Whitechapel rooms on foot. A carriage, especially a ducal carriage, would surely attract attention in that ragged part of London. They'd ridden in the carriage until the neighborhood turned seedier, and then proceeded on foot.

Being in Whitechapel made tightness clutch at Cassandra's shoulders, and her arms felt chilled. It was so like Southwark and the grimness of the Marshalsea.

Packs of barefoot, bedraggled children ran through the narrow streets. She'd been one of them, hungry and angry. Men and women stood in groups, watching and weary as another day passed without the prospect of work or wages. The buildings leaned into the street, as if exchanging gossip, and debris lay piled up in indiscriminate heaps. An early twilight settled over the lanes, heavy with smoke. Despair could be tasted on the tongue, stale and sorrowful, and Cassandra fought a rising panic at being back where she had started. She kept her hand light and loose on Alex's arm, though she wanted to dig her nails into him and hang on for dear life.

"I'm never coming back," she muttered under her breath.

"Our business here will be quick," he assured her, clearly thinking she meant she would avoid Whitechapel in the future.

She didn't correct him. Now was not the time to tell Alex that she would never return to places like Whitechapel or Southwark or St. Giles, or even the slums of Paris or Rome. Yet they beckoned to her, waiting for her to slide back into the desperate poverty of her youth. No one who grew up in squalor ever truly forgot it.

They turned onto Hope Street. It was a short little avenue with a few run-down shops and private rooms lurching above. No one lingered on the curb or leaned out of windows. An air of loneliness hovered over the packed earth and strung between the buildings like a cobweb.

In the middle of the block stood the chandler's shop. And above it, if Becky had been telling the truth, was Martin.

Her footsteps hesitated.

"Wait here, and I'll see to Hughes," Alex said.

She shook her head. "It's my face he needs to see. The hurt and danger he's caused me. There's no easy way out for him."

Alex nodded and guided her to the stairs beside the chandler's. The steps were falling down like a mouth full of rotten teeth. It took some agility to climb them, but soon they reached the hallway on the next floor. They were greeted with peeled paint and stained floorboards and holes in the wall.

Cassandra hoped Becky Morton did sell her necklace and start over in Grimsby. No one deserved to live like this.

They walked across the creaking boards to reach the third door on the left. Behind it was Martin, the missing money, the answer to everything. Yet her hand froze in midknock. She exhaled, long and shaky.

"This is stupid," she whispered to Alex. "I should be glad to face him and put this behind me. But I'm . . ." She searched for the right word, the right feeling. "Scared. Sad."

"Not stupid," he said lowly. "Understandable. It's natural, feeling conflicted. Hughes is a bastard who did you a great wrong. It's unforgivable. Doesn't mean it will be easy to confront him." His gaze warmed. "Yet if anyone I know can meet this challenge, it's you."

He reached down and squeezed her hand. Warmth coursed through her.

Everything could change at this moment. Once they had Martin, the idyll they shared would be over.

Lifting her hand, she knocked. Someone moved inside, steps on the floorboards, and stood on the other side of the door.

"Who is it?" a man snapped, his words tight with caution.

She glanced at Alex. Martin's voice. He truly was inside.

Calling on her ability to change her accent, she said in a rough, guttural voice, "Got a delivery for ye. From the fishmonger."

"I didn't order any fish," Martin barked.

"A dame called Becky said to drop it here."

There was a pause, and then a clicking sound as the door was unlocked. Cassandra braced herself.

The door creaked open. Martin's familiar visage peered out. His eyes went round when he saw Cassandra and Alex. His gaze met hers. They stared at each other for a moment.

I'm sorry, his eyes seemed to say.

I don't care, her own gaze answered.

Then the moment was over.

Instead of trying to slam the door to keep them out, he pushed past them.

Cassandra stumbled backward, but Alex snared Martin by his collar and dragged him back. Staggering, fighting to right himself, Martin threw a wild punch at Alex. His fist clipped Alex's temple as Alex sidestepped the brunt of the blow. A ring on Martin's finger scratched a shallow cut at the corner of Alex's eyebrow. Alex launched a punch of his own. His fist collided with Martin's jaw, and Martin fell backward onto the crumbling stair railing, his expression dazed.

"Damn," Alex growled, shaking his hand. "Got a jaw of iron."

"Shut up!" someone in a nearby flat shouted.

With no ceremony, Alex grabbed Martin's arm and half dragged him into Becky's flat. Cassandra shut the door behind them and locked it so no prying eyes could watch.

Becky's flat consisted of two chambers, one that served as a modest parlor and another that held the bed. The rooms were run-down, but clean and tidy. Here and there were pictures torn from periodicals, tacked up on the walls for color and cheer. Martin's belongings were heaped in an open trunk in the bedroom, his prized shaving set on a table with a ewer and basin.

Martin himself lay sprawled on the floor, partially on a threadbare rug, cradling the side of his face. He glared up at Alex, who stood over him, but when his gaze fell on Cassandra, his look softened and his eyes pleaded.

He swayed to his knees. "Cassandra, Cassie," he implored as quickly as his swelling jaw would allow. He held out a beseeching hand. "I meant to, you understand. I meant to include you all along."

"Was that the plan the whole time? To take the money and leave me hanging?"

His shamefaced expression said that that had been precisely his intention. "You're like a daughter to me. I'd never leave you in the cold. Cassie, please—"

"Stow it," Cassandra said through clenched teeth.

"If my heart has hardened against you, there's no one to blame but yourself."

Clearly sensing that his pleading was getting him nowhere, Martin tried another tactic. His expression turned stern and commanding. "You owe me, Cassandra." He reeled to his feet, and Alex widened his stance, his hands loose and ready. But Martin didn't try for another attack. Not a physical one. "Look around you. Look at this filth." He flung a hand toward the window and the poverty beyond. "This is where I found you. And this is where you'd still be—if you weren't dead from the pox already—if it wasn't for me. *I* was the one who saved you. *I* rescued you and made you into a fine lady. Everything you are is because of me and me alone."

Heat rushed into her face, but she pushed on. "Whatever debt I owed you has been paid in full. It was forfeit the moment you walked out that door in Piccadilly with all the money and without a word. Your betrayal wiped the slate clean."

Martin dropped his imperious look and once again played the pitiful wretch. "Be kind, Cassie. Be kind to an old man."

"Enough," Alex snapped. "You'll find no mercy here. Cassandra was almost killed because of you, and for that," he went on, his voice deadly and low, "I'll never show you a thimbleful of compassion." He took a step toward Martin, who flung up his arms to shield himself. "Either you pay up now," Alex continued, "or else I'll have you transported."

"You transport me, and no one will see a ha'penny," Martin flung back.

"Then you'd better produce the cash," Alex said coldly.

Martin looked quickly between Cassandra and Alex. She saw the calculation in his expression, running through the different tactics to take. Pleading, fighting, begging for sympathy. But what he saw in their faces must have convinced him that they both spoke truly. Neither would show him kindness or sympathy.

At last, he slunk toward the bedroom. Cassandra and Alex followed, standing in the doorway as Martin went to a portable writing desk sitting atop a table. He opened a drawer, and then pressed on a panel. The false bottom of the desk popped open, and a sizable bundle of cash fell out into his waiting hand.

He shook as he handed the wad of bills to Cassandra and winced when she snatched it up.

"Some has been spent already," he said mournfully.

Quickly, Cassandra counted the bills. Then counted again. It was the most amount of money she'd ever held in her life. Once, she would have thought of keeping it all for herself.

But she wouldn't now. That chapter had ended.

After counting the cash once more, she found that everything they needed to pay the rest of the investors was there. For the short time it had been operational, the gaming hell had turned a good profit.

After tucking the money into her reticule, she turned to Martin. "Pack. Now. Whatever you can carry."

"Where am I going?" he cried.

"We're putting you on the next coach to Dover," she said. "Then you're taking the first foreign-bound ship you can find. People are looking for you, so you'll have to stay hidden and not draw attention to yourself."

It would have been satisfying to drag him before the swindlers of London and have them wreak their vengeance on him. But she was done with violence and done with revenge.

"If I ever hear of you back in England," Alex added darkly, "I'll be sure to have you thrown onto a prison hulk with no chance of release."

Martin swallowed audibly. He held his hands out once more. "Forgive me, Cassie."

Her heart ached, but she straightened her shoulders. "I can't." She gazed at him pitilessly. "You'll have to live with that."

"But . . ." His eyes brimmed. "I love you."

His words were a thin blade slipping between her ribs. She fought from wincing.

She'd never once heard those words spoken to her before. But they meant nothing now. Not from him. And she couldn't let him see how much he wounded her.

"Love means giving," she said, gazing at Alex, "not taking."

Chapter 20

$\mathcal{T}$he yard at the coaching inn bustled with movement: vehicles coming in and out, passengers embarking and disembarking, luggage everywhere, dogs barking, the din of countless voices, horses being changed, tired travelers hurrying to take a fast meal in the taproom, and a hundred small exchanges that turned the yard into a swirl of muddy chaos.

But Alex cared only about the fate of one passenger on one vehicle. He and Cassandra waited, both of them crossing their arms over their chests, with their gazes fixed on the Dover-bound coach. Martin sat at the window of the vehicle, sending them baleful glances. Alex studiously ignored those looks. He didn't give a damn about Hughes or anything he might be feeling. He wanted him gone from England, never to set one traitorous foot on its soil again.

"I can still have him arrested," Alex said to Cassandra.

Her expression was deliberately blank, as it had been

ever since Hughes, the bastard, had claimed to love her. Alex imagined she didn't hear those words very often, and having them come from one who had deliberately hurt her must have wounded her deeply.

"For all that he's a son of a bitch," she said flatly, "having him rot in prison would only gnaw at me. This solution is cleaner for my conscience."

Whatever gave her the most ease was the solution he favored. He didn't want her troubled in any way by Hughes's fate.

"If ever you change your mind . . ." Alex said.

"You'll be the first to know," she answered. "I don't want to know where he is, what he's doing. If everything lines up properly, I never will."

Alex hoped Hughes would meet with a sad and bleak end. The swindler had nearly gotten Cassandra killed, and no fate was grim enough. If only they'd been alive fifty years ago, he wouldn't have hesitated to exercise his prerogative to shed blood in the name of the woman he loved.

A shock ran through him like a sizzle of lightning.

He loved Cassandra.

His anger had turned, first into tentative caring and then to a consuming passion. And love was there now, as steady and sure as an oak with its roots thickly woven around his heart. He'd altered completely from the man he'd been a few weeks ago—because of her. Sensations of freedom and benevolence coursed through him.

Even here, in this mud-spattered and anarchic coaching yard, he looked at the world with fresh eyes and saw beauty in the mundane. The dog touching noses with one of the horses. A mother straightening her child's cap. The man giving a farewell kiss to his daughter as she climbed aboard a coach. He wouldn't have seen these moments before, but now, now he was someone else entirely. Someone better. Who lived more fully, who did more than move through the world like the prow of a ship carving through waves. He felt, he saw. He wasn't duty personified, but a thinking, feeling man.

She had done that. With her intelligence and bravery and sly humor and boundless passions. She had unlocked him, freed him. And he felt both huge and humble, ennobled and deferential. More than the Duke of Greyland, he was *himself*.

He couldn't speak of any of this. At least, not here, amidst the din and commotion. And he didn't know what would come of this new discovery of love. After all, they were fated to be apart. There was no surmounting that obstacle.

"The driver is calling for the final passengers to board," Cassandra noted.

A few more people squeezed into the Dover-bound coach. Some even sat on the roof, clinging tightly to keep from being thrown off. The driver slammed the door shut, then climbed up to his seat and snapped the reins. With a lurch, the coach rolled into motion. Hughes, seemingly resigned to his fortune, turned away from the window with a disconsolate expression.

Alex and Cassandra waited until the coach was no longer visible before turning toward his own waiting carriage.

As they walked to the gleaming vehicle, Alex said, "It's done." He scanned Cassandra's face for signs of sorrow, but found only exhausted resignation.

"He'll find a way to land on his feet," she said wearily. "He always does. All I have is hope that he doesn't trick some poor fool into caring about him." She exhaled. "That wound lingers longest."

Alex took hold of her hand and stroked his thumb over her wrist, where her pulse beat steadily. "He won't always have a hold on you."

"He won't," she agreed. "And now it's time to make everything right."

Cassandra's mouth had gone dry, while her palms were damp. A rushing sound echoed in her ears. She was about to give away a tremendous amount of money—but it wasn't hers. There had been a time when she would have schemed a way to keep that money for herself, but that was behind her. Now she only wanted everything made right.

The Union Hall was filled with every sort of swindling character known on the London streets. They jostled for a view of the "parlor," a large section of the warehouse that served as the main gathering place. Seated around the parlor were over a dozen investors, including Rose Donovan. Men and women who ran the criminal networks that made up the city's thriving other life. They ranged in age, but all of them had the same hard-won wisdom and cynicism in their eyes and faces.

Cassandra stood in the center of the parlor. She glanced over at Alex, standing at the periphery of the room. He gave her an encouraging nod, and the fear swirling in her belly calmed.

She lifted her hands, and everyone within the Union Hall quieted.

"I'm here to make good," she announced. "To each and every one of you."

"Ye want us to believe ye?" demanded Kitty Norham.

"Trustworthy as an adder, that one," Rose Donovan noted.

To prove it, Cassandra pulled out the sheaf of cash and held it over her head. There was a collective inhalation, a hundred criminals eyeing a fat prize.

"We'll go one by one," she continued.

"Make sure you count it so no one gets fleeced." George Lacey shouldered his way through the crowd, looking smug and self-satisfied.

Fear and anger welled up from deep within Cassandra. "You're not needed here."

"Couldn't resist seeing the last act played out." He smirked. "You're a naughty one, Cassie. If I don't keep you on the level, who will?"

She looked at Alex, whose expression was stony. The way a muscle ticked in his jaw, he was barely holding himself back from pounding Lacey into porridge.

"Get. Out," she said levelly.

"Fine talk from a gel who was begging for her life last night." Lacey advanced toward her, his serpent-headed walking stick raised high.

She flung up her arms to protect herself, yet the blow never came.

A bang rang out. The crowd gasped and dropped to the ground, but Lacey stayed on his feet. Both he and Cassandra looked to the only other man still standing.

Alex held a pistol to the ceiling as smoke curled from the muzzle of his weapon. His eyes were hard and dark as he stared at Lacey.

"You missed, toff," Lacey sneered.

A cold smile curved Alex's mouth. "I didn't."

Cassandra spotted movement toward the back of the crowd, and her fear gave way to vicious satisfaction as men in dark uniforms swarmed the building. Alex's shot must have signaled them to rush forward.

"I believe these men are here for you," she said to Lacey.

A thickset man with a substantial mustache stepped forward. "George Lacey, I am the local magistrate, and

I arrest you on the charge of kidnapping and threatening to commit murder."

Lacey froze as two even-burlier men approached him with a pair of manacles. Before they could reach him, Lacey darted to the side, trying to evade them.

The next moment, he lay sprawled on the ground, his eyes rolling back. Alex shook out his fist as he stood over the prone form of George Lacey.

Cassandra's heart swelled even as regret stabbed her. One of England's most esteemed peers had turned into a brawling ruffian—for her.

"Thank you, Your Grace," the mustachioed man said. "I appreciate the advance notice. Usually, we get there when it's too late."

"Make certain he gets no visitors or privileges as he awaits trial," Alex commanded.

"Of course, Your Grace."

The unconscious Lacey had his hands manacled. He was only just starting to come to, groaning as he was dragged from the silent Union Hall.

Deadly silence filled the space after Lacey's exit. Even Rose Donovan had nothing to say. Alex strode to the center of the parlor, until he stood beside Cassandra.

"You'll be repaid today," he announced to the crowd. His look was thunderous. "But if *anyone* thinks to pull a stunt like Lacey, if *anybody* touches this woman, Lacey's fate will seem like a holiday compared to what awaits you. Am I understood?"

"Yes," the crowd unenthusiastically chorused.

"Excuse me?" Alex demanded.

"Yes, Your Grace," everyone said, much louder.

Alex nodded. "Now queue up, and don't say another word."

Docilely, the crowd obeyed. Rose Donovan led the pack, but she was a decidedly more humble woman when she accepted her share of the money.

Soon, most of the cash had gone, and Cassandra tucked the remainder of it in her reticule. Exhaustion sapped her. When Alex placed his hand on the small of her back, she wanted nothing more than to lean into his solid strength.

Instead, she kept her chin high as she announced, "I hope to never see any of you again."

"Good luck, Cassie," Rose said with something akin to fondness.

"Goodbye, Rose," she answered.

With Alex beside her, Cassandra left the Union Hall. For the last time.

"How did you know?" Cassandra asked as they climbed the stairs of Alex's home.

"Know what?" He hadn't stopped touching her since the Union Hall.

"That Lacey would be there today."

Alex looked grim. "Because bullies like him can't resist tormenting people. Makes them feel big." He shook his head. "I've seen my share of that in Parliament. But there's not much difference when it comes to men with power." He exhaled. "I sent a quick note from the coaching inn, informing the authorities as to when and where to find Lacey."

Cassandra waited until they had reached his room before she spoke again. He closed the door behind them, and she waited by the fire. When he stood before her, she looked into his eyes.

"Thank you," she said simply. "For what you did with Lacey."

"It was for my benefit as much as yours," he answered. "I didn't want to be tried for murdering that son of a bitch."

"What a beautiful thing to say," she murmured, and kissed him. He returned the kiss hotly, his mouth demanding on hers. Heat curled through her, and she felt in every part of her body how long it had been since they'd made love.

She broke the kiss. "My work isn't finished."

He raised a brow in curiosity.

"My debt to you," she said.

Cassandra stepped away to pick up her discarded reticule. She pulled out the remainder of the money, then walked it to him. "Here," she said, holding the cash out to Alex. "Plus what you paid Lacey, and interest, that's everything I owe you."

She exhaled. This would set everything right and mark the end of their time together. She felt no relief, only emptiness.

He looked at the cash for a long time. So long that Cassandra pressed the bills into his hand.

"Take it," she urged.

He gently pulled his hand away.

"What are you doing?" She thrust the money at him. "This is yours. Everything you wanted."

"That's not what I want," he answered.

"What is?" Desperation edged her voice. She had to finish this, before she lost her strength.

He gently closed her fingers around the cash. "I want you to be happy," he said softly.

She gazed at him, bewildered.

"Take it." He held her hand between his. "Take it and start over. A new life. Wherever you want to go. Anything you want to do."

"I . . ." Her eyes grew hot, and tears threatened to spill. He was giving her this. Releasing his hold on her. "Alex."

"I've got one requirement." He looked at her with such sadness, such tenderness. "Stay away from gaming hells and racetracks."

She gave a small laugh, but knew that his words held so much more than what he'd spoken. "I will."

"Now put that money away so I can make love to you good and proper."

Her pulse throbbed, and heat spread through her at his words. Cassandra did so, tucking the cash back into her reticule. "And your revenge?"

$\mathcal{A}$LEX stared at her for a long time, and she felt the shock reverberating through him. "Good God, Cassandra, after everything? You'd ask me that?"

"You're a man of your word," she countered. "When you say you're going to do something, I believe it."

Alex continued to hold her gaze, looking into the eyes of the woman he loved but who had been hurt many times. Mistrust might always be part of her. He couldn't be angry with her for that. Not when everyone she had ever cared about caused her suffering.

"Words of a man deeply wounded and lashing out in pain." He looked at this strong, powerful woman who had turned his life into chaos, and he loved her for it. "You cut me. Severely. I needed some way of balancing the scales. But if I once felt that way," he continued firmly, "those feelings have changed now. I swear to you, Cassandra, hurting you is the last thing I desire."

A flush rose up in her cheeks. "What *do* you desire?"

"You," he answered simply. "Your safety. Your happiness. That is all I want now."

"I . . ." She swallowed. "I've been so bad for so long. I don't know if I'm worthy."

"But you are," he said fiercely. "You deserve security. And joy. And—" He stopped himself, the word *love* perilously close to his lips. "And caring," he finally added.

Her eyes took on a sheen, and she blinked furiously.

"Maybe I do," she allowed, though she did not sound entirely convinced.

There was only one way to reach her, one way to show her what she deserved.

He wrapped her in his arms, pulling her close, and kissed her.

CASSANDRA sank into him, feeling his warmth, his protection, the solidity of his body, and the strength of his heart. Hot and needy, they devoured each other, lips and tongues searching and claiming.

He pulled back slightly. "I want you so much," he breathed, his gaze fiery and his hands burning as they curved on her waist.

"Let's not wait a minute longer," she whispered.

They pulled off clothing, letting garments drop heedlessly to the floor. She held his look as she stripped, their gazes locked. He stared at her as if she was the center of the world, as if she was all he ever wanted. Inch by inch, they bared themselves. He was so lean and strapping in the firelight, tightly muscled and very aroused. His cock curved up toward his belly, and it twitched when she dropped the last of her clothes and stood before him, nude.

He strode toward her, animalistic and raw in his nakedness. His mouth captured hers in a long, drugging, wet kiss. She felt the press of his hardness against her belly and loved that she could make him feel this primal, visceral desire. Her own need was a wild thing, clawing her from the inside out as she ran her hands all over his taut body, tasted his mouth, and heard the rumbles of need and pleasure resonating deep in his chest.

She felt herself being walked backward, until the wall met her back. He took hold of one of her thighs and hitched it high over his hip, his fingers digging wonderfully into her soft flesh. Her quim pressed snug against his cock. It was thick and firm against her wetness. And when he dragged the length of it through her folds, she gasped aloud.

"That's it," he growled. "That's my love."

Holding tight to his shoulders, she clung to him as he teased her with his cock, stroking her but never delving inside. He would circle her opening, yet didn't thrust in, rubbing her clit with the head of his cock, driving her into a frenzy of need.

"Alex, now," she moaned.

"What do you want?" The cords of his neck stood out and he was hard everywhere.

She practically wailed with desire. "Fuck me, Your Grace."

"Yes, my lady." He angled her body slightly, then sank in all the way to the hilt.

The wall at her back kept her standing as he thrust into her. She held tight as he stroked the length of his cock in and out, building sensation, shaping ecstasy.

"Remember this," he breathed hotly. "Remember me."

"Always," she gasped. "Forever."

Her climax exploded, filling her with bright, heart-breaking pleasure. She cried out, her eyes pressing tightly as she lost herself in the wonder they created together.

He wasn't finished. The moment her last tremors subsided, he pulled free from her body and led her to a nearby chaise. Soft and pliable with release, she allowed him to position her on the chaise so that she was on all fours, with her knees braced at the edge of the sofa. He stood behind her, aligning them, with his hands tight on her hips.

"*Yes*," he hissed when she pressed her still-soaking quim against his hardness. He plunged into her in one thick thrust, feral sounds coming from deep within him. He took her like an animal, and she adored it. She watched over her shoulder as he fucked her, his body shining with sweat and need, his eyes mere slits as he looked at her, too, in this primal coupling.

Reaching around her, his fingers found her firm clit. He stroked her in tight circles, and pleasure climbed to unknown heights. She didn't care who heard her scream with release, the orgasm as infinite as time itself.

Then he pulled back, and she felt the heat of his seed spilling on her. He made such gorgeous growls, so free, so lost to desire.

As she panted, still shaking with her climax, he leaned close and kissed her.

"Don't forget me, Cassandra," he murmured.

"Never," she vowed.

CASSANDRA knew they were deliberately trying to create memories. Yet it didn't matter the *why* of it, so long as she and Alex had plenty to draw from in the long years ahead.

They slid between the cool sheets of his bed and immediately found each other, holding close, flesh to flesh. Mouths met hotly, insistently, their tongues lapping and stroking. His hands were everywhere, shaping her, caressing as though recording the feel of her body. Because time was short. Because there was no future for them together.

All the while, she felt the words burning her throat. *I love you*. Words that couldn't be spoken aloud, since they served no purpose other than to cause pain. They'd both suffered enough. Now was for pleasure. Tomorrow was unknown, but certainly lonesome.

Throughout the night, they made love. Sometimes they were tender and quiet. He slid into her gently and their motions were soft and slow. Release would come as delicately as a sigh. Other times, a hard need pushed them to verge on roughness, gripping and straining and moving with urgency. They made guttural, animal noises and cried out loudly with their climaxes. And all of it, all of it she adored, trying to remember this night for the rest of her life.

A considerate servant left a tray of food outside his door. She and Alex supped at midnight, feeding each other, kissing between bites. And then they made love again because they couldn't keep from touching each other, and touch led to desire, which burst into a consuming flame.

Sometime in the small hours, they lay wrapped in blankets in front of the fire, watching the dance of the flames as they held each other.

He stroked her hair and she nearly purred. She soaked up every sensation, knowing they wouldn't last.

She exhaled, ruffling the hair on his chest. Such good, manly hair. She'd miss running her hands through it. She'd miss everything about him. But a swindler from Southwark and a duke had no hope of anything but a temporary liaison.

"I don't want to think about tomorrow," she said softly.

"We won't talk of it," he answered.

She didn't know what awaited her. Every road was open. Yet for all that, she wasn't afraid. Maybe even hopeful. Terror didn't claw at her when she thought of her limitless possibilities. She even felt a rise of anticipation like a beam of light falling on the floor, illuminating the darkness.

Yet sorrow was hope's twin, living side by side. He'd take a wife someday. He was too responsible not to continue the line. And she couldn't be around to witness that, to know that he visited some other woman's bed, that he gave her children and they would be a family together. She couldn't face that.

"Stay in London," he suggested, wrapping some of her hair around his finger and releasing it in a curl. "An abundance of opportunities here."

"Such as what?" she asked. She wouldn't resume her life of swindling, and the city held so many dark memories. And—she couldn't admit out loud—even in a place as large as London, it was too close to Alex, and that would be a torture, to have him so near and so unattainable.

"We . . . care for each other, you and I," he said slowly.

Care for was a paltry way to describe what she felt for him. But even now, after everything, she couldn't bring herself to say the words *I love you*. They were too immense, too terrifying.

"Now that the debts have been paid," he went on, "why should anything come to an end?"

"A mutually satisfying arrangement," she concluded. "Become your mistress."

He sat up a little and spoke earnestly. "You'd have anything and everything you could ever want. A house. Servants. I'd settle an annuity on you that would never stop, even if . . ."

"Even if you married," she finished.

"I have to," he said somberly.

"I realize that. But it doesn't mean I'd be content, knowing you'd be sleeping with her and having babes to carry on the name of Greyland." She smiled sadly. "The money doesn't matter. But my heart does."

He was silent a long while, still and grave. "I understand," he finally said.

She cupped the side of his face and kissed him. "We both knew I was going to say no. But you had to ask."

He returned the kiss, and there was no mistaking the urgency or sadness in his lips. "I wish," he said lowly between kisses, "I could see what someone as strong and intelligent as you are capable of, with your talents applied to lawful enterprises."

"It will be a discovery," she agreed. "But don't count on any letters. My handwriting is awful."

It was clear they both knew her poor penmanship was only an excuse. When she left him, it would be for good, with all connections between them severed. It would be easier—less painful—that way.

With words exhausted, they made love in front of the fire. After their breath had returned, their bodies cooling, they made their way back to bed and fell asleep in each other's arms.

Cassandra awoke before dawn. Propping herself up on one elbow, she watched Alex as he slept. His dark slashing eyebrows folded down as if he was puzzling through something in his dreams. She wanted to run her fingers over the hawkish blade of his nose and the curves of his lips, but that might wake him.

She whispered the words, "I love you, Your Grace," before slipping noiselessly from the bed.

After dressing quickly, she hurried to the door. She

would pack up her few belongings and start off for her destination. But she couldn't resist one last, lingering gaze as she stood at the door to his bedroom.

Do it quickly. Like cutting a purse string.

She turned and fled.

Chapter 21

$\mathcal{A}$lex had heard her whispered words before she'd left him. He'd feigned sleep because the alternative, facing the anguish fully, would ruin him.

He saw now it didn't matter. Pain lanced him, hot and unforgiving.

She had gone again, as they both knew she would. He hated that the world was as it was, where people of certain classes could only be with people of the same class. In the gray light of morning he readied himself for the day, slowly armoring himself for the hours ahead, for his ducal responsibilities too long neglected, for a life without Cassandra. The social hierarchy seemed a ludicrous, woefully out-of-date concept that had outlived its usefulness—if ever it had a purpose. He railed against it. He wanted to run to Parliament and argue that anyone should be able to join their lives to whomever they wanted, rank be damned.

He'd finally been given love, but fear kept him from voicing the words he wanted to speak. Fear of pain, fear of the impossibility of their future together. And so he'd been silent, letting her go.

Once shaved and dressed, he found himself striding to Cassandra's room. He stood in the doorway and gazed at the bed in which she had slept—some of the time. The past few nights, she had been in his bed. Even so, he paced into the chamber, hunting for something she might have left behind, the smallest token that she'd been here. A glove, a hairbrush, a button that had come loose and fallen from an article of clothing.

Nothing. He searched the floor, the dressing table, her pillow, yet she'd been thorough in wiping away all traces of herself. He smoothed his hand over the counterpane, to no avail. She had been economically minded, unable to part with anything in her accoutrements.

He strode to the cold fireplace, holding her pillow. Unable to resist, he pressed his face to the fabric and inhaled. It bore the faintest trace of her scent—rose and vanilla. It wouldn't take much to erase that fragrance. A few more days and it would disappear with only the memory of her scent left to linger. He set her pillow back at the head of the bed.

Where would she go? What would she do? Would she be afraid? Lonely? Would she make friends? Meet a man?

The last thought made his body hot and tight all over. He hated the idea of her with another man. Yet he could make no claim on her. All he could offer was becoming his mistress, but they'd both known she wouldn't take his offer.

Even knowing she would refuse, it felt like hell.

His father's voice was noticeably quiet when it came to heartbreak. The old duke knew nothing of that feeling. Or, if he did, he refused to acknowledge it. Dukes had to set their hearts aside for the greater good, after all.

But Alex was far more than his title. Through their voyages into the underworld, he'd learned to step off the narrow path of his life. He'd been wild and reckless and seen his own darkness. He'd ached with desire and given in to need, and she had been with him through every step. Cassandra had shown him that he could be so much more than a duke. And now she was gone. Gone forever.

A footman appeared in the doorway of the bedroom. "Beg pardon, Your Grace. Your men of business are here and await you in the study. Shall I send them away?"

"No, I'll see them." He would bury himself in work. Lose the pain by immersing himself in his many responsibilities. Seemed a sound plan.

He gave one last look around before leaving Cassandra's bedroom. Just in case, he'd ask the maids to keep watchful eyes out for any little token left behind. There was no harm in that.

Downstairs, a trio of men met him in his study. They carried portfolios and sheaves of paper, their faces clear and bright, their minds on business. He'd neglected his duties for some time. The backlog would keep him busy for days, weeks. Thank God. Numbers and laws and crops could shelter him from the cavernous sorrow that wanted to rip him apart.

Hours passed. He industriously applied himself to mountains of work, stopping just long enough to eat quickly—though he had no appetite—before returning to writing letters, drafting bills, and considering proposals.

"A duke is never idle," his father had frequently proclaimed. "He is—"

Ah, the hell with you, Alex thought, cutting off the memory. His life was his own, not something created out of his father's template. He was his own man, and, if he ever did have a son, he wouldn't advise him on the proper way of existence for a duke. Rather, he'd concern himself with showing his son how to be a better person. How to live generously. How to treat others. How to love.

"I love you, Your Grace."

Bent over a proposal for a new circulating library in the village near one of his estates, he shook his head slightly. She loved him. At last, he deserved love. Yet she had chosen herself over him, as he knew she would and must. He'd never offered her the prize of love, fear holding him at bay. He couldn't blame her for walking away. That didn't stop the hot grip of pain in his chest whenever he thought of her, however.

The day waned. His men of business excused themselves to return to their families. He was alone.

Ellingsworth found him by himself in the study as he stood looking out into the garden. A footman announced his friend, but Alex didn't turn to greet Ellingsworth as he entered. Instead, he gazed toward the gazebo, where he and Cassandra had kissed.

"Given the funereal pall over the place," Ellingsworth's voice said behind him, mercifully free of its usual sarcastic humor, "I'd venture that the Cheltenham widow has decamped."

"She has," Alex acknowledged. Dusk shadowed the garden. Soon, he wouldn't be able to see anything out back, just darkness.

Ellingsworth's footsteps were muffled on the carpet as he came to stand beside Alex.

"I won't mouth platitudes about how it's for the best, et cetera," his friend said, also looking at the garden. "I've a feeling if I did, you'd only give me a fist to the face for my trouble."

"Appreciate your discretion," Alex noted drily. They were quiet together for a handful of minutes before he broke the silence. "First it was Lady Emmeline, now it's Cassandra. Both left me. Am I not enough?"

Ellingsworth placed a hand on his shoulder. His friend's grip was strong. He tried, without success, to give Alex a slight shake. "Never question your value, Greyland. With Lady Emmeline, you both knew in your hearts that you weren't right for each other. She would have been acceptable as your wife, but neither of you would have been truly happy."

That much was true. Alex acknowledged it by inclining his head. He couldn't mourn the loss of Lady Emmeline when she had been a concept, not a person. But Cassandra . . .

"I love Cassandra," Alex admitted softly.

"Even a dullard like myself can see that," Ellingsworth said.

"She went anyway."

"Did you tell her of your feelings?"

"Not in so many words." He'd held the words back, like a fool.

"She might need them. I don't know the woman," his friend said thoughtfully, removing his hand, "so I can only guess at her motivation for leaving. But if she did go, her reasons were not because of you."

"It's my sodding title," Alex muttered. "Had I been Alexander Lewis, mercer, and not the Duke of Greyland, she might have stayed."

"There's nothing to be done about your birthright." Ellingsworth moved away from the window and walked toward the cabinet that held an assortment of spirits. He poured two drinks, then walked the glasses back to Alex. "Whiskey makes all men equal."

After taking his glass, Alex threw back the drink, finishing it in one swallow. He couldn't drink Cassandra away, but might give it a damn good try.

"I don't know what love is," Ellingsworth acknowledged. "Hell, I doubt I ever will. But I know that hiding inside your lair like a wounded beast won't ease your sorrow."

"Been working all day," Alex said, nodding toward his desk crowded with papers.

"Work!" Ellingsworth snorted. "That serves one purpose—to make us miserable. What you need is a better distraction."

Alex set his glass on a table. "I've no taste for actresses or opera dancers. Not tonight. Not any night." The idea of touching any woman besides Cassandra was abhorrent. He shrank within his skin just contemplating it.

"There's a ball at the Collchesters' tonight," Ellingsworth said. "Dance with a few debutantes, listen to moldy jokes by their fathers, and smile politely at their mothers' attempts at flirtation. Will it cure your suffering? No. But it gives you something to do besides howl and lick your wounds. There will come a time when your loss will lessen. Bit by bit. Until it's as wide as a well instead of a chasm."

"You've become awfully sagacious," Alex said wryly.

Ellingsworth made a face. "All the damn Romantic poetry I've been reading. Soon I'll be weaving crowns of flowers and sniffing my lovers' pillows."

Alex coughed and looked away, in case he gave himself away as a fellow Romantic. "I'll meet you at the Collchesters'."

"Oh, no." Ellingsworth crossed his arms over his

chest. "Go upstairs and change. I'm taking you to supper. The beast won't be alone tonight."

$\mathcal{F}$EW hosts could claim evenings as fine as those held at the Collchesters' mansion in Bryanston Square. The *ton*'s most glittering personages filled the ballroom, exchanging pleasantries and brokering political alliances. The best musicians played as people moved across the dance floor in country dances and the newer waltz. French chefs toiled in the kitchen, preparing the finest dishes for guests to consume, and the wine was also undoubtedly French. Nothing was wanting. Everything was perfect.

Perfect. The word haunted Alex as he spun on the dance floor with Lady Mary Hudson. The young brunette was vivacious, pretty, and from a good family. She had all the hallmarks of an excellent prospective bride.

She wasn't Cassandra. For that, he could only muster courteousness as he turned Lady Mary in time with the music.

Not that long ago, he'd waltzed with Cassandra. It had been a dance of explicit desire, timeless in its intent, seductive in its power. The location couldn't have been more dissimilar. At the Collchesters', the dance was entirely different. It was a mating ritual, to be sure, but so bloodless and calculating. Ennui was a thief, stealing away any interest or enjoyment he might have felt.

They had been dancing together in silence for several minutes. Alex ought to make polite conversation, but asking Lady Mary to dance had exhausted his reserve of words.

This was his world. Where he belonged. With men and women of his station, his rank, his breeding. Not in union halls for swindlers. Not prowling the streets of Whitechapel.

Yet everything here was false and hollow. An illusion where the rest of the city was the reality. He was energized when breathing in the smoke-choked atmosphere of East London, facing off against hired muscle. He was fully in command of himself when people didn't defer to his title, but cared only about what he could do in that instant.

He was alive when he was with Cassandra.

"The music is very fine, is it not?" Lady Mary offered.

"Yes, fine," he answered mechanically.

"And the room is commodious without being overlarge," she went on. "I do hate it when there's a crush and you cannot take a lungful of air."

"True," he murmured without thinking.

She looked discouraged by his rote responses, but he couldn't bestir himself to alter his behavior.

Finally, she said, "There's a cut over your left eye."

His hand began to rise to touch the souvenir from his scuffle with Hughes. He stopped himself in midgesture. "Riding accident."

"Does it hurt?"

The question reverberated through his mind, his body. Did it hurt? A life without Cassandra felt like an eternity, absent of all pleasure and feeling, scoured clean of happiness, an ache that would never go away—no matter what Ellingsworth said. Her absence was a wound that would never heal. Alex hated the thought of being with any woman other than her. His duty to his title felt like a yoke, tying him to a destiny he didn't want. What did any of it signify? Life was brief. The mystery of love came to only a few lucky ones.

"I love you, Your Grace."

He'd grasped love, but had let it slip through his fingers. Like a fool, he'd turned away from it, because he'd believed in rules that didn't matter, not where the heart was concerned.

Being without Cassandra was an unspeakable agony.

And if he didn't move quickly, he'd lose his last chance at happiness.

"Forgive me, Lady Mary," he said, releasing his dancing partner. He bowed. "There is an emergency I must attend to."

He barely heard her response as he walked quickly away. He hurried out of the ballroom, down the stairs, and out the front door. Ignoring Ellingsworth, who called to him, he hastened to his carriage. But he didn't get into the vehicle. Instead, he stood at the foot of the waiting driver.

"Where did you take her?" he demanded.

The driver looked confused. "Pardon, Your Grace?"

"Miss Blake," he explained impatiently. "I made sure the carriage was at her disposal when she left this morning."

"Oh, aye," the servant recalled. "She wanted us to drive her to the docks. To an inn. I'm sorry, Your Grace, but I can't recall the name of the place."

Alex climbed into the carriage. "Take me where you took her. And be fast about it."

"Yes, Your Grace."

In an instant, they were heading southeast, to the docks. To ships that would take Cassandra far away—if she wasn't gone already. As the carriage rocked with speed, Alex prayed he wasn't too late. He vowed that he'd find her. No matter what happened, even if she had set sail, he'd pursue her across the globe to distant shores. He would do anything to pledge himself to her, from now until the end of time.

Chapter 22

Cassandra sat at a tiny desk in her cabin aboard the *Elizabeth*. Her quill paused above the sheet of paper in front of her, then she continued to painfully write, making sure her handwriting was at its most legible.

You will find Mrs. Cassandra Blythe to be an excellent companion, well versed in ladies' accomplishments, as well as amenable to any task asked of her. While she was in my employ, I could not have asked for a more agreeable companion. Indeed, I consider it a tremendous blow that Mrs. Blythe has decided to leave England and seek employment in Buenos Aires . . .

She set her quill down and shook out her hand, which was cramping from the effort of making her penmanship resemble something akin to a fine lady's elegant script. It would have to do.

This will be my last falsehood, she vowed. It was a small one, and would see her set up for a new life in a new place.

The prospect didn't excite her. At best, she could only summon a dull kind of nervousness. But it didn't matter what happened to her on the voyage or once she landed. Nothing really mattered anymore, now that she had left Alex. Going to Argentina ensured that she would never see him again, and hopefully never hear of him or his existence without her. Eventually, she might receive some gossip about his wedding, or the birth of his heir. With any luck, she would be deadened to any feelings that might stir up.

But now, the thought was a sharp, barbed pain, digging deep and holding fast. She'd been given what she wanted—someone to care about her—but she'd turned away because in the cold light of day she knew it wouldn't be enough.

She'd done right by refusing to become his mistress. Hadn't she? Or was it better to take what she could, content herself with crumbs when she wanted a feast.

Cassandra covered her face with her hands, suppressing the tears that had been threatening all day. If she gave in to the need to weep, she might never stop. And she owed it to herself to survive. She deserved that much.

But it would be hard without him. Hopelessly difficult. She would endure, but it would be a shadow existence, free of joy. Of pleasure. Of love.

It will be better once we've set sail. Wouldn't it? The last tie severed. Her final connection to Alex. But not entirely. His comb snuggled in the pocket of her pelisse. She shouldn't have taken it, yet it had been impossible to leave without grabbing something, some small item for herself.

The ship's midnight departure was only an hour away. The *Elizabeth* would sail off, and that would be that. The end of happiness.

A firm knock sounded at the door. Was it a steward, checking up on her?

"Come in," she called.

The door opened and she rose slowly to her feet, unable to believe what she saw before her.

"Alex." He was here. Aboard the ship. Wearing his elegant dark evening clothes, looking stern and magnificent.

He stepped in, closing the door behind him, then strode to her and stopped just short of their bodies touching. His breath came fast and hard, as though he'd been running.

"How did you find me?" she asked softly.

"Searched every dockside inn within five miles," he panted. "A porter at one of them told me he'd taken you to this ship."

There had to be dozens of inns in the area, and he'd gone to all of them. In pursuit of her.

"What . . . what are you doing here?" she managed. Understanding struck her like a leaden weight. "You said you didn't want the money back. Or . . . is it about the comb?"

"This isn't about money," he said lowly, "or a damn comb." His dark, possessive eyes never left her face. He drew a slow breath. Finally, he straightened to his full, imposing height. "I love you."

Her heart jumped and her nerves came alive. She struggled to make sense of what he said. "You can't," she said, stumbling over her words.

"Of course I can," he said imperiously. "I love you, Cassandra. Without you, my life is a husk."

"Oh, Alex." She forced herself to turn away and stare at the porthole and the dark river beyond. "It's impossible for me to be your mistress."

Gently, he turned her around to face him. "I don't want you for my mistress. I want you for my wife. If you'll have me," he added.

Her pulse was thunder in her ears, and she couldn't catch enough breath. "I'm a nobody."

"Not to me," he answered, his eyes glittering with intent. "You're the woman I love. Courageous. Strong. Wickedly intelligent." He touched his fingertips to the underside of her chin, holding her reverently. "I want all of you. And I want to give you all of me."

Eyes hot, dizzy with wary joy, she gulped. "I love you, Alex."

"This morning, you said, 'I love you, Your Grace.'"

Her eyes went wide. "You were awake. And you didn't stop me."

"I was afraid. And I thought we were an impossible match." He shook his head. "But my fear is gone, and *impossible* means nothing to people like us."

She gave a watery, tentative smile, then it faded. "My father died in the Marshalsea. I picked pockets and swindled people. How can I be your duchess?"

"Because you *are* my duchess," he answered confidently. "I have a plan for us. You'll see."

She had to believe in his confidence. He was the Duke of Greyland. The world shaped itself to his demands.

"I bring you nothing," she felt obliged to say.

"You bring me yourself," he said, lowering his lips to hers. "The greatest gift any bridegroom ever received."

$\mathcal{T}$HE clock in the parlor ticked a full minute before either Ellingsworth or Langdon spoke. Both of them looked from Cassandra, perched on the edge of the settee, to Alex, standing behind her, his hand upon her shoulder. The two men wore looks of equal disbelief.

But not disgust. That was what she feared most.

"This woman," Ellingsworth said, waving his hand at her, "as polished as a gem, the very picture of gentility . . . she's a . . . a . . ."

"A swindler," Cassandra filled in for him. "And one-time pickpocket."

Langdon, standing by the fireplace, crossed his arms over his chest. "I don't believe it. You're having us on."

"Has there ever been a time when I've *had you on*?" Alex wondered archly.

"Well . . . no . . ." Ellingsworth admitted. "But this could be a facet of your personality we've never seen before."

"I think I know how to convince you," Cassandra declared. "Lord Ellingsworth, would you oblige me by walking from the doorway to the sofa?"

With a puzzled look on his face, the blond man left his position by the window and began to stroll from one side of the parlor to the other, as she'd directed. Cassandra rose from the settee and strolled past him. As they came abreast of each other, she stumbled. Immediately, his hands went to her shoulders to steady her.

"Are you all right?" he asked, sending a worried glance in Alex's direction. Alex glared back, clearly unhappy that his friend was touching his intended.

"Perfectly well, thank you." Cassandra straightened and glided past him, until she stood in the doorway. Turning, she faced the three men, who all stared at her, mystified.

"What did that prove, other than Ellingsworth was damned eager to put his paws on you?" Langdon wondered.

Cassandra held up a shiny gold pocket watch, beautifully engraved.

Ellingsworth's hands immediately went to his waistcoat pockets. He appeared stunned. Then, slowly, a grin spread across his face. "Nicked it, you clever gel."

Langdon approached, also beaming. He gazed at Alex with wondrous appreciation.

"Old man," he said, shaking his head, "you grow more fascinating by the day."

"This is why we need your help." Alex crossed the room to pour four drinks. He handed one to Cassandra, then to his friends, before finally taking a glass for himself. "We'll need both of you to get the word out about Cassandra. Tell everyone the story we proposed."

"Meaning, we're supposed to *lie* to the *ton*?" Ellingsworth demanded.

"Well . . . yes," Cassandra ventured.

Ellingsworth and Langdon looked contemplative for a moment, before Langdon raised his glass high. He smiled widely. "To dishonesty!"

"To dishonesty," Cassandra and the others echoed. They moved closer and chimed their glasses against each other. Everyone drank.

After downing her whiskey, Cassandra locked eyes with Alex. He gazed at her as if she was the long-lost answer to the enigma of life. Soon, they would be wed, their lives joined until breath left their bodies.

He loved her. Not the lady she had pretended to be, but her truest self.

Two years ago, she had stolen from him. Now he was the thief who had taken her heart.

Epilogue

$\mathcal{T}$he front door closed behind the last guest. Finally, Cassandra and Alex could be alone. They sat on the carpet, side by side in front of the fire in the drawing room, hands interlaced, content to watch the flames and listen to the firewood pop.

"Felicitations on your first dinner party as the Duchess of Greyland," Alex said, raising her hand to his lips and planting a kiss there. "A roaring success."

"It rather was, wasn't it?" Cassandra smiled to herself. "Even Ellingsworth and Langdon looked entertained, despite the fact that there wasn't a single opera dancer to be found."

"Miracle upon miracle," Alex confirmed.

Three months earlier, Cassandra had made her official social debut as Alex's intended. Langdon and Ellingsworth had done their work, circulating the story that Cassandra was the daughter of a deceased obscure baronet, and was the widow of an old school friend of Alex. It had been a surprise, but also *not* a surprise, how willing the *ton* had been to accept this story. They had been quite amenable to believe whatever the Duke of Greyland told them.

Soon after, she and Alex had been wed by special license. A month-long wedding journey to Tuscany had followed. They had spent that time making love, eating, and strolling the rolling Italian hills. It had been with some reluctance that they had returned, but Alex's duties could not be put off indefinitely.

With the wealth that came with the title, she'd learned something about herself. She wanted to give back, to help others. She had been considering the idea of founding a school in the heart of Southwark. Cassandra hoped to help alleviate the grinding poverty and hopelessness of the area, to give girls and boys like her more roads to travel besides the ones leading to crime. Tomorrow, she was to meet with some of Alex's men of business, to expand the idea into a reality.

She was now one of the wealthiest women in England. She had come from nothing, and now . . . everything was different. It might never become easy to accept. But if she could affect real change with her newfound power and fortune, then she would gladly take on the role of duchess.

"We're to dine at Carlton House tomorrow," Alex said as idly as one might say, "We're going to pick out new curtains."

She swallowed hard. "I'm meeting the Prince Regent?"

"He's been asking to make your acquaintance for months." Alex sighed. "He's a bore, but the rest of the company should be worthwhile. They're all eager to meet the woman who ensnared my most virtuous heart," he added with a smile.

A nagging thought urged her to speak. "We're not being truthful, pretending that I'm something I'm not. A righteous duke might be bothered by that."

He leaned close, so that she was surrounded by his scent, his presence. "Only one truth matters—how we feel about each other. Everything else is inconsequential." He kissed her, gently, but with heat and purpose.

"You talk very nicely," she murmured against his lips. "Perhaps you should consider speaking in the House of Lords."

He smiled softly. "I'll argue that all men and women, regardless of their rank, should be able to love whomever they want. Without conditions, without limits." He brought their lips together again. "As I love you."

At Avon Books, we know your passion for romance—once you finish one of our novels, you find yourself wanting more.

May we tempt you with . . .

- **Excerpts** from our upcoming releases.

- Entertaining **extras**, including authors' personal photo albums and book lists.

- Behind-the-scenes **scoop** on your favorite characters and series.

- **Sweepstakes** for the chance to win free books, romantic getaways, and other fun prizes.

- Writing **tips** from our authors and editors.

- **Blog** with our authors and find out why they love to write romance.

- **Exclusive content** that's not contained within the pages of our novels.

Join us at
www.avonbooks.com